FAKE
IT WITH YOU

FAKE IT WITH YOU

KANE BROTHERS BOOK 1

MAKENNA CLEAVER

Book Cover by Emily Wittig Designs

Beta, Sensitivity, and Proofreading by English Proper Editing Services

Editing by Jenny Sims of Editing4indies

First Edition 2026

ISBN 979-8-9945490-0-1 (paperback)

Published by Makenna Cleaver

To anyone afraid of what the future holds.
Don't let your future steal you from the present moment.
Only in the present, can we truly live.

CONTENT WARNINGS

This book contains explicit sexual content, profanity, and topics that may be sensitive to some readers. In the interest of preserving the reader experience and avoiding spoilers, I have listed all trigger warnings on my website. For a full list of content warnings, please visit: www. makennacleaver.com

1

SIENNA

*Thank you for your interest in the Architectural Associate
position at Pinewood Construction. At this time, we have
decided to move forward with other candidates...*

My last bit of hope shrinks down until it's nothing more than a crumb as I read the words on my laptop screen.

Exiting the email, I hit the trackpad harder than necessary as I reach for the small cup of coffee on the diner table and take a drink. It's bitter, bleak, and void of any joy (a.k.a. sugar). Just like my chances of graduating from college with a job lined up.

Grabbing the sticky maple syrup bottle from the table, I drench my stack of pancakes as I take a moment to collect my thoughts. I've spent the past few weekday mornings in this diner before my first class of the day.

Most college students would prefer a quiet environment or at least somewhere with more comfortable seating. But the library isn't walking distance from my apartment, and coffee shops don't serve stacks of fluffy pancakes like these. Most breakfast places in Portland don't serve affordable, edible food on a college student's budget.

That's what keeps me coming back here. The pancakes.

It's certainly not the ambiance. I jump slightly in my seat at the sound of a ceramic plate shattering against the tile floor. Grimacing, I do my best to ignore the high-pitched scrape as the two materials come into contact, and one of the servers begins cleaning up the mess. The grating noise mixes with the expletives from the kitchen as two of the chefs argue over something. The fighting is a daily occurrence that most diner patrons watch through the pass-through window behind the bartop.

My throat warms as I sip my coffee, looking at the many business cards and advertisements laid out under the clear plastic tabletop. I remember a few of these businesses closing over the years, and I'm surprised this diner remains standing. Given the tear in the red-and-teal booth seat across from me that seems to grow each day I visit, I'd assume they are close to meeting these other businesses' fate sometime soon.

As I take a substantial bite of my carb-loaded breakfast, I think back to the crisis at hand. Five companies have turned me down for architecture jobs this week. That's not including the other ten that turned me down this month and the fifteen I didn't hear back from. I'm still waiting on a few responses from other companies, but I'm starting to run out of jobs to apply to.

It's the beginning of May, which means I have six

weeks until I graduate with my bachelor's degree in architecture. If I don't secure a respectable entry-level job, I'll never be able to build the career I want, I'll never be able to make the kind of money I want, and I'll end up like—

"You doing okay, Sienna?" The perky voice of my server, Jane, catches me off guard. She's come to learn my name, given that I sit in the same booth every day.

No, the world is about to open up beneath my feet and swallow me whole.

Considering it's not socially acceptable to dump your existential crisis on your unsuspecting server, even if you do consider her a familiar acquaintance, I nod and give her the most polite smile I can muster at the moment. It must've come across less polite and more "I'll murder you in the woods" than intended, judging by her grimace and the speed at which she walks from my table to the kitchen.

Thankfully, she tops off my coffee mug before taking off. But it's safe to say she won't be coming back around anytime soon for another refill.

My attention is briefly pulled outside when I hear rain begin to softly tap against the glass of the diner window to my right. Growing up in the Pacific Northwest, I've never cared for spring. As I got older, I started to grow tired of Mother Nature's indecisiveness during the second quarter of the year.

A cold, rainy morning usually ends with the sun high in the sky, reflecting off the many puddles that accumulate throughout the day. Sunglasses are a spring essential around here. Without them, you're sure to be blinded by the sun's reflection in the pools of water. Not to mention, the Portland State University sweatshirt I'm currently bundled up in is going to be unbearably hot by the time I'm finished with my late afternoon class.

Thankfully, the apartment I share with my best friend, Beth, is within walking distance of campus, so I can run home and change if needed. Sometimes the perks of living in a walkable city outweigh the weather's variability. Although, as I stare out the window, I still find myself counting down the days until summer is in full swing.

Watching the rain pour down as people rush to nearby buildings, I note who is using an umbrella and who isn't. It's a fun little game I like to play called "Spot the Tourist." Spoiler alert: none of us PNW natives use umbrellas. It rains year-round here, so we've all learned to embrace it.

Shaking off my moment of procrastination, I turn my attention back toward my laptop. Just as I'm beginning to regain my focus on job applications, Jane flies by, frantically trying to deliver a strawberry shake to a family a few tables down from mine. Between the scowl on the woman's face, the way the man cowers behind the menu, and the young child throwing crayons across the table, I'd bet they were about two seconds away from asking to speak to the manager.

Stabbing my fork into the last bit of my pancakes, I savor the bite as buttermilk and maple flavors fill my mouth, all wrapped in a fluffy package. This place might be run-down, but they know how to make a damn good pancake.

I glance down at my smart watch, 9:13 a.m. The cheap, pseudo-gold link band serves as another reminder to regain focus on my job search. Taking one more sip of my bitter coffee, I set it aside. Only forty-seven minutes until I need to leave for my first class of the day. I'll be damned if I leave here without having submitted every possible application to any company that will have me.

Pushing past the numbness growing in my fingers, I hit submit on my tenth job application. I continue my search through various online job boards as I hear the high-pitched chime of the diner bells mounted on the top of the entryway door.

"Table for ten!" a man yells excitedly at the host. "No wait, eight...No...ten!"

Glancing up, I roll my eyes at the group huddled in the entryway. Judging by their stance and the way they sway and cling to each other, it's clear they're running on fumes from whatever frat party they attended the night before.

I silently say a prayer that they will be seated far away from me, preferably around the corner behind the kitchen, so I can continue to be productive for the last eleven minutes I have here.

When they're seated at the table right next to me, it can only mean one of two things: I was a very bad person in a past life and this is a result of my karmic cycle, or Jane requested they be sat here as a result of the unpleasant smile I gave her earlier.

The latter is confirmed when Jane saunters over to their table and giddily takes their orders. Honestly, I can't be mad at her. I may not have time for a man right now, but she has my full support if she's on the hunt for one. If you look past the "I'm either still drunk or very hungover, but I'm not sure which" look on their faces, most of them are decent-looking, I guess.

I just wish this display of testosterone didn't have to happen right next to me, distracting me from the very important task of making sure my life doesn't completely fall apart before it even starts.

After placing their orders, the cavemen decide it's a great time to play paper football. As if the volume in which they are speaking wasn't enough to drive me mad. Unfortunately for me, I'm seated right behind the "goalposts" one of them makes by holding up their hands.

Pushing through the distractions, I try to ignore them, but I end up misspelling a word on this application when I hear the front bells chime. Again. I know it's impossible, but I swear the bells are louder this time.

After fixing my spelling mistake, I hit submit on the application just as one of the paper footballs hits me in the side of the head and gets stuck in my curls. The small white triangle isn't hard to find against the deep brown of my hair, but my annoyance grows as removing it catches a few of my curls in my small gold hoop earrings.

Annoyed, I turn to the table, still trying to untangle my curls from my earring. "Do you mind?"

The majority of them wince at the expression on my face. It's a healthy mix of irritation, anger, and disgust that appears only when I'm extremely overstimulated.

The table erupts in a soft chorus of frantic, mumbled apologies just as a smooth, low-timbre voice interjects from beside us, "You guys are such assholes sometimes." By the way he laughs through the statement, I'd assume he finds their antics more amusing than disrespectful.

I pay no attention to the mystery man as my irritation grows. Whoever he is, I'm sure he's responsible for the bell chime that made me mess up on my last application anyway.

"THEO!" the chorus of men yell, causing me and a few others in the diner to jump.

Feeling eyes on me, I finally give attention to the man they call "Theo," glancing in his direction. He's staring at me, a slight tilt to his head as though he's waiting for me to say something. I don't say a word. If he's associated with these, as he deems them, "assholes," then I can safely assume he's one too.

"They're harmless, I swear." He flashes me a wide grin, and my brain short-circuits. While charming, there's a hint of recklessness in his smile, and the combination is intriguing.

Asshole or not, it's one hell of a smile.

I continue to stare at him as I sit there, saying nothing. I haven't even so much as smiled at him. I should probably say something.

Just move your fucking mouth, Sienna.

"It looks like you're busy. We'll try not to bother you." Theo winces and points behind him. "They usually seat us in the back."

Finally coming to my senses, I respond, "I'm fine. I was just about to leave anyway." Shutting my laptop, I decide I can push my schedule up by five minutes today. I don't think I can get many more applications filled out with my current table neighbors, anyway.

My jeans scrape against the cracked leather seat as I slide out of the booth, creating the most god-awful noise. There's absolutely no graceful way to slide out of a diner booth seat, and my cheeks heat. I could not have a worse audience for a moment like this.

I'm apparently on a mission to make this the most embarrassing morning in the history of mornings, and my laptop slips out of my hands. Theo, witnessing the disastrous chain of events, catches my laptop with one hand moments before it meets its untimely demise.

He straightens as I finally wiggle my way free of the diner booth seat. At five-foot-seven-inches tall, I'm average for my height, but Theo is *tall*. I have to crane my neck up just to make eye contact. Looking straight ahead only gets me a view of his noticeably broad shoulders.

When he takes a tentative step toward me, holding out my laptop, the light catches in his eyes. Hazel green with swirls of brown as though he was born of the forest itself. When I reach out to grab my laptop from him, my fingers accidentally graze his hand, and my breath hitches against my will at the touch.

"Theo!" A slightly shorter blond man approaches Theo, slapping an arm around him. "Come sit down. Pancakes have arrived, and the girls will be here any minute." He appears less hungover than the rest of his breakfast companions, but not by much.

"Matt, chill. I'll sit down in a sec." Matt gives me a look up and down that unsettles the pancakes in my stomach. Walking back to his seat, he winks at Theo with a half-cocked grin on his face.

"Thank you. I should really get going." I work to shove my laptop into my backpack and push past Theo, heading toward the door.

"Hey, wait." Theo's voice stops me in my tracks just before my exit. "Wouldn't want to forget this."

Theo holds out my planner. Or more accurately, the one thing I can't live without. I was in such a rush to get out of here that I must've left it on the table.

"Thanks," I mumble as I put the planner in my backpack. Theo doesn't walk away as I swing the backpack over my shoulders. The bells above the door chime again, a reminder I should be exiting. Yet my feet are slow to move.

"I also go to Portland State. You graduating next month too?" My eyebrows furrow in confusion. *How did he know I...?* He points at my sweatshirt.

You know, after all those murder podcasts I listen to, you think I'd know better than to proudly wear merch that states what school I'm currently attending.

Before I can respond to his question, a thin blond woman pushes past me, all but shoving me into the coatrack next to the front doors. Her eyes are locked onto Theo as she reaches out, placing a hand on his chest.

"Hey, Theo," she says in a honeyed tone. I guess the women Matt referenced earlier have arrived.

Theo's eyes are still on me when I turn toward the exit, not saying a word.

"Maybe I'll see you around sometime?" Theo reaches

a tentative hand out to stop me, but his ability is limited by the woman still clinging to him.

Looking once at her, then pointedly back at him, I respond, "Yeah, see you around," lacing sarcasm into my tone. Not wanting to linger any longer, I turn to exit the diner.

I can feel forest-green eyes on me as I push through the doors, but resist the insistent urge to steal a glance behind me. I refuse to be distracted for a minute longer than I already have been this morning.

As I walk to my first class of the day, the rain feels like a much-needed cold shower to remind me that the last thing I need is to be distracted by a *man,* of all things.

Refocusing my thoughts, I think through my to-do list for the day and go through my mental checklist: apply for more jobs, attend architectural design studio class, make final touches on my senior capstone project, hazel-green eyes with a smile that could blind the sun itself.

Well, shit.

2
THEO

A pillow hits me square in the chest, knocking the air out of my lungs and causing my phone to fly out of my hand.

"What the fuck, man?" I say through a grunt to my friend Matt sitting next to me. Leaning down, I pick up my phone and inspect it for cracks. I really can't afford to break another phone.

"We're planning our last party of the year. We have to make it big, and you're not even paying attention," Matt scowls at me from his side of the couch.

"When was the last time you got laid? You've been tense for the past two weeks." He throws his hand my way, as if I didn't feel his aggravation through the sheer force of the pillow that just hit me.

"Finals. Just stressed." I wave him off. I don't like lying to my friends, but they'd laugh at the real reason I haven't been able to take my eyes off my phone lately.

"There's plenty of time to study for finals. We have one chance to throw a final banger of a party," Matt says, throwing a grin my way. I flip him off, then go back to scrolling on my phone. The fucker's lucky he didn't crack my screen. Otherwise, he'd have to deal with Roman.

"Would you two focus? We only have two weeks to plan this party for graduation, and I'm not doing it myself." Jessie sets down a plate of mini corn dogs on the living room table as he slinks down in the cracked leather chair across from where Matt and I sit.

"As I was saying, before Theo rudely interrupted my ideas by ignoring me." I side-eye Matt as he continues, "I think a pool party is the way to go. No one can get in unless they are wearing a swimsuit, and we can have a Slip 'n' Slide in the back, a kiddie pool in the living room—"

Jessie raises his hand. "We are absolutely *not* putting a kiddie pool in the living room. I'll be damned if I have a bunch of drunk people near water, running around my house with no shoes on."

"Your house?" I look up from my phone at Jessie, raising an eyebrow at him. I admire his confidence in phrasing it that way, but we both know damn well that this isn't his house.

"You know what I mean." Jessie brushes off my question and grabs a corn dog off the shared plate. Technically, the townhouse we live in is owned by Jessie's dad, not Jessie.

Despite the low square footage, we're all very grateful for Jessie's dad, who has been letting us rent the place for next to nothing while we're in school. At least there are three bedrooms, so no one has to share.

Just big enough for all three of us to get on each

other's nerves but not quite small enough for us to go to prison for first-degree manslaughter.

Jessie and I have been best friends since preschool because our moms were close. Following the death of my parents when I was in kindergarten, Jessie's parents helped my brothers and me as much as they were able. We met Matt in English 101 during our freshman year of college and haven't been able to get rid of him since.

"We're not throwing a pool party in a fucking townhouse that doesn't even have a pool in the back. It's Portland. It'll probably be raining in mid-June anyway," Jessie says to Matt.

"Yeah, that's true. I always forget the summers can be so emo here sometimes." Matt shudders. With his swept-back blond hair, preppy style, and insistence on using an umbrella every time it rains, he doesn't exactly fit the Pacific Northwest mold. Matt grew up surfing on the West Coast down in Cali rather than hiking to see the mountain views like Jessie and me.

"If you guys bother to visit me over the summer, I'm taking you to all the pool parties. Then you'll understand." Matt shoves a mini corn dog in his mouth.

Jessie and I both roll our eyes at Matt. He's been telling us for years that "not only is the weather hotter in California but so are the women," and we haven't been able to see him in his "prime" yet. Which apparently happens at these pool parties.

Jessie's curly black hair, dark brown skin, and athletic build, combined with Matt's blond surfer boy hair, slim build, and height, usually make them a dynamic duo for picking up women. That is, until Matt opens his mouth.

Standing from the couch, I stretch my limbs, needing some space from the cramped living room we're currently crowded in. For most people, it's not too small, but for someone of my stature, any room that isn't big enough to fit at least a four-person sectional feels suffocating after a while.

"You guys want a soda?" I ask my friends.

Jessie shakes his head at the same time Matt responds, "Yeah, but you'd better come back. There are details to discuss."

Making my way through the cramped dining room to the kitchen, I squeeze past the small round table, only big enough to seat four. The fact that there are only three mismatched chairs around the table is a testament to how many parties we've thrown since living here.

Once I've reached the kitchen, I grab two sodas out of the fridge. The sun shines through the window at the back door, just to the left of the fridge, painting the tile floor in a yellow glow. The moment takes me back to the woman I met in the diner a couple of weeks ago.

Sienna.

That was the name stitched in cursive across the front of her planner. I didn't consciously take note of it, but for some reason, her name is burned into my brain. It's not like me to be so caught up on one woman, but something was so intriguing about her. It's why I haven't been able to get off my phone. Unfortunately, I still haven't been able to find her on social media.

I keep replaying the way her dark curls framed her face. The way her deep bronze skin glowed under the morning sun. The sun hit her doe-shaped eyes in such a way that I swear they actually sparkled.

When her lips parted every time I flashed my smile at her, I found myself not able to look away. Not to mention how amusing it was to watch her tell off my friends. If Matt hadn't invited the women from the party to join us at the diner, I might have actually gotten Sienna's number.

Maybe then I wouldn't be obsessing over my phone so much.

Shaking my head, I make my way back to the living room. It doesn't take me long before I'm handing Matt his soda and cracking open my can.

I'm just about to sit back down when my phone rings.

"Sorry, guys. It's Roman," I say, flashing my phone screen at them. "You know I have to answer, or he'll have the whole city looking for me within the hour."

"Your brother is such an overbearing prick some-times," Jessie says, half smiling.

"Yeah, and you love him anyway!" I yell as I'm exiting the room, heading back toward the kitchen. Once I'm out on the small back porch, I answer the call.

"Hey, Roman." I lie back on the outdoor sofa, fluffing the pillow behind my head, locking in for whatever lecture he's about to give me this time. I should've been out here earlier. The sun could do me some good in getting Sienna off my mind for once.

"Why the fuck aren't you answering the group chat?" Great, he's already agitated. I swear he gets grumpier every year. If Matt thinks I'm pent-up, then I don't know what word he'd use to describe Roman.

"I didn't even notice. I've been swamped with finals—"

"So you've been studying?" he asks, a hint of suspicion lacing his tone.

"Of course, what else would I be doing?" I haven't exactly started studying for finals yet, but Roman doesn't need to know that. For someone who didn't go to college, he sure has a lot to say about my grades.

To my relief, he decides not to press further and changes the subject. "We're setting a date for the lake house this summer. Leo has that cooking trip in August. Alex said his training schedule is booked for all of June. I'll have to move some stuff around, but it looks like July is our only option. After the Fourth. Does that work for you?" Some papers rustle in the background, reminding me I still need to have another conversation with my brother.

"Yeah, that's fine. While I have you on the phone, I was thinking since I'll be graduating next month—"

Matt bursts through the back door, followed by Jessie, and they're both yelling, "Togas! Togas! Togas!"

Matt gets close to my face. "A toga party, bro! Isn't it perfect?" I push him off me, and they laugh as they leave through the side gate of our less-than-average-sized backyard.

"Really, Theo? Another fucking party?" Roman's stern voice snaps me back to our conversation. Shit. I forgot to cover the phone when Matt came outside. That will make what I have to say a lot harder.

Roman hasn't been impressed by my "recent lifestyle choices." He's the oldest of my brothers, and to say we have a complicated relationship is an understatement. I try not to complain too much, given the fact that he raised my brothers and me at only nineteen years old after our parents died. But sometimes I wish he acted more like a brother than my guardian.

I try to play it cool. "It's just a small get-together with some friends to celebrate graduation. I *am* graduating with my bachelor's degree in business administration. Do you not think that's worth celebrating?" Lacing sarcasm into my tone, I'm annoyed he still doesn't trust me despite my being this close to having a college degree.

Average grades be damned, I've still made it to graduation.

"Oh, I'm sure it's just a small get-together." Based on his tone, there's no need to question where I get my sarcasm from.

To deter the conversation away from my "less than savory party lifestyle," as Roman likes to put it, I go back to what I was originally trying to say.

"Anyway, I'll be free in July. Unless you think you'll be needing me in the office. I know—"

"I already told you, you're not taking a position at my company." Once again, he shuts me down.

Roman is currently the CEO and owner of Kane Construction. A company he took over from our father when he passed. I've been working for months to convince Roman to sign me on as a partner. I have ideas to grow the company into something much larger than what it is, but he's never interested in listening to what I have to say. Considering my last name is also Kane, I have just as much right to work for Dad's company as he does.

I have a little money left over from the nest egg our parents left each of us. It would've been more had I not just bought a new car, but purchasing this car moves me one step closer to being treated as an equal to my brothers.

Kane Construction is a multi-million-dollar company; my brother, Leo, is a top chef in the city, having worked at several Michelin-starred restaurants; and Alex owns his own boxing gym. Most of the time, I feel miles behind all of them, especially considering I'm the youngest and the college path doesn't allow for many business ventures.

Roman claims I'm not mature enough to work with him. I call bullshit. Sometimes I wonder if he just wants to keep what Dad left us all to himself.

"I'm twenty-two, Roman, going to a few parties here and there is part of the deal. I'm graduating next month. What else do I have to do to prove I'd make a good business partner?" I run my hand down my face, trying to find a reprieve from my eyebrows being pinched together for too long.

"Considering you called me drunk off your ass at two o'clock just last Wednesday morning, I'd say you still have some growing up to do."

"That has nothing to do with my business sense. I told you, we could expand Kane Construction to make it more profitable. We have the residential sector locked down, and together, we could break through to the commercial space, which you know is huge in this market."

Not wanting to hear my ideas for the twentieth time,

he says my name in the "dad" tone I rarely hear him use with my brothers.

"Theo, I've heard all about your 'ideas.' Your degree isn't comparable to my time as CEO. Maybe in a few years we can—"

"I-I have a girlfriend." What the fuck did I just say?

"A what?" I don't think I've ever heard Roman so shocked.

"A...A girlfriend. Been going steady for about six months now. She's really helped me change into a more responsible version of myself." I guess we're going with it.

When the other end of the line is silent, I continue, "She's helped me set some goals, cut back on the partying, and even has me going to bed at a decent time every night. Last week was merely a slip-up. She chewed my ass out for it too."

There's a long pause. When he finally speaks, his response makes my head spin. "Well, I can't wait to meet her at the lake house this summer."

It's my turn to be silent now as he continues, "I'd love to meet the young woman who has helped my little bro become such a responsible young man. As a matter of fact, I'll make you a deal." My grip on the phone tightens in anticipation. "If you prove to me over the summer that you truly have become more responsible, with your new girlfriend in attendance, of course, then I will *consider* letting you work for my company."

"Deal." I accept his offer with a little more desperation than I intend. "I can't wait to sign the offer letter that comes my way at the end of the summer. My girlfriend will be so excited she's invited."

"It's settled then. You and your new girlfriend will be in attendance when we visit the lake house in July. I'm sure Alex and Leo will be thrilled to hear about this development." Fuck, Alex is going to give me so much shit for this.

He ends the conversation with, "Answer the fucking group chat next time. Love you." I respond with a quiet "love you" before he hangs up.

Now, where am I going to find a woman I can convince to visit a secluded lake house with my three brothers and me this summer without her thinking I'm going to end up burying her in the woods?

3

THEO

It's been roughly two weeks since my talk with Roman, and I still haven't found a woman who's willing to be my fake girlfriend. It's not exactly the easiest thing to ask a woman, even one who I have a history with. I'm not sure I can even remember the last time I had a serious girlfriend, if ever.

Sitting at the dining table, the words in the textbook in front of me start to blur as my mind begins to wander. I take a bite of the sandwich I've made for lunch as I contemplate how to spend the next hour. I should probably focus on my finals, but it's hard to do when I'm running out of time to find a fake girlfriend. I still have a little over a month before the lake house, but I have a feeling I'll go through a few rejections before I find a woman who will agree to my proposal.

Deciding to take a break from studying, I open the dating app on my phone. I swipe left on any woman whose profile photo is of them at a party. While I have nothing against those women, that isn't exactly what I'm looking for. Knowing Roman, he'd see right through me if I picked a party girl to be my girlfriend.

"Why'd you swipe on her? She was hot," Matt says out of nowhere, standing next to me. He's eyeing my sandwich as I take a few chips off my plate and bite into them. A toasted turkey with Swiss cheese and every vegetable I could fit on it. I may not know how to cook as well as my brother Leo, but I know how to make a mean sandwich.

I wave Matt off as he takes a seat next to me. "I agree, but she didn't look like the type of woman who'd agree to a fake-dating scheme."

He chuckles. "I still can't believe you told Roman you have a girlfriend. What were you thinking?" He grabs half my sandwich and takes a bite, following up with a handful of chips that he also takes from my plate. Looking at him, I can tell by the sweat stains on his gray T-shirt that he just got back from the gym. Having food around Matt after a gym session, you really can't expect to keep more than half for yourself.

Grabbing my plate, I slide it away from Matt, explaining, "The only reason I said anything was because *your* dumbass decided to get in my face and yell 'TOGA PARTY' when I was on the phone with Roman." I make a show of looking like I'm contemplating my next words. "So really, this is all your fault if you think about it."

Jessie comes through the back door, making his entrance by exclaiming, "You find a girlfriend yet, Theodore?" His favorite way of fucking with me has always been to call me by my full name. He learned that little habit from my brothers.

Ignoring him, I move from my seat to help him with

the grocery bags he's just brought in. Matt follows shortly after he sees me pull out his favorite protein bars from one of the bags. Jessie has been out since this morning getting the supplies we need for the party next weekend. With graduation in a couple of weeks, it's the last weekend we have before we're all thrown out into the "real world."

As I'm unpacking the party supplies, I realize something. "Jessie. You only got seltzers, beers, vodka, and Jell-O mix. What exactly is everyone supposed to eat at this party?"

"Relax, man, there's a bag of chips somewhere." He frantically dumps out all the reusable bags sitting on the small kitchen island, and a few apples fall to the tiled floor. Realizing there are, in fact, no chips, we stand there for a few seconds staring at the pile of non-party food and alcohol.

"Shit, man, I thought I had some chips here. They must've gotten left at the store or something. But I have a date in a couple of hours that I have to get ready for, so I can't go back." Jessie rubs his forehead, a nervous tic he's had since we were kids.

Matt, trying to find a solution, says, "Don't worry about it, I'll go get the chips from the store while you—"

"Yeah fucking right. There's no way in hell you're driving my car again after you wrecked it the last time," Jessie explains, shaking his head at Matt. He turns to me. "Theo, can you go?" Reaching into his pocket, he grabs his keys and holds them out to me.

"Yeah, that's fine, but I'm not making the Jell-O shots." I grab the keys from him.

"For sure. Matt will do it." He motions his thumb to Matt standing beside him.

"The fuck? I get one tiny scratch on your car, and I somehow end up having to make all the Jell-O shots?" Matt exclaims.

Jessie responds, but I don't hear it as I'm already heading out the door. Better to leave now before I get roped into their fight of the day.

I would've taken my car, but since I don't have tags yet, I'd rather not get a ticket. Pulling out of the driveway, I can't help but think about Sienna. Part of me hopes I'll run into her again. If for nothing but closure, at least, so I can move on with my life.

I've just finished loading up the cart with every variety of chip in the chip aisle when I remembered I also didn't see any chasers when unloading the bags with Jessie. With my extensive experience in attending and throwing college parties these last four years, I've found there to be three types of drinkers: the type who want chasers, the type who don't want them, and the type who only drink chasers. Without soda, we'll disappoint over half of the party population.

Rounding the corner to the soda aisle, I pull out my phone to text the group chat.

THEO

Any requests? I'm not making a second trip.

MATT

No thx.

Maybe you'll run into your "girlfriend" while you're there. 🙃

I'm looking at the three dots on my phone screen, waiting for Jessie to reply, when I accidentally ram my cart right into one of the shelves in front of me.

"Ow, son of a bitch." Wait, not a shelf. A person. Shit, did I just hit a person with my cart?

Looking up from my phone, I confirm my suspicions.

Such an asshole move, Theo.

"Oh shit, I'm so sorry." I throw my phone in the pocket of my hoodie as I move to the front of the cart to check on my victim and...it's her.

Her face, the one I haven't been able to get off my mind for weeks, is twisted up into an expression of pain as she holds her ankle. My feelings are at war with themselves. On the one hand, I feel awful that I've just attacked the one woman I haven't stopped thinking about with my cart. On the other hand, I'm just happy Sienna is actually standing in front of me.

I thought seeing her again would provide me with some closure to finally get her off my mind. But I fear it will do the opposite. Her curly dark hair is thrown up into a bun. The sweatshirt she's swimming in makes her look tiny, but I can tell from her leggings that she's fairly toned, and the exposed light brown skin on her neck is complemented by the tiny gold chain that disappears beneath the sweatshirt.

I spend way too much time looking at that particular

spot on her neck. Thoughts of what it would be like to kiss her there, to taste her, to touch her…

I shake my head, trying to free those thoughts from my mind. Matt was definitely right. I need to get laid.

Before I can apologize again, I'm hit on my right arm with a cereal box. By someone half my height and who I think I recognize.

"What the fuck is wrong with you?" *Slap.* "You just hit my friend!" *Slap.* "You need to watch where you're fucking going." *Slap. Are those Froot Loops?*

Officially placing a name to the face I recognize, I confront the cereal abuser. "Beth? I think we had a marketing class together last semester. You go to Portland State, right?" I point at myself, still hoping I can save this interaction. "Theo."

"Oh, hey Theo. I didn't recognize you. You look different in class than when you're trying to run my friend over with your cart." She punctuates her sentence with a sarcastic smile. It hurts, but I'd be lying if I said it wasn't deserving.

Looking toward the woman who has been plaguing my mind for weeks, I say, "Sienna, right? Theo, from the diner a few weeks back. Is your ankle okay?" I look down at her ankle and let out a relieved sigh when I realize she's standing on it. At least it's not broken.

"Mm-hmm. You just caught me by surprise is all." She waves me off with a smile that doesn't quite reach her golden-brown eyes. I notice she's still avoiding eye contact with me in a very similar fashion as in the diner. Interesting.

I take note of Beth still half-cocked with the cereal

box, ready to unleash it on me any second, so I take a slight step away from her and closer to Sienna.

"Between my friends in the diner and the mark I've definitely left on your ankle, I've been a real asshole. Is there any way I can make it up to you?" I'm not sure why the question leaves my mouth, given the fact that I was looking for closure, not...whatever this is.

"You don't have to make it up to me. I'm fine." Turning to Beth, she gestures for them to go.

It's strange, but watching them walk away feels wrong. I feel an involuntary pull toward Sienna as her distance from me grows. I don't understand the feeling, but it's uncomfortable. I hate being uncomfortable.

That's when it hits me. From the very little I've gathered about Sienna, I can tell she's calm and polite, yet there's a quiet strength to her as well. She's exactly the type of woman I've been looking for. Having Sienna by my side would surely convince Roman I've become more responsible. After all, in my experience, women like her never date men like me. Not unless we're willing to settle down. She's perfect.

Leaving my cart behind, I catch up to them in only a few strides. As I cut in front of them and block their path, I wince at my mistake. By Sienna's startled look and Beth's protective stance, I realize I could've gone about this in a less aggressive way.

"I share a place with two of my friends, and we're throwing one last party before graduation as a big farewell. You should come." I realize I'm staring at Sienna when I remember that her armed-and-dangerous friend is with her. "Both of you. We'll have plenty of snacks and drinks." Smiling, I motion to my cart that was left at the scene of the crime.

Neither of them says anything, so I continue to ramble, "No pressure to be there, I just wanted to offer my apologies and was hoping an invite to my party would be the start of that." I hold up my hands as a show of innocence so I don't get whacked with the cereal box again. Alex put me through an intensive arm workout the other day. My biceps have had enough abuse.

Sienna hesitates. "I don't know. We have finals to study for before graduation."

I can feel her slipping through my hands. Along with her goes my chance of working with my brother.

"Let me grab your number, and I'll text you the details. The party is next weekend, so you'll have plenty of time to think about it." I grab my phone from my sweatshirt pocket and open a new contact page. Handing it over to Sienna, I'm surprised when she types her number on the screen.

"Great. I'll text you the details," I say, stepping aside so I'm no longer blocking their path to the exit.

Sienna gives a silent nod before they take off. I don't usually text a woman this quickly, but I can't stop myself from texting her as I head back toward my cart.

THEO

Sorry again for the cart incident.

This is Theo btw.

I'm making my way down the soda aisle when my

phone vibrates in my pocket. Pulling it out, I see a notification from Sienna.

SIENNA

All good. Nothing a little ice can't fix.

I let out the breath I didn't realize I was holding. At least she texted me back. Now I just have to figure out how to ask her to be my fake girlfriend for the summer.

4
SIENNA

Kicking off my shoes, I toss my bag on the floor in the entryway of my apartment. Too tired to place the bag neatly on its rightful hook, I head toward the couch. Falling face-first into the plush navy-blue cushions, I wish my problems away as I sink deeper. The smell of coffee invades my nose, and I wonder if I'm going to smell like this permanently.

"How many times were you asked for a cappuccino with no foam today?" Beth asks me from where she sits in her emerald-green swivel chair next to the living room window.

"Too many to count, but enough to lose brain cells." My response is muffled by my face buried deep into the couch pillows.

I don't have to look up to know that Beth watches me with a sly grin on her face. We've known each other since kindergarten, so I've memorized her facial expressions.

Beth is my opposite in many ways, but that's part of what makes us such great friends. Take fashion, for example. Where I struggle, Beth excels. She never fails to find the perfect outfit for any occasion. Especially since the many tattoos that decorate her body elevate any clothing item she wears. I've failed to see the day she doesn't find something that perfectly complements her light skin tone, brown hair, and blue eyes.

Although she constantly reminds me that her success in finding clothing items is more due to the fact that the fashion industry caters heavily to that specific combo, rather than her talent. I think it's a bit of both.

Unfortunately for me, where I'm taller and slimmer, she is shorter with a textbook hourglass body type. Which means I'm usually more likely to wear an old sweatshirt from my closet than I am to find something in hers that will fit me.

"Did you hear back from any companies today?" I sit up as Beth continues the conversation, and she sets her newest romance read on the coffee table.

Beth has always been a voracious reader. In first grade, she was reading at a fifth-grade level. I've always preferred movies to books, but I love hearing about her latest read. She's only about halfway through the one she just put on the coffee table, but I know she'll have it finished by tonight.

"Yes, but they all hated me," I grunt, burying my face in my hands.

The couch cushion sinks as Beth sits next to me. She doesn't say a word, and for a few moments, we sit in silence. I've always appreciated Beth and her ability to let me have my self-pity moments when needed.

Gathering my thoughts, I think about the shitstorm of

a day I've had. My water bottle already sits on the walnut coffee table in front of me, and I reach out to take a drink. Setting the bottle down, I lean back on the couch. It's days like these that I'm thankful Beth and I were able to be resourceful enough to make this place somewhat decent.

Thankfully, we can scrounge up enough money each month to afford a two-bedroom. During our freshman year, Beth and I tried sharing a dorm room but quickly realized—despite how much we love each other—sharing a space that intimate just doesn't work for us.

We snagged this place during our sophomore year. Since it was the only two-bedroom we could afford near campus, we didn't have a choice. The appliances are run-down, two of the stove burners don't work, and we both have mini fridges because the one in the kitchen is too small to hold all our groceries. Don't even get me started on the plumbing. I had to create a shower schedule to make sure we both get hot water.

We have enough money to get by between my job at the small coffee shop just down the street and Beth working at Powell's Books. It's not an uncomfortable life, but I can't help but think there has to be more to life than this.

Hence, my very specific ten-year plan to achieve success. I long for the days I don't have to grab my breakfast from a mini fridge or smell like coffee even after I shower.

My phone rings, and I hit the silence button. I don't need to look at the screen to know who's calling. I know I shouldn't be dodging his calls like this, but it's just not a conversation I want to have right now.

"How's the bookstore planning going?" I ask Beth in an effort to steer the conversation away from my crumbling life.

Beth sighs. "Amazing and awful at the same time. I have too much to do, but I can't get started until I find a place to actually house my bookstore. I just want the space to be perfect. I was hoping to find a place by the end of the summer, but I'm okay waiting if it means I find the perfect spot..." She stands and continues talking as she paces about the living room.

She walks over to the bookshelf by the TV opposite the couch and fidgets with some of her books, making sure they're perfectly aligned on the shelf. Since living with her, I've noticed it's a tactic she uses to calm herself when she's stressed.

She continues talking as she rearranges the classic novels she has on display. The movement brings my attention to the top shelf, where my cacti sit next to our small flags from last summer's pride parade. Hers is the unmistakable pink, blue, and purple bisexual flag, and mine is the less recognizable ally flag.

I'm having a hard time focusing on her words when my phone rings for the second time. I hit decline call again.

"Don't even get me started about a color palette, or a tagline, or fuck, taxes..." She continues talking as my phone rings again, prompting me to hit decline call one more time.

"You should get that. He'll just show up here if you

keep dodging his calls," Beth says, noticing my phone in my hands.

"Sorry." I grimace. "I just can't talk to him right now. Today was rough. I don't need his words of wisdom to be the cherry on top of the shit sundae." I slump deeper into the couch.

"Just answer his next call, get the conversation over with, and then we can make up a tray of junk food and watch a marathon of your favorite movies tonight." It's an offer she knows I can't refuse.

As if on schedule, he calls again, and I finally answer, heading out of the living room and into my cozy bedroom, only big enough to house a twin bed, a small desk, my mini fridge, and a nightstand. If I put anything else in here, I wouldn't be able to walk around.

"Hey, Dad," I say, answering the phone.

"Pumpkin! Finally, I've been trying to reach you all day. How are you? They aren't working you too hard at that coffee shop, are they?" Despite my shit day, I can't help the smile that spreads across my face at his greeting.

You eat half of a pumpkin pie at the age of eleven at Thanksgiving dinner, and it becomes your nickname forever.

"No, Dad, they aren't working me too hard. I could do without some of the self-centered customers, though." He chuckles, the sound simultaneously rich and light-hearted.

I sink onto my mattress, relaxing at the comforting sound of home.

"How's Mom?"

"Better than ever. Her strawberries are growing very

nicely. She says she can't wait for you to try them. She's out in the garden now," he responds.

I stare at the framed family photo on my nightstand. My parents stand on either side of me in my high school graduation cap and gown. We're in my mom's garden as she insisted her flowers were the perfect background for a family photo.

My father, John, is a tall man with dark skin and a smile that never fails to bring out a sparkle in my mother's eyes. He's an accountant at a small accounting firm downtown, not too far from my apartment. I'll occasionally stop by his office for lunch when our schedules align, but I've been so focused on applying for jobs lately that I haven't been by in a few weeks.

My mother, Sara, is shorter than my father but not by much. Her skin is paler compared to my dad's and mine, but the dark brown curls cascading down her back leave no question that she is, in fact, my mother. We share the same light brown eyes and an affinity for clumsiness. She is a beautiful force to be reckoned with when she's in her element. Her element being her home garden, or the small plant nursery where she works part-time.

Pushing past the feelings of homesickness, I look away from the photo. I'm surprised my dad hasn't brought up the reason for his call yet, but I humor him and reply, "I can't wait. I'm excited to see both of you next week at graduation. Did you get the tickets okay?"

"Us too, pumpkin. We got the tickets, but to be honest, I didn't call to discuss graduation."

Here we go. The conversation I was dreading. "Have

you heard back from any of the companies you applied to yet?" I suppress the eye roll.

"Yes, I have. I haven't received any offer letters, though. But I've been applying to multiple jobs every day and—"

"Have you thought more about *my* offer?"

Ah yes, his offer. The one that requires me to "take some time off, move back home, and relax for a change." My dad is the sweetest person alive, but he's also one of the most determined people I know. Lately, he's been insistent on getting me to throw my plan out the window and go along with his idea out of the fear that I'm trying to do too much too fast.

"Dad, I've told you before, I can't take time off. I'm on a strict ten-year plan, and that plan relies on me getting a job by the end of this summer." I wince at my tone, but I'm annoyed that I have to explain this again.

I'll be graduating next week with my bachelor's in architecture. While all of my classmates have big internships and jobs lined up for the summer, I have nothing. No matter how many times I explain it, my dad never seems to understand the importance of my plan.

My parents provided me with a good life. My mom stayed home until I was in school, then took a part-time job at the plant nursery, and my dad has worked for his accounting firm since graduating from college. Being an only child, I never had to worry about sharing anything, including my parents' attention. We had mundane Christmases and family trips to the beach. It was a steady childhood, and as a kid, I was never left wanting anything.

That is, until I grew older.

By the time I reached high school, I realized there was so much more to be attained in life. Instead of road trips to the beach, I wanted to take flights and explore other countries. Instead of shopping the discount racks, I wanted to buy clothing items at full price. Instead of fake jewelry, I wanted *real* gold to adorn my fingers and wrists.

I'm grateful for the steady life my parents provided, but I believe I am capable of achieving more than what I grew up with. I refuse to settle in the same way they did.

"Hmm...Okay, I'll keep sending you applications as I come across them. Just promise me you'll give my offer some more thought. I'd hate to see you burn out at such a young age."

"Thanks, I will." I feel gross lying to my dad, but I'm tired of having the same conversation with him over and over again.

"We'll see yo—oh, oh no." My dad cuts himself off, and I hear a rustling on the other side of the phone.

"Pumpkin, I have to go. The sprinkler is going haywire on your mom again. Sara, I'll be right there. I love you. Keep an eye out for my emails, okay?" he says. With an "I love you too," our conversation is over.

Sitting on my bed, I contemplate my dad's offer for a split second before brushing the idea off. There's just no wiggle room in my plan to take a few months off after graduation. My dad is usually right, but he's wrong this time. There's no way I'll burn out. I'll be fine.

My phone pings in my hand, and I tap the incoming notification on the screen.

THEO

Here's the address. Party is on Saturday.

The three dots are loading, and I wait for the next incoming message.

THEO

How's the ankle I so brutally ran over?

Again, so sorry about that.

A giggle escapes my throat of its own free will at his triple texting. I'm not sure why I gave him my real phone number, considering he slammed into me with his cart. I'm also not sure why I decided to text him back. I think part of me still wants to thank him for saving my laptop and planner the day I saw him in the diner.

Yeah, and the other part of you has spent the past four weeks thinking about his smile.

Shutting up my thoughts, I type out my reply.

SIENNA

All better, thanks to a bag of ice and a tub of ice cream.

THEO

lol there's nothing a bowl of cookie dough ice cream can't fix.

I smile at his mention of my favorite ice cream flavor. I'm just thinking of my response when Beth appears in my doorway.

"How pushy was your dad this time?" she asks.

"Not as bad as last time, but that's only because the

sprinkler broke on my mom again, and he had to cut the conversation short."

"Oh Sara," she says, clutching her hands to her chest. "I just adore your mother."

Standing from my bed, I grab my favorite sweatshirt off the back of my desk chair and slip it on. "I was promised junk food and comfort movies, and if I don't get that within the next hour, I might have a complete breakdown."

"Right, I think we still have some cookie dough ice cream left," Beth gushes as she exits my room, all but running out into the kitchen.

Grabbing my phone off my bed, I read the chain of text messages with Theo again.

I'm not even sure we'll be attending the party this weekend. Usually, when I attend parties with Beth, it's during a school-sanctioned break. Parties on a random Saturday night aren't typically my thing.

Especially not when they're being thrown by a man with forest-green eyes and laptop-saving reflexes.

Nevertheless, there's no point in attending a party that only serves as a distraction from my job search. Before I can throw my phone on my bed and ignore it the rest of the night, it pings again.

THEO

Hope to see you this weekend ☺

He's certainly not going to make avoiding this party easy, is he?

5
SIENNA

"Hair up or hair down?" Beth bursts into my room, a hand around half her hair, holding it into a ball on top of her head.

"What?" I say, too busy recovering from almost poking my eye out with my mascara wand to process what she just said to me.

"Hair up?" She motions to the hair at the top of her head. "Or hair down?" She lets it fall. Waiting for a response from me, she does this about five more times without saying a word.

Eventually, I put her out of her misery and respond, "You know you'll look good either way, but I say hair down. You always end up taking your hair down after your third drink, once you find an elevated surface to dance on, anyway."

Sitting next to me on the bed, Beth smooths out the yellow-and-pink quilted comforter covering my mattress.

"I don't always find an elevated surface to dance on." She scoffs.

I give her a pointed look, silently calling bullshit on her statement. We don't go to many parties, but when we do, she always ends up dancing on some*thing* or some*one*.

Refocusing on applying my mascara in the lighted rectangular mirror that sits on my nightstand, I say, "You know you do, and I love you for it. All the way until the moment you try to drag me up on said surface with you."

I pull an eye shadow palette out of my makeup bag, knowing she'll be asking me for it any second now, and hand it to her.

"I still can't believe you talked me into going to this party in the first place."

"Oh please." Beth waves her hand. "With the way you were looking at Theo even *after* he ran you over with his cart, you practically begged me to drag you to this party."

"I did not." I point my mascara wand at her through the mirror.

"Did too. It was all in the eyes," she says with a dramatic wiggle of her eyebrows. "I know I beat up on him a little in the store—"

"A little?"

"Feeling protective?"

I scoff. "No." But I did feel bad seeing the look on his face when Beth was hitting him with the cereal box.

She laughs. "I had a class with him last semester, and he seems nice enough. Charming too. And the way he was looking at you, oh my *god*. I might as well have been invisible."

I make a show of rolling my eyes as I move to my closet to pick out my shoes for the night. Being that it's mid-June and the warm weather has officially hit, I'm wearing one of my favorite summer dresses. A blue-and-brown paisley printed dress with straps that sit off my shoulders, a cinched waist, and a flowing hem that reaches just above my knee. Beth helped me pick it out last summer, when I had some extra cash and could actually afford to buy an item off a rack that didn't have a huge "Sale" sign on it.

Typically, I'd wear it with a pair of sandals, but I learned my lesson sophomore year at a welcome-back party. Let's just say there was a lot of pushing, drinks spilled, and I ended up spending the rest of the night cleaning Fireball off my bare feet.

Shuddering from the flashback, I grab my brown Converse from my closet. I don't plan on being there for long tonight, and it's probably in my best interest if I avoid seeing Theo altogether. I can't afford the distraction with graduation next week, especially when I still have no job prospects. Not sure how it'll work, considering the party is at his house, but I'm willing to give it a shot.

"I don't really understand how you expect me to get in the 'party' mood when I have absolutely no future ahead of me," I say. Beth gives me my small gold pendant necklace and moves to hand me my signature gold hoops.

Waiting for her response, I take a moment to admire Beth's outfit. Once again, she's nailed it, and I rejoice in the fact that I have such a fashion-forward friend. She's donned a more casual look than I have, with high-waisted jean shorts that are cut off mid-thigh, a white crop top, and a loose red button-down I'm pretty sure belongs to an ex-fling of hers.

"That's exactly why you should go to this party. It wouldn't hurt to get your mind off things for a minute. Besides, I'm hoping to find someone tonight who can take my mind off things for a minute as well." She gives me a knowing look at her obvious innuendo.

"Still not ready to settle down, huh?" I tease.

"Please, you know me better than that." She waves her hand. "And don't even think about asking me if I'll be bringing home a man tonight. You know I've sworn them off forever." She juts up her nose, playfully snubbing me.

I raise my hands in an effort of defeat. I know better than to joke about Beth dating a woman, let alone a man. Beth has, to put it bluntly, commitment issues. Those issues multiply tenfold when a man is involved. Hence, her decision to swear off them forever. I decide to keep my mouth shut, as I've seen, on occasion, a man leaving her room in the middle of the night over the past few years. But to her credit, her visitors have mostly been women.

"Hey, I won't bug you about your love life if you don't meddle in mine." I point a finger at her, and she smiles.

"I'm not meddling. I'm simply pointing out that Theo's hot, and you could use a night off from applying for jobs." She raises one eyebrow, and it has me questioning if she's been talking to my father recently.

"While you might need a distraction, I certainly don't. I need to be focused on building my career. Once I've become a senior designer at a respectable company, then I can look for a husband." I reach for my bag on my bed, pulling out the essentials for the party and making sure my phone is fully charged. I also check that my portable phone charger is charged because Beth will inevitably need it tonight.

"No one said you need a husband, Sienna. But a six-foot-five man with luscious brown hair, green eyes, a sharp jawline, toned muscles—" I cut her off before she starts giving me any ideas.

"Your point?"

"A man like that is one you bang and then move on. You don't need to become his wife. You'll still have plenty of time to apply for jobs tomorrow, even if you take the night off," she responds.

"I was actually hoping to use this party as a networking opportunity. See if anyone has any ins with some companies that might be hiring." I shake my head in defeat, slightly embarrassed by my plan.

"If you ask a single person for job info instead of asking them to play seven minutes in heaven or grind on you, then I will personally ensure you spend the rest of the night doing Jell-O shots with me."

She knows I detest Jell-O shots with my entire being, and I gasp at her threat. "You wouldn't."

"I would." She links her arm through mine as we head out to the parking lot to catch our ride. Once we're outside, my phone pings again.

THEO

What's your favorite Jell-O shot flavor?
I'll be sure to save you one.

I show Beth the text, and she laughs as she squeezes

her way into the back of the sedan. She directs the driver to where we are going, while I think of a reply.

I consider asking our driver to turn around and cancel this party altogether when another text comes through.

THEO

Excited to see you tonight.

6

SIENNA

We arrived at the party thirty minutes ago, and I've already been separated from Beth. She's stuck on the other side of the living room, talking to the blond woman she met half an hour ago. By the look on her face, I can tell she's exactly where she wants to be.

Had Theo told me this was a toga party, I definitely would've canceled. The majority of the men are dressed for the theme, and as a result, I've bumped into more male bare chests than I'm comfortable with. Drink in hand, I've slunk into the nearest corner I could find between the dining room and the kitchen.

As I'm scanning the room for someone I might know, I'm startled when the group gathered around the dining room cheers as a ping pong ball makes it into a red plastic cup. Glancing into the kitchen, I shudder as another group downs Jell-O shots like they are about to expire. Across the room, Beth and her new friend have moved to the couch, where their seemingly PG conversation has quickly turned PG-13.

No signs of anyone I know, and definitely no signs of Theo.

Downing the last of my seltzer drink, I question why I seem to care so much about seeing Theo tonight. On the entire ride here, I had myself convinced that I wouldn't give him the time of day to avoid any and all distractions possible. Now that I'm here, I can't help but wonder where he is. It is his house after all.

Shaking the empty can in my hand, I move toward the kitchen to find the recycling bin. I squeeze past the Jell-O shot group and round the corner, narrowly avoiding the couple making out by the fridge. I spot an open door next to the fridge and figure the bins must be outside. Even if they aren't, I could do with some fresh air.

The doorway is tucked into a small corner of the kitchen, so I can't see when I move through the threshold and run directly into a wall.

No, not a wall. Walls don't smell this good. I've just run into a man. A very tall, very attractive, rock-hard-bodied man. Thankfully, one who isn't wearing a toga.

Theo.

I back up once I realize I've been clinging to him for longer than is socially acceptable. Busying myself to avoid further embarrassment, I hold up the can in my hands to check the alcohol content. It's too dark to read, but I decide I'm done drinking for the night regardless. I've hit my two-drink limit, and I especially shouldn't keep going if I'm taking note of how Theo smells.

A mix of fresh laundry, citrus, and the ocean breeze. I'm definitely done drinking for the night.

"Hey, you made it!" Theo shouts over the music filtering outside from the kitchen. "Are you looking for something?"

"Recycle bin!" I yell. He leans closer to me, indicating he didn't quite hear me, so I opt to shake my can in front of him instead. He nods, then motions for me to follow him beyond the threshold of the door, farther into the small backyard.

Theo leads me to the recycle bin near the fence gate, and I toss my can in while he holds the lid open for me. The music isn't as loud outside and only filters in softly to the backyard. As I'm standing next to Theo, the sudden change of volume feels suffocating. A few people have gathered around a small firepit on the other side of the yard. They stare at the fire as they each take a hit of the blunt being passed around. Even with the quaint size of the yard, they're still far enough away that we can't hear them. I think they're already too high to have even noticed we're out here.

Taking a deep breath, I relish the summer night breeze that kisses my bare legs when it flows through the hemline of my dress.

Theo must catch me surveying the backyard as he says, "Jessie's dad owns the place. Matt, Jessie, and I all live here. Have since our sophomore year of college."

I give him a polite smile when I respond, "It's a nice place. Beth and I just have a small two-bedroom apartment. It can get pretty cramped, especially with her housekeeping tendencies."

He chuckles. "The guys would probably say the same about me."

I contemplate taking the chance to leave during the few moments of awkward silence that follow his statement, but for some reason, I can't seem to pull myself away. It must be the alcohol. That's the only logical explanation.

"Hey, about the other day in the store. Again, I'm really sorry I ran into you. Hopefully, your ankle isn't too fucked. I'm happy you came to the party instead of trying to have me arrested or something."

"My ankle's fine, but the jury's still out on getting you arrested." When his smile matches my own, I can't help but continue, "Or maybe I'll sue you for negligent driving of a shopping cart."

We laugh together, but when our eyes lock, I'm entranced by the swirls of green in his irises again. When he glances down at my lips, I look away, suddenly finding the sky is more interesting than anything he has to say. Considering we're in the city, no stars are in sight, but I can at least make out the moon. I've already let my thoughts stray from my plan enough as it is.

I'm just about to make an excuse to leave, grab Beth, and get out of here when he says, "So what are your plans after graduation?"

I laugh. "Not much, considering every company I've applied for has turned me down. I'm starting to think I'm meant to be a barista my entire life." I steal a glance at him, catching a glimpse of the intensity with which he's looking at me, and quickly look away, afraid that I've dumped too much on him.

He must notice my embarrassment because he responds with, "I'm sure something will come up soon. What are you majoring in?" There's a flicker of something behind his eyes when he asks me this, but it must just be a reflection from the moonlight.

"Architecture. I've applied to just about every architecture, design, and construction company around here just to try to get my foot in the door." I pause to think before continuing, "Well, except for the big ones that I know I'd probably just be wasting my time applying to."

"Which big companies?"

"The obvious, Callaway Designs, Rose City Designs, Kane Construction...what?" I stop listing companies when his smile grows tenfold. My stomach flutters at the sight. It's more radiant than I remember the first time I saw it.

"Kane Construction, you say?" he asks with a hint of amusement in his voice. I nod while waiting for his response.

With a laugh, Theo sticks out his hand. "I don't think I properly introduced myself. Theodore Kane, youngest brother to the owner and CEO of Kane Construction. It's a pleasure to meet you." He wiggles his hand like he's waiting for me to shake it, appearing to be very pleased with himself at this big revelation.

I grab his hand and give a tentative shake as I'm trying to wrap my mind around what he just told me. My efforts are stunted when I can't seem to take my mind away from the fact that his hand engulfs mine. When I try to pull away, he squeezes again just slightly, not enough to hurt but enough for me to take notice. Just like that, our hands are separated, and mine is suddenly cold from the absence of his touch.

"You know, I've been meaning to ask you something." He wags his finger at me as his eyes squint in concentration. The whole motion comes across a little wobbly, indicating he's had a few drinks tonight as well. Despite the alcohol running through both of us, I swear I can see the wheels turning in his head.

"You, Sienna...." He motions toward me as though he is trying to get me to say my last name.

"Parker," I confess.

He continues, "You, Sienna Parker, should be my girlfriend!"

"I should *what*?" I say the last word loud enough that it catches the attention of the group by the firepit. I move to stand out of their sight line, but being the klutz that I am, I step on a rock and fall toward the ground. Saving the day once again, he catches me. Grabbing hold of my waist, he puts his other hand on my shoulder to balance me.

Our lips within inches of each other, speaking only loud enough so the two of us can hear, he says, "Be my girlfriend." Not a question, a command.

There's a rush of heat low in my stomach at his low-timbre voice, and I push him away.

"I'm not sure where this is coming from, but how did we go from talking about plans after graduation to this?" Taking a few steps away from him, I put some distance between us.

His eyes grow wide then, and he scrunches up his

nose in a wince, "Oh shit, my *fake* girlfriend. I meant to say my fake girlfriend."

"Why do you need a fake girlfriend? What about the woman from the diner?" The second question comes out with more jealous undertones than I meant. I really need to find a way out of this conversation before I dig myself deeper.

"She's one of Matt's friends. No one to me. Why, jealous?" He smirks, and I immediately roll my eyes, trying to save face.

"Alright, I think it's time for me to go home. Happy I could stroke your ego, though." I turn to leave and feel his hand land on my elbow as he gently pulls me back to him.

"I'm sorry, this is all coming out wrong. Let me start over. I also don't have a job lined up for after graduation. My oldest brother is convinced I'm not mature enough to take on a position as his business partner. Long story short, I lied to him and told him I have a girlfriend in an effort to obtain a job offer."

Crossing my arms, I interrupt Theo. "So you lied to prove to your brother how mature you are?"

"It doesn't sound so good, does it? I thought I could move past it, but then he told me to bring my 'girlfriend' with me to our lake house this summer, and as long as he sees a change in me, he'll let me work at the family company starting in the fall." He winces, as if hearing how it sounds out loud for the first time.

"And this helps me how?" I ask, not seeing the point.

"Come with me," he says. "Be my fake girlfriend for the trip, help me convince my brother that I'm mature enough to work with him, and I can use his connections to get you a job starting in the fall."

My eyebrows shoot up. "Are you serious? You want *me* to be your fake girlfriend for the summer? We're practically strangers, and there's no way you can even guarantee a job for me."

"I wouldn't call us strangers. At minimum, we're acquaintances." He flashes another smile at me. "I don't think we're hiring anyone at Kane Construction, but my brother has strong connections with Rose City Designs. We could start there."

I stare at him, dumbfounded. Rose City Designs is my dream company. They are one of the top architecture and design companies in the entire nation. Their designs inspired my entire portfolio, from clean, modern lines to characteristic vintage details. I've written several papers about their buildings. I just never thought I'd get a chance with them so soon. They weren't factored into my plan until five years from now.

"Think about it. I get to prove to my brother that I'm mature enough, and you end the summer having had a fun vacation at a lake house and a job lined up. What do you say?"

"I say the chances of you being a serial killer are increasing by the second." I've watched too many crime documentaries to know there's no way I'm going to a lake house with a man I barely know who just hit me with his cart a week ago. Heart-melting smile or not, I won't be starring in the next crime documentary to go viral.

He chuckles, the sound taming my nerves in a way that I don't care to acknowledge.

"Sienna, I'm not going to murder you. Just think about it. I know I might be a little tipsy, but I actually think we could help each other here."

I humor him by nodding. Saying my goodbyes, I all but book it into the house to find Beth. Dragging her away from the blonde, with her all but kicking and screaming, I call a ride so we can get out of this party. This night has taken a turn for the strange, and I don't have any intention of humoring the universe any further.

On the ride home, I scroll through all of the rejection emails I've received over the past few months on my phone. There are a few more companies I'm hoping to hear back from. But with each rejection email I read through, Theo's proposition looks more promising by the second.

I shake the thought from my mind. No, there's no way I'm desperate enough to accept his offer. Something else will come up, I know it will.

7

SIENNA

Graduation has come and gone, and there is still no job offer in my inbox. I sit on my bed, staring at my degree sitting in the ridiculously large frame that cost almost as much as the degree itself. I've been led to believe that once I had this piece of paper in my hands, I'd feel a great sense of accomplishment, or purpose, or the sense that my real life could begin.

Instead, it serves as a reminder that I've fallen behind my peers. A reminder that my plan continues to fall apart with each passing day. Not being able to look at my name scrawled across the piece of paper any longer, I shove the frame underneath my pillow. If I can't see it, then maybe it will stop mocking me.

You always have Theo's offer to consider.

The voice in my head coos at me for the tenth time this week. He texted me after the party to let me know he'd need an answer after graduation, and it's already been a week since we walked across the stage. I hadn't crossed paths with him there since my parents dragged me out as soon as the ceremony ended to make our dinner reservations.

Every logical part of me screams not to accept his offer. But a small, annoying part urges me to take a chance. It's probably a lost cause anyway. I'm sure he's found someone else by now.

Sighing, I make my way back out to the living room. The sun shines through the sheer floral curtains draped across the large window. Beth lies in her reading chair, basking in the sunlight, frantically typing on her keyboard.

"Still hunting for a place for your bookshop?" I ask, grabbing my laptop from the coffee table and taking a seat on the couch.

Looking up from her screen, she throws her arms up. "Since when did Portland become so expensive?"

"Since always," I deadpan.

"Everywhere is either too small, or too expensive, or too small *and* too expensive." She throws her head back onto the armrest of the chair.

"You'll find a place. I'll help you look. I just need to check my inbox first."

Motioning to my laptop, she replies, "Please, one of us needs good news today."

Taking a deep breath, I open my laptop. My email tab is already open on the screen, seeing as how I've barely used my laptop for anything other than job searching the past few weeks. I stare at the three unopened emails sitting in my inbox. These are the last three companies

I've applied to. If they've rejected me, I officially have no other options.

That's not true, Sienna. There's still one option you've yet to consider.

I silence the voice in my head before clicking to open the first email.

Thank you for taking the time to apply with us.
We're sorry to inform you...

Fine. Not a big deal, considering their employee satisfaction rating was below 2.5 on all job-rating platforms.

We're sorry, but you have not been selected for an interview...

I feel a small ping in my chest. This one hurts a little more than the last. I had reached out to a former classmate of mine who had an internship there last year. She said she would put in a good word for me, but it must not have been enough.

Holding my breath, I click on the last email.

Thank you for your application. At this time, we've decided to focus on other candidates for this role...

Closing my laptop, I bury my face deep into the cushions of the couch.

"On second thought, who needs good news anyway? Bad news just means we have an excuse for another movie night." Beth's voice comes through, muffled by the pillow I've hidden my face under.

Finally emerging, I prop my head up on the armrest of the couch. Looking at Beth, I say, "They all rejected me. I've officially run out of options to find a job in the one field I've studied for the past four years."

"Well..."

"Beth, no."

"You aren't *completely* out of options," she says, pointing out the one option I've been trying and failing to ignore for the past two weeks.

"Ah, yes. *The mysterious case of Sienna Parker: How a young woman went missing after she was stupid enough to follow a man she barely knew into the woods.* That'll make for great television." Sitting up, I make a show of my hands as though I'm unveiling the title of the future crime documentary featuring myself.

"A little exaggerated, don't you think?"

Ignoring her comment, I respond, "How about I just work at your bookstore instead? You'll be opening it soon anyway."

"Sienna, I still haven't even found a spot for my bookstore yet, and when I do open, I'll only be able to afford to pay myself a salary of frozen meals and water." Giving me a stern look, she says, "Call him."

"There's no point. I'm sure he's already found someone else anyway. And there's still no guarantee that going along with his plan will result in me being employed."

"You have no other choice, babe. You've gotta call him.

He's a Kane, and he has huge connections within the architecture industry." She pauses for a second before continuing, "Not to mention, a little fun in the sun could do you some good. If you wind up any tighter, I'm afraid you're going to snap, and I certainly don't want a documentary with my name in the title."

Pulling out her phone, she makes a show of waving it at me.

Chuckling, I pull up Theo's contact on my phone, her comment giving me an idea. "Fine. I'll call him. But you have to go with me."

"Uh, what now?" she asks, perplexed.

"I'll call Theo and agree to go to his lake house with him, but you have to go with me. That way, if he does turn out to be a murderer, he'll have to kill both of us, and we'll either die together or be trauma-bonded for life." I stick my nose a little higher, asserting the fact that I'm dead serious, no pun intended.

"I don't even have a place picked out for my bookshop yet. I need to continue searching for places. I have my logo to design, I need to look into setting up my business license—"

I lift my hand. "Well then, it sounds like you could use some 'fun in the sun' as well," I say, throwing her own words back at her.

Her eyes squint, and she's silent for a moment before she finally responds, "Fine, I'll go with. Just call him already."

Before I give myself a moment to hesitate and inevitably change my mind, I hit the Call button. The sound of ringing on the other line fades into white noise as I anxiously await his answer.

If we're going to do this, we will need a set of ground rules. There's no way in hell this will turn out like one of Beth's romance books. I need to end the summer having obtained an offer letter, not a boyfriend.

8

THEO

I'm lying on my bed, scrolling through my phone when Sienna's name pops up on the screen. I'm surprised she's calling me, given how I proposed the fake-dating scheme to her. When I first had the idea to ask Sienna to be my fake girlfriend, I hadn't exactly planned on drunkenly blurting out the idea to her.

Tapping the Accept button, I answer, "Hey, I was beginning to think I'd never hear from you again."

"Alright, I'll do it."

"Sorry, do what?" I know I'm playing with fire here, but I can't help but mess with her just a little.

"I'll be your girlfriend, uh, your fake girlfriend, I mean."

A smile slowly spreads across my face at her acceptance.

"Perfect, I think you're really going to like the lake house. It's—"

"Okay, look, if we are going to do this, we need some ground rules. And I have a ton of questions that need answers." My smile grows at her businesslike tone. She's cute when she gets serious about something.

At that revelation, I realize she's right. We will definitely need some boundaries in place if I'm having thoughts like that.

"Rules, hmm. Okay, let's hear them." Sitting up on my bed, an involuntary grunt slips from my lips.

"Is this a bad time?" Sienna asks.

"Not at all, just a little sore from the gym yesterday. So let's hear those rules."

There's a slight hesitation to her voice when she responds, "Okay, here's the deal, we need to keep things professional. Treat this like a business transaction. While we might appear to be dating in public, we need to be nothing but mere acquaintances in private."

"Sounds like a plan, boss." I try my best to match her professional tone, but it comes across as flirtatious.

"Okay, that right there, rule number one, no flirting unless we are in front of your family. And even then, we need to keep things light."

Unable to help myself, I try to lighten her tone a tad by responding, "Aw, but flirting with you is so fun."

"Theo, I'm serious. Actually, you know what? Never mind. If you aren't going to take this seriously, I don't think I can help you. Good luck finding another woman to agree to your plan." She responds with growing agitation in her voice, and I realize I've let the conversation get away from me.

"Sienna, wait, I'm just messing around. Seriously, thank you for helping me. I assure you I will help you get a job before the end of the summer. Besides, I think you'll have a lot of fun with my brothers and me." That came out creepier than I intended. For some reason, my usual charm keeps morphing into assholery whenever I'm around Sienna.

"Wait, exactly how many brothers do you have?" She's silent on the other line as she waits for my response.

"I have three older brothers—Alex, Leo, and Roman. I guess I should've mentioned that previously, huh?"

She chuckles, and I relax at the sound of her loosening up just slightly, "Probably would've been a good idea. But it's okay because rule number two is that Beth is coming with me. If she can't come, then no deal."

"The more, the merrier. Whatever you need." I try not to get stuck on how serious I am when I say the last part.

Sienna continues listing her rules. Making sure to reiterate that if I have secret plans for any nefarious activities, I should remember how dangerous Beth was with a cereal box, and then envision the damage she could do with a real weapon. The thought makes me laugh, but I'm smart enough to know she isn't kidding.

The next rules she lists out are as follows: No sharing a bed, she will be sharing a room with Beth. Only minimal touching will be allowed, focusing on our hands and arms only. Absolutely no kissing. Her final rule is that she can add additional rules at any point during the trip.

Without hesitation, I agree to each of her rules. If she wants to treat this as a business transaction, I will consider it practice for when I finally take a position at Kane Construction.

"I'll be sure to text you all of the details, but we'll leave the Sunday after the Fourth of July."

"Great. Two weeks is plenty of time for me to get packed. I'll wait for your text."

Before she hangs up, I stop her. "Sienna, one more thing before you go. I have another rule to add."

"Okay, shoot," she says.

"No falling in love with me." It's an obvious rule, maybe, but one I feel should be said out loud. Although maybe it's less so for her and more for me.

"Ugh, just text me the details." She hangs up, and my pulse instantly escalates at the thought of visiting the lake house this year.

I just hope my plan actually works. For both of us.

9
SIENNA

E leven days until the lake house.

SIENNA

What kind of activities can I expect?
Casual summer attire okay?

THEO

Yes and also activewear, a bathing suit,
and something you can get dirty ☺

Seven days until the lake house.

THEO

Been thinking.

Wouldn't make sense if we drove
separately. We can take my car.

SIENNA

Sounds good. Give us time to go over
our backstory.

> Remember, Beth and I will be armed and dangerous.

THEO

You sure you aren't the serial killer?

SIENNA

> Highly unlikely. Only one in six serial killers are presumably women.

THEO

Idk. You don't seem like the type of woman who'd let a statistic define what she's capable of.

Three days until the lake house.

THEO

Do you have any allergies? Leo wants to know. He usually does most of the cooking.

SIENNA

> No allergies but Beth cannot stomach fish.

THEO

Leo will hate that lol.

Alex will be happy he doesn't have to eat fish this year, though.

Zero days until the lake house.

THEO

Here. I'm in the Mustang out front.

Theo and I have been texting for the past couple of weeks leading up to our departure for the lake house.

You'd think it would have done something to ease my nerves, but my stomach churns as I read his text.

"You ready?" Beth asks as we stand in the entryway of our apartment. I nod, gripping my suitcase handle tighter than necessary before we head out the door.

Stepping out into the parking lot, I see Theo leaning against the side of a dark blue Mustang with one of those double white racing stripes down the center. As if my stomach wasn't wrecked enough already, the sensation of butterflies fluttering around overwhelms me when I lay eyes on him.

He's dressed casually, in a loose-fitting T-shirt, linen shorts that hit just above the knee, crew socks, and sneakers. Nothing too noteworthy other than the fact that Theo makes the outfit look remarkable. His chest muscles flex beneath the shirt, the loose fit doing nothing to hide them. The hemline of his shorts shows off the definition of his thighs, and his shirt is a shade of green that makes his eyes glow in the sunlight.

The logical part of me screams to turn around, go back upstairs, and start applying for every job I see. The other part of me, the one I'm hell-bent on ignoring, wonders what his abs look like and prays the wind picks up his shirt so I can catch a glimpse.

"You like what you see?"

My eyes snap to Theo's when he asks the question. I'm immediately embarrassed that I've clearly been staring at his body for way too long.

When I don't respond, Theo clarifies with a chuckle. "The car." He motions to the Mustang he's leaning against. "It's a 2009 Mustang GT. Just got this baby. What do you think?"

A sigh of relief escapes my lips. "It's nice, but will we all fit?"

Theo glances down at our bags. I have a respectable, medium-sized suitcase, and Beth stands next to me with the same, along with her backpack and gym bag. She doesn't plan to go to the gym. She's only bringing the bag because she ran out of room for all her shoes.

Moving to grab our bags, Theo says, "We'll be fine. As long as one of you doesn't mind taking the back seat."

"I don't mind," Beth says before I can volunteer, "as long as you have AC."

"Oh, for sure." Theo smiles at Beth, closing the trunk after just barely fitting our bags in next to his. As Theo helps Beth into the back seat, I silently scold myself for the way my teeth clench when he smiles at her.

Once we are all in our respective seats, Theo turns to us. "Buckle up, we've got a two-hour drive ahead of us."

When the engine roars to life, I double-check that my seat belt is buckled. Tightening the seat belt as far as it can go across my lap, Theo must notice out of the corner of his eye because he begins to laugh.

Quiet enough for only us to hear in the front seat, he says in a low voice, "Don't worry, I'm an excellent driver."

"I'll be the judge of that, thank you." My response prompts his smile to grow wider, and I look out the window to avoid blushing any more than I already have.

Something tells me this is going to be a long car ride.

Forty minutes into the drive and Beth is passed out against the window. She never makes it through a long car ride without falling asleep in the first hour. Reaching back, I carefully take her book from her hands and mark her page with her bookmark. I'm sure to slip the book into her backpack for safekeeping.

When I bring my attention forward, I notice Theo smiling at me.

"How long have you two been friends?" he asks.

"Since kindergarten."

This is good. We need to focus on getting our story straight, and I could use some conversation to make this car ride go faster.

R&B music has been playing softly throughout the car, and at one point, I rolled down the window for some fresh air. Other than the music and the sound of the freeway, the silence has been suffocating.

"I have a friend like that, Jessie. I've known him since preschool. Our moms were best friends," Theo replies.

"Were?" I chuckle at his past-tense phrasing.

"Yeah." He pauses. "My parents died when I was six. It's just been my brothers and me since then. Well, and Jessie's parents helped out here and there too."

I feel like an absolute ass for asking. "I'm so sorry, I had no idea."

My hand touches his shoulder, and when he glances at our connection, I quickly pull away, worried that I've crossed a line.

"It's alright. That's what this car ride is for, isn't it? So we can get to know the basics?" I relax when he throws a grin my way.

My phone buzzes, and I force my attention away from Theo to check the incoming message.

DAD

Hey, Pumpkin, I hope you and Beth have so much fun at the lake house! Text when you get there. So proud of you for taking some time off and relaxing. Love you!

SIENNA

Thanks, love you too! Text you when we get there.

Wincing, I send the text message, then put my phone away to avoid any further communication from my parents for the rest of the car ride.

"My music choice isn't that bad, is it?" Theo asks.

"What? Oh no. It's not that." I pause, not sure if I should continue to complain about my very minimal issues with my parents after he just told me his have passed.

He continues the conversation when I stay silent. "Then what is it? Like I said, we have to get to know each other a little bit to make this work."

Sighing, I confess, "I sort of told my parents that Beth and I were renting a lake house with some other girl-friends for the next two weeks instead of telling them the truth."

He raises an eyebrow. "I take it you're not the type to lie to your parents?"

I hide my face in my hands. "No, never. My dad has begged me to take a break from job-hunting and use this summer to relax. He thinks that's what I'm doing when I will in fact be doing the opposite."

"Well, look at it this way. Yes, your main focus is to get a job, but there will still be plenty of time to relax over the next two weeks. So it's only a half lie if you really think about it."

I smile at his attempt to cheer me up. It's sweet that he would care about my feelings enough to do so. But then again, he's probably just doing it so I'm not in a weird mood when I meet his brothers for the first time. He's also getting something out of this deal after all.

A moment of silence spreads between us. Looking at Theo, another wave of envy washes over me as I wish I could be as relaxed as he is right now. His elbow rests on the window, and his hand keeps the steering wheel in place. His other hand reaches for his sports drink in the cup holder, and I watch as he brings it to his lips and takes a swig.

His throat bobs as he swallows, and the veins running down his hands and up his forearms flex under his skin as he lifts the bottle. Setting the drink back in the cupholder, the sun reflects off his lips as his tongue darts out to catch the remaining liquid lingering there.

My body heats as I watch the display, and I adjust the air vent so it's pointed directly at me.

Trying to regain focus on the task at hand, I say, "So tell me about your brothers."

"Let's see. Alex is only a few years older than me. He owns a boxing gym downtown and is by far the most competitive. We all think it has something to do with the fact that he's only around six foot, and the rest of us tend to tower over him." He smirks as though he's reminiscing about the many times he's teased his brother about his height.

Unable to stop myself, I ask, "And how tall are you exactly?"

He straightens in his seat a little as though he is trying to rise to his full height. "I'm six foot five. Why? Does height matter to you, Angel?"

"What's with the nickname all of a sudden?"

"I have to call you something, don't I? What would you prefer, sweetheart? Baby? Lovebug?" Another flash of that perfect smile, and I swear I melt a little in my seat. With summer now in full swing, I blame it on the heat and move on.

Visibly making a show of gagging at the last nickname he throws out, I respond, "God, no. I'm not sure I need a nickname. Just call me Sienna." I punctuate my sentence with a slight nod.

"Whatever you want, Angel." Theo winks, and I roll my eyes at his blatant disregard of my request. Although I can't say I'm too mad about his choice of nickname for me.

"You were telling me about your brothers," I say, motioning for him to continue what he was previously saying before the conversation got sidetracked.

"Right. The next oldest is Leo. He's a chef at some fancy restaurant that I can't pronounce the name of. But he's damn good at what he does, and he always cooks for us on these trips. That is, when he's not too busy antagonizing Alex."

"Do you take these trips often?"

He nods. "We took our first trip when I was eight

years old. It has become an annual summer tradition since then."

I suppress my giggle at the concept of four grown men having a summer vacation tradition. But I lean toward Theo as he continues, finding his words more interesting than I had expected.

"A few years back, Leo brought his boyfriend with him. He ended up saying some stupid shit about his cooking, and we immediately kicked the fucker out of the house. Leo hated us at the moment, but thanked us a few weeks later. We had to do the same with one of his girlfriends once, when he showed us a snippet of a song he composed on the piano, and she was looking at her phone the entire time. He hasn't brought anyone with him since."

"Sounds like you're a hard group to please," I say, my heart rate picking up at the thought of his brothers not accepting me.

"Not really. I just think we're all a little protective of Leo. Not sure any of us think there's a person out there good enough for him."

Theo lets out a laugh, and I join in, as I watch him watch the road in front of him. My smile doesn't fade as he continues.

"Then you know Roman. Or at least, you know of him. He can be a stubborn asshole sometimes. He's thirteen years older than me and basically raised my brothers and me when our parents died. We usually get along, but sometimes, we have our differences." He shrugs.

I must have the one question I've been waiting to ask

written all over my face because he looks at me and says softly, "You can ask. It's okay."

His small, reassuring smile is all I need to ask, "And your parents? Anything I should know about them?"

Theo shrugs. "I don't remember them too much, but I've seen photos. High school sweethearts, had Roman the year following graduation, then had the rest of us in later years. My dad started Kane Construction. One of the many things Roman and I disagree on. He likes to call it 'his' company, but it's the family company, even if Roman is the CEO. He's done great, but I still think there's room for growth. That's why I'm trying to convince him to take me on as a business partner. To help the business grow to its full potential, you know?" His slight change of subject from dead parents to work tells me that I shouldn't ask how his parents died. That's not a sore spot I want to poke, and not one I need to. If this drive is solely to learn more about each other, then all we need to learn is the basics.

Nodding, I respond, "I have a strict ten-year plan that relies on me getting a job by the end of this summer. Not exactly the same as your situation, but I get the feeling of wanting more than what's already in front of you."

"Exactly. Sometimes I feel like I'm falling behind my brothers and I'll never catch up."

"I understand the feeling. My parents married and had me young too. I'm not sure they realize how much they've settled on due to a lack of planning. I refuse to settle for anything less than my dream life, which is why I'm so strict about my plan."

"And what is your dream life, Sienna Parker?" He

glances my way, prompting me to look at the road ahead of us.

"Travel, seasonal clothing, not something off the sales rack, a new car, that sort of thing. I just want a life that doesn't require me to check my bank account every time I make a purchase, no matter how small. It gets exhausting after a while."

Theo nods his agreement. "Sounds like a nice life you've got planned."

I smile softly at him, "Thank you. I know I'm technically helping you here, but I appreciate you helping me get a job in return. I'm not sure I could take another rejection letter."

"Well, anyone who rejects you is a certified idiot in my eyes." As he responds, he places his hand on my knee, not an intrusion, but as reassurance.

The rough callouses on his hands graze against the top of my bare knee. I mentally send Beth a thank you for suggesting I wear shorts for the road trip. Heat begins to pool in my lower stomach, and a chill is shot up my spine when his thumb lightly brushes across my skin.

When I look up from our connection, our eyes lock, and his hand jolts away from my knee, snapping back to the steering wheel. Both hands are now in a tense 10 and 2 position. Beth begins to wake up from her nap and says she needs to stop for a bathroom break.

"There's a stop only ten minutes from here," Theo tells Beth.

Theo's hands haven't budged from the wheel, his knuckles turning white from his grip. Neither one of us says a word for the remainder of the drive.

10

SIENNA

I'm relieved when we finally pull up to the lake house. Since Theo's hand left my knee, the air in the Mustang has been cold, and it's not just because of the AC.

As we drive down the long, winding road into the driveway, I take in the stunning views of the house and the lake behind it. Given that Theo had said it's been here since he was at least six years old, I wasn't expecting something so grand. It's dated, sure, with older stone and traditional lines used on the pillars in the entryway, but it's gorgeous. The dark tones of the wood contrast with the evergreens surrounding the lake.

After parking, Theo gets out of the car as I help Beth out of the back seat, both of us fighting the front seat as she squeezes through the opening. Once out, we stretch our limbs, looking around the side of the house to steal a view of the lake. The late afternoon sun reflects off the deep blue water, making it sparkle. As birds fly across, they just barely tap the water as they go. In the far distance, the trees perfectly frame the snowy peaks of Mount Hood. The summer wind blows, ruffling my T-shirt as I take a deep breath of the fresh air.

If I refuse to take one thing for granted, it's the air quality of the Pacific Northwest. That, and our tap water.

"Theo, it's been too long." A man slightly shorter than Theo approaches, holding his arms out. He wraps them around Theo's shoulders, and Theo lets out a laugh.

"We saw each other a few months ago. It hasn't been that long." Theo rolls his eyes.

Waiting for an introduction, but not wanting to intrude on their catching up, I move to help Beth grab the bags from the trunk of the car. The trunk is empty once she pulls her bags out, and I look around for mine. Looking down, I see my bag by Theo's feet, next to his. He must have grabbed it when he first got out of the car.

Turning to me, Theo wraps his arm around the man's shoulders. "This is my brother Leonardo. Leonardo, this is Sienna, my girlfriend. And her friend Beth." He gestures to both of us, and I accept Leo's offering to shake my hand.

"It's nice to finally meet you. I've heard so much about you," he says with a smile almost as heart-stopping as Theo's.

"You're too kind. It's nice to meet you, Leonardo," I respond. I have to suppress a laugh at his politeness, considering I know there's no way he could have heard that much about me.

"Please, it's just Leo. Theodore here likes to use my full name just to fuck with me." He wraps his arm around Theo's neck and pulls him into a playful chokehold. It's when he decides to rough up Theo's hair a little bit that I decide I quite like Leo.

While Beth and Leo make their introductions, I notice the classic green Mustang parked next to Theo's. Considering it's the only other car on the lot, I'd assume it's Leo's. It seems fitting given his appearance. Medium brown hair with a small amount of wave, similar to Theo's, but chopped a little shorter. A loose light blue button-down T-shirt that brings out the blue of his irises, and tan shorts slightly shorter than Theo's. With his toned but slimmer build, clean shave, and dashing smile, he looks very fitting for his Mustang.

I'm analyzing Leo's outfit when fingers brush the inside of my wrist. My eyes are pulled to Theo, who has gently wrapped his hand around my wrist to get my attention. He opens his mouth to say something, but a loud noise cuts through the air before he gets the chance.

A high-pitched whine abuses my ears as the sound travels down to the lake from atop the winding road. Beth and I are quick to cover our ears as the noise grows louder.

When we see a red blur come into view, Beth yells over the noise, "Is that a car? How could anyone drive a car that sounds like that?"

I look at Theo and Leo to make sure they aren't offended by Beth's unfiltered question. Judging by the two Mustangs sitting in the driveway and what I can now see is a red Mustang headed toward us, I'd assume this is a family hobby. Not sure how easily I can secure a job if we offend the guys on day one.

To my relief, Theo and Leo are laughing, quite hysterically, at Beth's comment.

"That's Alex for you," Theo says, shrugging.

As if right on cue, the whining, bright red Mustang pulls into the driveway right behind Leo's green Mustang. Something resembling a WWE belt hangs out of the driver's side window as music blares through the open windows of the car. The bass is turned up so high that I can't make out the song.

Alex pops out of the driver's side window, his body half hanging out of the car as the music continues to play.

He raises the belt above his head, yelling, "Ready to lose to me again this year, motherfuckers?"

Without a second thought, Theo and Leo move toward Alex in an ambush, yanking him out of the car through the open window. Tackling Alex to the ground, they wrestle the belt away from him. Theo begins walking toward us with the belt, but not before Alex catches up to him. He catches Theo off guard and wrestles the belt back from him. They walk over to us, Alex with Theo in a headlock, the belt hanging over his shoulder.

Leo yells from the driver's side of Alex's car, "You two enjoy the feel of the belt in your hands while you have it 'cause I'll be the one going home with it this year."

I note that Leo hangs back to ensure the red Mustang is properly in Park and the keys are removed from the ignition. My ears thank him when the thumping bass finally stops.

"In your dreams!" Alex says to Leo over his shoulder.

Still holding Theo with one arm, Alex sticks a

tattooed hand out toward me, and I tentatively take it. When Theo had said Alex was shorter than the rest of them, I wasn't expecting him to tower over me as much as he does.

Theo finally pushes free of Alex. Standing, he adjusts his clothing as he introduces us. "Alex, this is Sienna, my girlfriend."

"It's nice to meet you," I say to Alex.

Compared to Theo and Leo, Alex has a darker, more chaotic presence. His hair is a shade darker brunette than the other two, with no waves to be seen. Despite the sun shining down on us, he's in dark clothing. A loose-fitting T-shirt in a distressed dark gray with a red logo I can't quite make out scrawled across the front of it.

He smiles, and while it's reminiscent of Theo's smile, Alex's has a hint of danger I find slightly off-putting. Unfortunately for Beth, he's her type to a T.

Given Beth is only five-foot-one, he has to lean down slightly when he offers her his hand to shake.

"And you are?" As Beth takes his hand, he adds, "Single, I hope."

Smooth, but if I know Beth...

"Annoyed with your shitty-sounding car, nice to meet you," Beth responds, shaking his hand firm and only once, then letting go. I hear Theo snicker beside me.

Alex smirks at her response. When their eyes lock on each other, refusing to break contact, I step in. Beth did say she's sworn off men after all, and I don't need Alex complicating my chances at securing a job.

"Beth. Her name is Beth." I smile and wrap my arm

around Beth's shoulders. I squeeze her slightly, hoping she'll get the hint from me to play nice.

"It's nice to meet both of you." His smile is devilish in a way that makes me wonder where Theo stands on the spectrum of sweet and dangerous, where Leo and Alex seem to be on opposite ends.

Alex looks at Leo. "Where the hell is Roman?" I can't help but wonder the same thing as he is the reason I'm here in the first place.

"He's at the grocery store. I was prepping for dinner and realized I needed a few things. He should be back soon. We can head in and wait for him. I made a few appetizers to hold us over until dinner is ready."

Alex and Leo start to turn toward the front door of the lake house when Alex stops in front of Theo's Mustang.

"Whose car is this?" Alex continues to stare at the Mustang in front of him.

"It's mine," Theo answers, a touch of pride in his voice. "It's the 2009 GT."

Alex looks at Theo then. "You didn't." I can't say for certain, but I catch almost the faintest glimmer of disappointment flash across Alex's face.

"What? I couldn't afford the Cobra like you have. Plus, this is the same—"

"We know what it is, Theo," Leo says, with a slight bite to his voice.

"Roman's gonna kill you, man." Alex pats Theo on the shoulder, then walks off into the house with Leo.

The prideful look on Theo's face falters at his brother's commentary. I feel a strong urge to reach out and comfort him, but I resist.

Without thinking, I ask, "What was that about?"

"It's nothing. Come on, let's get inside. I'm not sure about you, but I'm starving."

His smile has returned, but the light in his eyes remains dim. I'm so caught up in thoughts of how to make Theo feel better that I almost miss it when Beth brings up an important question.

"So is anyone going to explain the giant-ass belt he's carrying?" Beth asks Theo, pointing at Alex.

Theo's face lights up. "Oh, did I forget to mention that? Come on, I'll tell you all about it inside." Grabbing our bags, he takes off toward the front door.

Beth and I exchange a fearful look, questioning what we just got ourselves into.

11

SIENNA

"So basically the Summer Olympics, but the family version?" I ask, popping a grape into my mouth that I took from the charcuterie board Leo had made.

The design of fruits, cheeses, crackers, and various proteins is stunning. I never knew snack food could be presented so well. If this is any indication of how good a chef Leo is, then at least I know I have one thing to look forward to on this trip.

I'm sitting at the kitchen island when I ask Theo and Alex the question. I check on Beth by stealing a glance her way from where she sits at the dining table with Leo. They both checked out after the basics of the summer games were explained and are now talking about some actor they both love.

When I turn my attention back to the two men standing next to the island, I can't help but notice I'm not the only one stealing glances at Beth. Alex looks completely lost in what Beth is saying, an expression on his face that I can't quite make out.

Deciding to ignore Alex for now, I turn my attention to Theo, whose smile grows wider when our eyes meet.

"Something like that. We've always called it the Kane Family Games." I chuckle at the name, and he responds, "Laugh all you want, but we thought it was pretty clever when we were kids."

I throw my hands up to feign innocence, as Theo laughs. "I didn't say anything. Who's won the most times?"

"Me, obviously," Alex claims as he shifts his attention to me, though he can't help but steal another glance in Beth's direction.

Alex continues, "Roman started taking us here after our parents died. A couple of years into the tradition, we came up with the Kane Family Games. Nothing like a little summer fun to drown out the fact you're orphans," he says with a sarcastic smile. I look at Theo, my eyes widening slightly at Alex's response to my question.

He waves Alex off. "Don't mind him, he tends to have a dark sense of humor compared to the rest of us. We've fine-tuned the games over the years, but you'll be happy to know I've won plenty of times. I even plan on winning this year." He places his fists on his hips and puffs out his chest as though he's some kind of superhero. My giggle dies off when I notice just how muscular and defined he is. His loose-fitting shirt isn't doing much to hide the dips and grooves of his triceps when he flexes.

I'm the one who set the rules, so I really shouldn't be

thinking about whether he's strong enough to lift me, what he looks like naked, or how he might taste…

Busying myself in hopes of getting rid of the distracting thoughts, I look around the house. The wood floors flow throughout the open concept downstairs. They have that classic orange tint to them that was popular twenty years ago.

Alex moves to grab a glass from one of the brown wood cabinets to the right of the stove. I watch as he fills it with water from the fridge and comes back to join Theo and me as he sets the glass down on the white stone countertop.

He's still stealing glances at Beth, who sits in the dining space to the left of the kitchen. The evening summer sun shines through the large window just behind the dining table that seats six. Looking past Leo and Beth, I catch a glimpse of the lake, wondering how long it'll be before I can dip my toes into the cold water.

The large deck is furnished with plush outdoor seating. Accessible through a door just to the left of the dining space, I have no doubt that's where Beth will be spending the majority of her time. Curled up with a book, of course.

To my right is the living room, complete with a sectional so large it takes up most of the room. The dark brown linen couch complements the large brick fireplace. In true bachelor pad fashion, there is, what I would guess, a seventy-five-inch TV hanging above the mantel.

With the warm features, dark furniture, and black accents, there's barely any touch of a woman here. Except for the photo wall near the entryway to the right of the fireplace. The photos cascade all the way up the staircase wall. I'm trying to make out what the pictures are of when the front door swings open.

"Whose fucking blue Mustang is that?" I see the man standing in the entryway before his low-timbre voice registers in my mind.

It wouldn't be an inaccuracy to say this man is attractive. Many would probably call him so, but I'd describe him as intimidating upon first glance. He's about as tall as Theo and seems to get bigger the closer he approaches the kitchen. His biceps flex against the fabric of his shirt as the many grocery bags he's lined on his arms swing with each step. His jawline looks as though it could cut diamonds in half, and his sheer presence has me inadvertently holding my breath.

Setting the bags on the counter next to the stove, across from the island, he turns and meets Theo with a scowl so intimidating that it has me wondering if he's always this grumpy or if something happened between them in the past thirty seconds that I missed.

I lean a little closer to Theo in the presence of the man who I can only assume is Roman. With my proximity to Theo, his scent invades my senses, and I'm intoxicated by the smell of fresh laundry, citrus, and something reminiscent of a summer ocean breeze.

"It's Theo's," Alex says with a mischievous smile, pointing at Theo, before taking a handful of meat from the counter and moving to the opposite side of the island.

"Where the fuck did you get the money for it?" I sit there quietly as Roman questions Theo on his choice of vehicle. Even though I don't think a Mustang is the most responsible of car choices for the Pacific Northwest, I still find myself wanting to defend Theo. But I decide it's not my place as his fake girlfriend, so I keep my mouth shut.

Theo ignores Roman's clearly disgruntled mood and responds, "I had some money left over from my college fund. It's secondhand, nothing like the price of what *your* Mustang costs." Roman has one too? Damn, they must really love Mustangs.

Roman's jaw ticks, and his eyes dart toward me before he responds, "We can continue this conversation later when we don't have company."

Turning his full attention to me, Roman holds out his right hand, smiling softly. "Hi, I'm Roman. I hope my brothers have treated you and your friend respectfully while I've been away." He nods to Beth before side-eyeing Alex. The gesture makes Alex slap a hand against his chest in a "why are you looking at me" gesture.

I shake Roman's hand and respond with a smile. "Sienna. It's nice to meet you. They've been perfect gentlemen." Impressing Roman is first on my to-do list for this trip.

A familiar snort-laugh comes from my left. "Speak for yourself. What's with that one's Mustang?" Beth has joined us at the counter while Leo has begun unpacking the groceries. Beth points in the direction of Alex across the island from her. "It sounds like there's an animal trapped under the hood and he's torturing it every time he revs the engine." This gets a half chuckle from Roman, and for once, I'm envious of Beth for being charismatic in a way I feel I never could be.

"It would explain the color he chose, wouldn't it?" Roman says, leaning in toward Beth as though it's a conversation only for their ears. Great, while she's buddying up to every single one of these men, I can't seem to get more than a polite smile out of Roman. So much for my good impression.

"Clearly, you two don't know what a supercharger is," Alex says, in retaliation.

"Don't worry, I know what one is, and I have the better one." Roman throws a smirk toward Alex before turning his back on the group to help Leo finish unpacking the groceries. He gives Leo a small pat on the back as though he's saying hello. I can't help but notice the stark difference in how Roman greets each of his brothers.

Once the groceries are put away, Leo kicks everyone out of the kitchen. But not before double-checking that Beth and I don't have any food allergies. I appreciate his thoughtfulness as we move back toward the entryway to collect our bags. Classical music begins to play from the kitchen when Leo turns on a portable speaker, and I take a moment to savor the peace it brings.

"So," says that deep, grumpy voice from behind me, "why don't I show you to your rooms? Theo has never brought a woman home before. I'm excited you're here." His words contradict his less-than-enthusiastic tone. If I knew any better, I'd say his voice held a hint of suspicion.

In an effort to counteract whatever I'm picking up in Roman's tone, I grab Theo's hand in mine. "I'm very excited to be here as well. It was nice of you to let Beth and me tag along. We appreciate the hospitality." I flash a warm smile at him, hoping that I've convinced him that this is real. Roman just meets me with a scowl that would burn through my eyeballs if he could wield lasers through his.

After what feels like an eternity, he finally responds, "You're welcome. Follow me. Your rooms are just up here."

I go to follow him and realize I'm still holding Theo's hand. Letting go so we can grab our bags, Theo playfully knocks my hand out of the way when I go to reach for mine. Roman grabs Beth's bags from her at the same time. Beth and I follow the men upstairs as I shake my hand slightly in an effort to expel the lingering sensation of Theo's hand in mine.

As we ascend the stairs, I make the effort to look at the many photos on the wall. Most of them are four young boys, who I'd assume are the Kane brothers. One photo of a young Roman, in particular, catches my eye. He stands tall behind three much younger versions of Leo, Alex, and Theo. Judging by their apparent ages, I'd guess this was just before their parents passed.

They're all making a silly face with the exception of Roman. His smile is radiant as it resembles the ones I've seen from his brothers today. I can't help but notice the photo looks cut off on the edges, with what appears to be a woman's hand on Romans' chest, yet no woman is in the photo.

I continue up the stairs, hoping Roman's grumpy mood will fade as the days go by, morphing into something like what I saw in the family photo. A smiling Roman seems like an easier one to convince to help me get a job than the grumpy one I've had to introduce myself to.

Upstairs is a small hallway with six doors and what looks to be another staircase leading down toward the back of the house.

"How many bedrooms does this place have? It's gorgeous, by the way," I say.

Theo chimes in once we reach the top of the stairs, pointing at each door, "Five bedrooms total. At the end of the hallway is the main bedroom, Roman's. Then you have Alex and Leo's rooms to the left. Their rooms have a connecting bathroom. And over here on the right, my room, then the guest room, and the shared bathroom is the last door at the end of the hall."

All I can think is thank God we don't have to share a bathroom with all of these men during our stay. We head in the direction of the guest bedroom. It's surprisingly light and airy, with cream bedding, a large window on the far wall behind the bedframe, and a small beige chair with a footrest next to the bed. Beth throws herself down onto the plush comforter and begins searching through one of her smaller bags.

Reaching for my suitcase from Theo's hand, Roman stops me. "Beth, this is where you'll be staying. Sienna, I'm sure Theo would be more than happy to show you to his room." He gives Theo one hard pat on his shoulder.

"Oh, I don't mind staying with Beth. Honestly, this room looks so cozy." I reach for my bag again, but Roman stops me for a second time.

"Nonsense," Roman says, "the lake house can be quite romantic if you want it to be. Surely, you'd want to stay with your *boyfriend*." He puts a little extra emphasis on boyfriend, meeting me with a tone that's less than tasteful.

When Theo and I stay silent, Roman continues, "Unless there's a particular reason you two wouldn't want to share a room?" He looks between Theo and me. The rising panic inside me stalls slightly when Theo steps toward me.

"No, no reason. Sienna was just looking out for Beth. She's a sweetheart like that." I try to hide my wince at the stereotypical nickname he just used on me that we both agreed he would keep out of his vocabulary.

Roman looks at me to corroborate Theo's story. "Mm-hmm. Just wanted to make sure Beth is comfortable in a room by herself."

"She looks fine to me," Roman says, motioning his chin toward Beth. One look and I see Beth on the bed, already curled up in the pillows with her latest book in hand.

"Beth," Roman says to her, "you're good if Sienna sleeps with Theo, right?"

Beth waves her hand in a gesture telling us to get out of her newly claimed room. "Yeah, yeah, fuck whoever you want. Come and get me when dinner's ready."

My face heats at Beth's comment. To be fair, Roman did set her up for that one, and judging by the smirk on Roman's face, he's more than pleased with her response.

"She reads like Alex does," Roman says to Theo in a hushed tone almost too quiet for me to catch. "I'll be downstairs if you need me. Leo will call us when dinner's ready." Just like that, he takes off.

Theo guides me toward his room, just through the next door over from where Beth is staying. I linger in the doorway as I take it in. I can tell he's grown up in this room over the years.

The bed, no larger than a queen, is dressed with a plain dark-blue comforter and two matching pillows. A bay window to the left of the bed has a built-in bench decorated with blue-and-white-striped pillows. The room smells faintly of him, and I resist the urge to take a deep inhale.

I take a tentative step into the room as Theo sets our bags down on the bed. My attention focuses on the small desk to the right of the bed. It's cluttered with pens, pencils, and a toy airplane a cousin of mine used to have when we were kids. The sun reflects off a basketball trophy displayed on a nearby shelf, and I step closer, embarrassingly eager to read the year written on it.

"I used to play, but wasn't good enough for any college scholarships or anything," Theo says from the other side of the bed.

"That's surprising, given your height." I chuckle.

"You'd be surprised," he shrugs, "I wouldn't have wanted to go pro anyway."

"No?" I ask.

"No, there's not enough time to just chill out. I could never stick to that rigorous of a training schedule. I barely make it to half the training sessions Alex tries to put me through."

My mind flashes back to what's hidden beneath his shirt at that comment, and I look away from Theo, scared he can read my thoughts.

"I can always sleep on the floor if that would make you more comfortable," he says, looking at me tentatively.

My chest tightens when the realization hits me like a freight train. There's only one bed, and I'm going to have to share it with Theo. So much for not breaking any rules.

12

THEO

I can see the wheels in Sienna's mind turning as she stares at the single bed in the middle of my bedroom. She stays quiet, but the slight widening of her eyes and the lack of blinking tell me she's panicking on the inside. I should've known Roman was going to pull some shit like this. He might need more convincing than I originally thought.

The urge to rush to where she stands on the other side of the bed and ease her panic overwhelms me. But I'm cautious not to scare her away. We both need this arrangement to work in our favor. I feel like an idiot for not thinking through the sleeping arrangements, especially when it breaks one of her rules.

I instantly feel like an ass when my pulse kicks up at the thought of sleeping in the same bed as her.

Sienna continues to stare at the bed as I move tentatively toward her. "Sienna, if you want me to sleep on the floor, that's completely fine. Would that be more comfortable for you?" Now standing in front of her, I lean a little to obstruct her eyesight from fixating on the bed.

When she finally snaps out of it and looks my way, I let out a sigh of relief. For a second there, I thought she was going to make a run for it, and I'd never see her again.

"I won't make you sleep on the floor of your own home," she says, finally moving her body to push past me toward the bay window seat.

Pausing a moment before sitting down, I watch as she stares out at the lake. I might have the smallest room in the house, but there's no argument that I have the best view. As the late evening sun washes over her warm brown skin, I catch myself holding my breath. She looks as though she's glowing. She looks angelic.

Sitting down on the window seat, Sienna grips the edge like she might fall off any minute, and the motion pulls me away from my fleeting thoughts.

"I really don't mind. If it'll make you more comfortable, it's the least I can do." Walking toward her, I take a peek at the lake myself.

I'm still standing when she looks up at me, having to crane her neck to do so as I tower over her. The image of her on her knees in front of me flashes through my mind, and my cock twitches. Shaking it off, I take a seat next to her.

She's your fake *girlfriend, Theo. Get it together.*

"We're both adults. I'm sure we can handle sleeping in the same bed together." She juts up her nose a little bit as she says the words. I admire her attempt at confidence, though I can't help but notice how her voice wavers a bit as she talks.

Nodding my head, I respond, hoping to provide her some comfort that might ease her nerves. "If you change your mind at any point, let me know, and I'll make a bed on the floor. Or I might just curl up in this window seat." I pat the cushion underneath me.

Sienna laughs, my chest jolting at the sound. "Yeah, like you'd fit. You're practically a giant." Seeing the smile spread across her face and the sparkle in her eyes, I'm overcome with the insatiable urge to make her laugh again.

Bumping my shoulder playfully against hers, I say, "Thank you again for doing this. I know you're technically just using me to get a job"—she rolls her eyes at me, but I notice her smile doesn't fade—"but I appreciate you helping me out in the process."

"You're welcome. But I'm still keeping a close eye on you," she cocks an eyebrow. It's my turn to smile now.

"I thought we already established *you're* the one I have to worry about." Winking at her, I lean in slightly. The smell of summer strawberries and fresh salt water mixed with something so uniquely her invades my senses. I have to concentrate not to take a noticeably deep breath in her presence.

We break into laughter as she lightly shoves me out of her personal space. Any lingering tension breaks, and when the laughter dies off, I can't help it when my eyes dip toward her full lips. I grip the edge of the bench seat tighter, holding myself back from pulling her into my lap and kissing her until the sun sets.

We haven't even been here for a full twenty-four hours yet, and I've already broken several of her rules. I'm a good man, and I'll be damned if I break the no-kissing rule. That crosses a line I'm not sure we could come back from.

"Theo." My name is released from her lips in a soft warning. Despite my best efforts, my body leans closer to her of its own free will. It immediately makes me question how good a man I really am. For a split second, it looks as though she starts to lean in too when I hear a cough come from the doorway.

Sienna reels back. Standing up from the bench seat, she moves toward the bed. The air around me chills as she moves farther away.

Looking toward the door, I lay eyes on the fucker who scared Sienna away. Alex looks amused as he leans against the doorframe. I wasn't lying when I told Sienna I wasn't going to murder her. I said nothing about not murdering my brother.

"Theo, come help set the table, would you?" Alex's smug smile has my blood boiling. When his smile grows wider, I can tell he sees the anger written all over my face.

Sienna has busied herself by going through the items in her bags. Her back is toward me as she stands next to the bed, and I silently wish she would turn even slightly, so I can make out what she's thinking by the expression on her face.

"Sienna, do you—" I'm cut off when her cell phone rings.

She doesn't look in my direction when she says, "Sorry, it's my dad. I'll be down shortly."

Understanding she needs space, I head downstairs with Alex.

"So—" he says once we are out of earshot of Sienna.

"Don't say a fucking word," I snap. He looks at me with a shit-eating grin on his face that screams guilty as charged.

Joining my other brothers in the kitchen, I stay silent as I wrap my head around what just happened. I was seconds away from kissing Sienna before Alex interrupted us.

The distance from her helps me regain clarity. It doesn't matter how attractive I might find Sienna, if this plan is going to work, I need to follow her rules and keep my distance. Which means I can't be slipping up and almost kissing her. Or worse, actually kiss her.

Adding the finishing touches to the table, I make a mental note to build a wall of pillows between us tonight. The thought conjures an image of Sienna lying in my bed, her full lips slightly parted, dark waves spread out on the pillows as her back arches beneath me, causing her hardened nipples to graze my chest, flashes in my mind.

If only it were as simple to build a mental barrier as it is to build a physical one.

13

SIENNA

Sitting at the dining table, I'm surrounded by garlic and herb scents as I run my hand along the oak wood next to my plate. Just at the edge, a few small indents are forming a half circle. I smile at the realization that it's most likely a small bite mark from when they were kids.

"That's your boyfriend's doing," Leo says from my right at one head of the table. He motions his fork to Theo, who sits to my left. Hearing Theo referred to as my boyfriend kicks up my heart rate in a way that I'm quick to ignore.

My smile growing wider of its own free will, I whip my head to Theo, widening my eyes as a silent plea to hear more.

"You bit the table?" I ask when he doesn't immediately fess up.

"Hey, I only did it because that fucker told me to." He points at Alex, who is sitting across from him.

Taking a sip of his water, Alex smiles when he sets

his glass down. "I never told you to do it. I simply bet you twenty bucks that you couldn't bite a chunk out of the table." Roman chuckles from Theo's left, and I glance at Beth across from me, who looks as though she's holding back a smile as she watches Alex. When she catches me watching her, she averts her eyes, suddenly finding her plate more interesting than the conversation.

"Yeah, and I never got my money either," Theo says.

"To be fair, you didn't exactly take a bite," Leo says through a reminiscent laugh.

Theo smiles at his brother. "No, but I left a few marks. That's worth ten bucks at least."

"How old were you?" I ask Theo.

"Only nine, but Alex was twelve, so I'm still choosing to blame him." The laughter dies down a bit as everyone digs into their dinner.

Taking a bite, I resist the urge to moan from the flavors colliding in my mouth.

"This is delicious," I tell Leo. I'm hoping paying my compliments to the chef can win me some brownie points with Theo's brothers. He nods at me, giving his silent thanks.

Taking another bite, I attempt to savor every flavor. I never thought that something as simple as roasted chicken, potatoes, and vegetables could be so delicious. I've always been thankful I got my mom's cooking skills, not my dad's, since his food is barely edible. But I've never been able to cook something so simple that's packed with so much flavor.

Theo adjusts in his seat, and his scent fills my senses

when he leans close for a moment. I try to keep my focus on the food in front of me.

It's completely unfair that one man could smell this good. Having almost crossed a line with Theo earlier, I'm hesitant about how to proceed with our interactions moving forward. I have never been more thankful for a phone call from my parents. I had to take a moment to cool down from the sheer heat that radiated between Theo and me before making my way downstairs for dinner. Of course, the moment I locked eyes with him, the heat immediately returned.

I can feel it radiating from Theo now, and it's suffocating.

Trying to brush it off, I remind myself to stay focused. Securing a job by the end of this trip must be my sole focus. No way am I leaving this place without a job lined up. I have no time for distractions.

Even if the distraction comes with a smile as bright as the sun, a full head of lush hair, and a body that has me wanting to break every rule I made before agreeing to this trip in the first place.

"So, Sienna, where are you from?" The question comes from Leo.

"Portland, born and raised," I answer simply.

"Ah, a Pacific Northwest native like us." He makes a show of nudging me softly on the shoulder. "I knew I liked you."

I laugh with Leo, but the laughter dies down when I look at Theo. His jaw is tight as he watches Leo. I can't quite read the expression on his face, but I feel the need to comfort him. Copying his motions in the driveway earlier, I reach out my hand and place gentle fingers on his thigh.

Theo snaps his eyes away from Leo, instantly relaxing the tension in his jaw when they lock onto mine. Satisfied that he's relaxed again, I move my hand away and return my attention to my plate.

"So how'd you two meet?" Alex says before taking a bite of his potatoes. Another glance at Theo, and he's now glaring at Alex. I look at Beth, who stares at me wide-eyed.

When neither Theo nor I respond, Roman turns his attention toward Theo. "Well, where did you two meet? I'd love to hear the story of how my little brother met the woman who has been such a great influence on him." He punctuates the sentence with a smile so devious it makes my stomach churn.

"We met at—"

"There was a—"

Theo and I speak at the same time, both stopping when we realize we have no story to tell. Looking toward each other, Theo's eyes lock on mine. He must sense the panic in them because he places a gentle hand on my knee under the table, then turns his attention back to Roman.

"We met through Beth, actually. I had one of my business classes with her during the fall semester. We ended up at the same party, she brought Sienna with her, introduced us, and the rest is history." He gives my knee a little squeeze, which instantly calms the settling food in my stomach. I send a smile in Roman's direction. To be fair, Theo's story isn't a *complete* lie.

"Hmm," Roman replies before taking another bite of his chicken.

To my benefit, no one questions Theo and me for the rest of the dinner. Instead, his brothers discuss their careers.

Alex goes on to describe the renovations he's completed on his apartment, located just above the boxing gym he owns. He seems fairly pleased with how his business is performing, and the way he talks sparks my own motivation to pursue a career in the field I love.

The only complaint Alex has is that the older woman next door has moved out and taken her coffee shop business with her.

In his words, "No one makes a better cup of coffee than Betty."

Leo goes on to talk about the restaurant where he works. He complains about the owner but speaks highly of the customers. Roman doesn't say much, as he silently listens and only drops one-word answers here and there.

My favorite part of dinner is watching Theo laugh with his brothers. I can't help but sneak a peek at his smile every time he does. He's caught me looking a couple of times, but I know I can play it off later as just trying to sell the relationship to his brothers.

Once dinner is over, Roman and Leo head out to the back deck with a couple of beers while the rest of us clean up in the kitchen.

"Ice cream's in the freezer," Leo says over his shoulder as he and Roman head out back. "Save me one this time, Theo!"

"Did he just say ice cream?" I look toward Theo, a smile already spread across my face.

"Yeah, and if I know Leo, it's homemade too. It's guaranteed to ruin store-bought ice cream for you." He takes one of the plates Alex hands him from the sink to dry.

"So is anyone going to give us the details on this family Olympics thing you guys were talking about earlier?" Beth asks, putting away the last of the food in the fridge and taking a seat on one of the barstools.

"Yeah, what exactly are the 'games' you guys play?" I ask Theo, my curiosity growing. I'm silently hopeful it's nothing too athletic, but one look at these men tells me otherwise. My lack of hand-eye coordination will not do me any favors in these supposed "games."

"Let's see. We always start the summer off by tie-dying shirts. So we have something to wear for the subsequent games, of course." Theo hands me the last dry dish, and I put it away in the cupboard.

I turn around to look at him, startled at how close he is to me. I know I should move away, put some distance between the two of us, yet my feet don't budge.

"The four of you tie-dye shirts?" I was expecting something more athletic. Tie-dying shirts is something I could probably accomplish easily enough.

"Absolutely. I made a superhero design one year that turned out amazing." He leans closer with his last word. For a moment, it feels like it's just the two of us in the kitchen until Alex speaks up again.

"Your spider symbol looked like a blob, Theo. The shirt was a blur of red and blue." Theo gives him a small shove, laughing off his comment.

I can't help but bask in the joy of their playfulness. From what I've seen, Theo and Alex are fairly close. I'd assume because the two of them are the youngest. There's something about it that reminds me of the closeness I have with Beth. The thought pulls me away from Theo, and I finally move my feet to stand next to Beth on the other side of the kitchen island. Simultaneously enjoying and hating the reprieve I get from being in proximity to Theo.

Theo moves toward the fridge, "We also have a water balloon fight, a best burger competition, we play flag football, and then one final game of Uno."

I can't hold back the wince that overcomes my face at the mention of Uno. The success of these games is shocking, given they play the game that could split up any loving family in just one night.

"I know, I know, but trust me, it's not as intimidating as it sounds. And we usually keep Uno pretty civil." Theo starts pulling the ice cream sandwiches out of the freezer. They look better than I could even imagine.

Taking turns grabbing a sandwich from the container Theo set on the counter, I take a bite and am immediately transported to dessert heaven. Beth lets out a tiny moan when she bites into hers, and Alex chokes on his at the sound.

"Holy shit, these are delicious. Your brother is basically a food god, Theo," Beth says to him.

"Trust me, we know," he says, before taking a bite of his sandwich as well.

After taking a few bites of the ice cream sandwich Leo clearly laced with something addictive, I say to Theo,

"Did you want Beth and me to participate? I'd hate to spoil any tradition." I'd also hate to make an ass of myself in any of the athletically charged games.

Having recovered from choking on his ice cream, Alex chimes in with, "Of course you'll be joining in. After all, you and Theo must be pretty serious for him to bring you along on this trip. There's never been a better time to start adding people to the games."

He takes another bite of his sandwich and turns his attention to Theo. "Unless there's a reason you wouldn't want her to join in?" He cocks an eyebrow at Theo.

"Nope," Theo says to Alex through gritted teeth. He turns his attention back toward me. "It'll be fun, trust me. I'd love to have you join in. Both of you."

My gut reaction is to say no, we didn't sign up for this on the trip. But the sincerity in Theo's eyes when he says he wants to include us is too sweet to deny.

"Of course, we'd love to." I give Theo and Alex a soft smile.

On the bright side, maybe these games will help me distance myself further from Theo. After all, how much touching could a water balloon fight or tie-dying shirts require?

When we head out to join Roman and Leo for a quiet night on the patio, I'm feeling good about the prospect of using these games as a distraction from my attraction toward Theo.

That is, until I remember we have to share a bed tonight.

14

SIENNA

The walk upstairs is excruciatingly silent. We use the second staircase located at the back of the house, near the dining room. After dinner, we all enjoyed ice cream sandwiches on the back porch while we watched the sunset. Theo and I are the last ones to go to bed. With everyone retired to their rooms, the only sounds that can be heard in the house are the creaking steps beneath our feet and my ragged breathing. Yes, just my ragged breathing. Of course Theo wouldn't get winded from the stairs. God forbid he has any flaws.

The moon is our only source of light as it shines through the many windows of the lake house. As we approach the top of the stairs, the moonlight is snuffed out, leaving only the faint glow of the small night-light in the middle of the hallway. Not bright enough to illuminate the top step, I confirm, as my foot catches on the edge and I stumble face-first toward the hardwood floor.

Before I can break my nose and knock out a few teeth, Theo's very large, very strong hands circle my waist. They stop me before I have the chance to catch myself with my own hands.

"Careful," Theo whispers in my ear with a chuckle. "We don't need you hurting yourself before the fun begins." The sound of his deep voice whispering in my ear sends a rush of heat low in my stomach.

Dazed and confused by his hypnotic voice, I respond, "Fun? What fun?" I internally kick myself for how breathy it sounds.

Theo smiles at me, adjusting his hands, keeping one on my lower back. A few of his fingers find purchase on the skin between my T-shirt and my shorts. He gently guides me to his room.

Once we are inside, he shuts the door, still whispering. "The family games, of course. What did you think I meant?" He squints his eyes slightly when he questions me, and my cheeks heat at the very dirty assumptions I was making in my mind.

"Right, of course. That's what I thought. Just wanted to double-check." *Smooth save, Sienna.*

"Are you sure you're okay with me sleeping in the same bed? I have no issue sleeping on the floor."

His tone, more serious than before, has me questioning whose comfort he's concerned about. After all, hadn't I already stated I'd be fine with sleeping in the same bed? I guess it was ridiculous to think he wouldn't be as uncomfortable with the idea of sharing a bed as I am.

"Yeah, I'm sure. Unless you want to sleep on the floor?" My question comes out hesitant, unsure of how he'll respond.

"No, but why don't we put a few pillows between us instead? That way, we're both a little more comfortable." He says it so matter-of-factly that a small twinge of pain starts in my chest at his tone.

"Sure, that'll be fine." I try my best to keep my voice steady when I reply.

Shaking off the feeling of rejection, I remind myself he's not my *real* boyfriend. This is what I agreed to. A simple, mutually beneficial business transaction between two acquaintances. There's no reason to feel hurt that he should want a wall between us all night.

As he grabs the pillows from the window seat, I watch him from the other side of the bed. He's bathed in the moonlight streaming in through the window as a strand of hair falls against his forehead, and my breath involuntarily hitches at the sight.

I can admit that Theo is an attractive man. Attractive enough to drum up an insatiable need to reach my hands out and run my fingers through his hair or inhale his scent every time he gets close.

But I refuse to let anyone get in the way of me securing a job that puts me back on track to complete the plan I set forth years ago. I won't throw away my dream career for a mere attraction to this man.

As he moves back toward the bed, many pillows in tow, he catches me watching him. I can't quite read the expression on his face, and I look away quickly, not wanting to make him feel uncomfortable.

For a moment, I think whatever attraction I'm feeling toward him is mutual, but I'm quick to push past that thought. To think this man would be remotely attracted to me the same way I am to him is ridiculous. He's using me to get a job, the same way I am with him. I already feel like I'm compromising my moral code by getting a job this way. There's no way I'm going to sleep my way into my dream career.

Theo throws the pillows on the bed, and I begin to make the wall Theo so enthusiastically suggested we build. Grabbing a few items from my suitcase at the end of the bed, I set them on the nightstand.

"What're you doing?" Theo asks me, crossing his arms as he stands on the other side of the mattress.

"Getting ready for bed," I say, motioning toward the pillows.

He smiles. "Okay, but that's my side of the bed." He points at where I'm standing on the left side of the mattress.

I look between him and the bed. "You can't be serious," I say, shocked that he sleeps on the same side of the bed as me. He was so willing to sleep on the floor, yet the possibility of me taking his side of the bed seems to be a problem.

"You also always sleep on the left side of the bed?" I ask, not convinced that someone like Theo would be so particular about this.

"No," he responds. Well, what the hell then? I've been told I'm weird for this, but it's part of my nighttime routine. I always sleep on the left side of my bed. Even in my twin-sized bed back home, I sleep more toward the left than the middle or the right side.

"I don't always sleep on the left side," he says.

"Well, okay then, you can take that side," I say,

motioning to the other side of the mattress, a little irritated he brought this topic up to begin with.

"I can't," he claims. "That side"—he points at where I'm standing—"is closest to the door. Therefore, I have to be the one to sleep there. Considering you're so worried about being murdered out here, I would think you would've thought about that." He takes a few steps around the bed, reasserting his insistence on the subject.

"Fine," I say, moving to the other side of the bed. "You're right, if an axe murderer breaks in, I'd rather him take you first." I smile at him as I grab my bonnet and hair care products from the nightstand and move toward the other side of the bed.

"Don't worry, Sienna. I'd happily take an axe through the heart for you." Theo smiles at me as he pulls back the covers on his side of the bed, and my stomach flutters at his words. I watch as the mattress dips beneath his weight, the muscles in his thighs flexing beneath his shorts. Thankfully, I chose to change into athletic shorts and a T-shirt before dinner so I could avoid having to change in front of Theo tonight.

I'm prepping my curls for the night when Theo asks, "So, why architecture?"

The answer comes to me as easily as my name. As I pile my curls on top of my head, securing it with a loose silk scrunchy and working it into the silky fabric of my bonnet, I reply. "There's something really beautiful about the makeup of a building and the intricate details that go into a design. Architecture is art, but with structure. It allows me to express myself creatively, but it also imposes specific rules that must be followed. The duality of the field made me fall in love with it."

I cringe at my use of the word "love" with Theo, and to avoid any more charming remarks from him tonight, I continue, "What about you? Why work at the family company?" Once my curls are secure for the night, I pull back the covers and crawl into bed next to Theo. Well, next to the wall of pillows.

Theo sighs, and I catch a glimpse of his arm being thrown up to rest on top of his head as he relaxes into the bed.

"He may be an asshole at times, but I look up to Roman. All my brothers, really. It's less about working at the family company and more about working with family."

I hum my understanding, waiting for him to continue. When he doesn't, I decide to continue the conversation to avoid the long stretch of silence growing between us.

"I don't think Roman likes me very much. I'm worried I've made a bad impression. Are you sure he's going to help me out?"

"Roman's grumpy," Theo says, and I chuckle as some of my anxiety dissipates. "I'm sure he likes you. He just doesn't warm up to people easily. I'll talk to him soon. Try not to stress about it," he reassures me.

I nod, and a yawn overtakes me before I'm able to say thank you.

With a soft touch to my shoulder, Theo says, "Good night, Sienna." He rolls away, instantly chilling the air around me the moment his back comes into view.

Rolling in the opposite direction, I fidget a little in an

attempt to get comfortable on the side of the bed that I'm not used to sleeping on.

"Good night, Theo," I whisper.

Eventually, I fall asleep staring out the bay window, watching the moonlight dance across the lake as I listen to the calming sounds of Theo's breathing.

15

SIENNA

"The rules of the game are simple, ladies and gents," Alex declares as he explains the tie-dye competition game rules.

We're gathered outside in the large patch of grass that separates the back deck from the lake. I look down at the supplies on the table in front of me. Various dyes, rubber bands, plastic bags, pens, and other tools I didn't realize were required for tie-dying shirts are laid out across the table. Theo towers over me as he stands to my right. He looks excited as he listens to his brother explain the game, as though he hasn't done this every year since he was a kid.

I was surprised to have slept through the night even though I was on the wrong side of the bed. Waking up with the lake in view and the sun shining through the window, I felt better rested than I have in months. However, I'm still trying to ignore the disappointment I felt when I woke up and found Theo's side of the bed empty this morning.

Eventually, I ventured downstairs to find Theo in the kitchen with his brothers, setting up a spread with what seemed like every breakfast food imaginable. After dishing up a plate, I joined Beth outside on the back deck, where she was already sitting with her book and a half-eaten omelet. The guys stayed inside while we had breakfast together, allowing us some quality time this morning.

It was peaceful, quiet, and for a second, as I sat with Beth, I forgot all about my career troubles. The moment was fleeting.

"I still can't believe you guys do this," I lean over and whisper to Theo. To our right stands Beth and Leo sharing a table, and to our left, Roman fidgets with some of the bottles, seemingly taking his color choice very seriously. Alex stands in front of all of us, continuing to explain tie-dying techniques for us "newbies" as he called us.

"It was Leo's idea when we were younger. He liked the thought of us wearing matching clothes." Theo whispers back, leaning in closer, "Our mom always got a kick out of dressing us alike." I smile at the thought of these four grown men matching with one another.

"Hey, lovebirds!" Alex directs the comment at us. "Anything you two want to share with the class?"

My skin heats when all eyes turn toward us. One glance at Beth and I see she's donned her signature mischievous smile that I match with an eye roll. I catch a rubber band flying through the air out of the corner of my eye. Following its path, I watch as it hits Alex right in the chest.

"You think you're the only one who can make a rubber band gun, you little shit?" Alex says, directing his comment toward Theo as he picks the rubber band up from where it landed by his feet.

"Alright, enough," Roman booms before Alex can escalate the situation. "I'm sure Beth and Sienna know how to tie-dye a shirt. Let's get on with this. We'll vote tonight once the shirts are done drying." With one motion of his hand, Alex ends his lecture, and we're off to start dyeing our shirts.

Leo leans over to Theo next to me, and I just barely catch him say, "I swear, he gets grumpier every year."

"You think it has anything to do with—"

Theo's response is cut short when Roman calls their names. Even if Theo hadn't told me, I wouldn't have a hard time noticing that it's clear Roman is the one who raised them. He's by far one of the most intimidating men I've ever met. A pit opens up in my stomach when I think about having to ask him for help securing a job by this summer. Part of me still hopes Theo will do most of the work convincing his brother to help me.

Brushing past that feeling, I take a deep breath, focusing back on the plain white T-shirt in front of me. Thankfully, Leo snagged a couple of smaller sizes for Beth and me so we don't have as much material to work with. Everyone else has already started tying up their shirts. Not wanting to be left behind, I pick up a rubber band and pretend I know what I'm doing.

"I don't think I'm doing this right," I say to Theo, after a few minutes of struggling with twisting my shirt and a few rubber bands snapping in the process. I stare at the mess of white fabric and broken rubber bands before me, embarrassed that I can't do something everyone else seems to be so skilled at.

I'm immediately overwhelmed when I take a look at Theo's shirt. It's tied in ways I didn't know were possible. He's manipulated it to look like a star, no longer recognizable as a shirt. Theo chuckles as I stare at what he's created.

"There's no 'right' way to tie-dye a shirt. You're doing great." Looking at him, I raise one eyebrow, calling bullshit on his statement that I'm "great" at this. His laughter grows, and he sets down his shirt as he steps closer to help me with mine.

Grabbing a rubber band, he takes the fabric lying in front of me, twists it at one of the bottom corners, and ties it off.

"See, you just twist and tie. A beginner-friendly design is to just make random tie-offs, then apply color where you want it." He passes a rubber band to me, and I stare at it, not knowing where to make my next twist.

You'd think I'd have an eye for design, given my architecture degree, but shirts and buildings are wildly different. When I'm working on my designs, I usually have time to plan, to make blueprints, mess around with renders, experiment with different colors, and really home in on a vibe. Having to design this shirt on a whim without any plan is wiping my mind of all creative ideas.

Taking the opposite corner of the shirt, I try twisting

the way Theo did. I let out a frustrated grunt when the shirt slips out of my hands, not doing what I've willed it to do.

"Here, let me help you," Theo says, placing his hand over top of mine. He makes eye contact with me before continuing, a silent question about whether this is okay. I respond with a small nod of my head. I could use all the help I can get right about now.

Breaking eye contact, we focus on the shirt in front of us. Well, he focuses on the shirt. I'm focused on how small my hands look in his. His palms cover the backs of my hands as he helps me work the shirt into a proper spiral, asking me to hold it in place here and there so he can secure it with rubber bands.

Theo places his hands on mine again to help me secure the rubber band. Our fingers move together, inter-locking to secure the knot. When his fingers linger on mine, I can't help but look over at him, having to squint given his height and the position of the sun. When our eyes meet, the world around us begins to blur as I lose my way in Theo's irises.

My phone dings from my pocket, breaking whatever trance Theo just put me under. His hands pull away, and I shiver from the cold chill that runs up my arm in the absence of his hand on mine.

"There we go. Now all you have to do is apply color where you want it. Easy, right?" he says, smiling down at me.

"Right," I say, avoiding eye contact, pulling out my phone to see who's texted me.

DAD

Hey, Pumpkin. Just found out that one of my clients at JR Construction is looking for a receptionist. Here's the application link. He said he can guarantee an interview if you submit an application.

But think about my offer before applying. You could stay with us through the holidays while you take some time off.

I stare at my phone, wide-eyed, unable to move. My dad has been sending me a few applications here and there over the past few months. This is the first time, though, that he's presented me with something decent.

Having already downloaded my résumé to my phone, I click the link my dad sent. Taking a few moments to fill out the application, I let out a sigh of relief when I hit submit.

Fresh air is snuffed from my lungs when I look up from my phone to see Theo staring at the screen. His eyebrows are scrunched together, and his mouth forms a flat line. Noticing he's been caught, he focuses back on his shirt, striking up a conversation with Leo.

I send a quick reply to my dad, letting him know I've applied, but my stomach twists as I set my phone down. I don't like the thought that Theo could be mad at me, but this is an opportunity I can't pass up. An opportunity that sets me on track for completing my plan.

Besides, I've only sent the application. An interview doesn't guarantee a job offer.

After a day lounging by the lake, we're back by the tables to vote on the best shirt. The sun sets behind the lake, disappearing behind the expanse of trees and hills that surround it.

Halfway through the day, I received an interview offer from JR Construction. Although when I accepted the interview, my excitement was bogged down by Theo's determination to avoid me all day. I'm not sure if it was our moment of sexually-charged eye contact or the fact that he clearly saw me submit a job application, but things between us have been tense since this morning.

Standing next to Theo now, I push past the suffocating silence between us as I focus on the shirt in front of me. The soft mix of pink, red, and orange in the sky is the color scheme I was aiming for on the fabric. Looking down at the shirt I hold in my hands, more brown covers the shirt than the original colors I used. At one point, I tried to add blue, inspired by the environment around me. I see now that was a mistake.

"It's nice." Theo hesitates at his compliment, his tone contrasting with his words. His bicep flexes as he rubs the back of his neck, seemingly unsure of the words he just used to describe my unsightly shirt. It's clear he's not impressed, but at least he's talking to me again.

I throw a glare his way, daring him to give my shirt another compliment when I say, "Don't patronize me, Theo. It's awful."

"Here, take mine." He takes my shirt out of my hands, swapping it with his that he's yet to unravel.

He holds the shirt up to his chest, the smaller size looking cropped on his frame. "I've always thought brown was a good color for me." He throws a playful smoldering look in my direction that makes me break into a fit of laughter at the sight. He follows suit, and I appreciate the distraction from my failures.

Unraveling his shirt, I hold it up, revealing the perfect blend of blue, purple, and yellow, intricately molded into a heart that spreads from the center of the shirt.

Smiling, I say, "Wow, you're clearly better at this than I am."

"I've had a lot of practice. Give it time, and you'll get better at it." He says it so nonchalantly that I don't have time to mull over the implications of his comment before Alex stands in front of us, instructing everyone to show off their shirts.

Beth's swirl design is a vibrant combination of pinks, blues, and purples. Roman also did a swirl design, which I've learned from the others is what he does every year. He just picks new colors each time. Except this year, he went with one color—black.

Alex holds his shirt up, showing off a zig-zag design made from a mixture of reds, oranges, and yellows. The combination is reminiscent of fire, the shirt fitting for both him and his Mustang. Last, when Leo holds his shirt up, my jaw hits the floor. My shirt may be in last place, but his definitely takes first, no question. Who knew you could make a plaid design out of tie-dye? No wonder he had so many rubber bands on his shirt.

A vote isn't necessary for us to come to the unanimous decision that Leo wins by a landslide. Last place, however, causes a bit more of a debate.

"Is that actually your design, Theo? The shirt looks a

little small, doesn't it?" Alex questions Theo. Not wanting Theo to come in last place because I don't know the first thing about color theory, I open my mouth to speak up, but Theo beats me to it.

"Yeah, it's mine. The dye must have shrunk the shirt," He shrugs at Alex, taking full responsibility for a shirt that clearly is about to come in last place.

"Alright, well, you know what last place means." Alex drops his shirt in front of Theo on the table, the others following suit.

My eyebrows scrunched together. I look up at Theo, less blinding now that the sun is setting.

"Last place has cleanup duty," he says to me.

"I can help you clean up. It is my shirt after all." I stay with Theo as the others start to head inside for dinner. Well, everyone except for Alex, who has lingered for some reason.

"Don't worry about it. I'm sure you have more important things to do anyway," Theo replies. I try not to show the hurt on my face.

"Is this about the application I submitted?" I ask. "I wanted to talk to you about that—"

I'm cut off when Alex joins the conversation. "I'll help him clean up. I wanted an excuse to talk to this fucker anyway." Throwing his arm around Theo's shoulders, he has to extend, considering their small height difference.

When Alex smiles at me, I get a strong feeling that leaving the two of them to clean up alone isn't up for debate. Honestly, it's a relief. The farther away I can get from the tie-dying supplies, the better. Although I can't help but feel worse as my distance from Theo grows.

I'm surprised Theo seems upset over my decision to apply for this job. After all, the goal of this trip is to secure a job offer. Theo couldn't possibly have a valid reason to be upset if I received a job offer through a means other than him.

16

THEO

It wasn't my intention to avoid Sienna all day, but the thought of her getting a job by other means left me more irritated than I'd like to admit. She doesn't seem like the type of woman who would go back on a deal she made. Then again, we don't know each other that well.

I was looking forward to getting to know her better over the course of this trip more than I care to admit. If she got a job offer only two days into this vacation, she'd have every excuse to leave.

If she left now, not only would it ruin my chances of Roman hiring me but I'd also have no excuse to see her again. For some reason, not seeing Sienna again scares me more than losing out on a job.

Pushing those feelings aside, I decide it's an issue to be dealt with later and stare at the pile of shirts in front of me. The shirt she designed is pretty bad, but I couldn't bring myself to admit it to her face. The pout that over-took her when she unraveled her shirt was so cute, I had to repress a smile at her failure. That's when I first noticed the carnal piece of me that would do anything to see her smile, even if it meant relinquishing my chances at beating my brothers in the games this year.

There was nothing in her rules about not making her smile. I see no harm in indulging in that impulse. As long as I don't indulge in my urge to kiss her every time her eyes dart toward my lips. I may have a history of partying, but I've never crossed the line of violating a woman's boundaries. I don't plan on starting now.

"I give it until day five." I jump at the sound of Alex's voice beside me. I had forgotten he stood next to me as I stared at the pile of shirts on the table.

"Day five until what?" I turn to him, taking the shirts from the table and putting them into a basket for the wash. I move away from him toward Roman's table, not sure if I want to hear his answer.

"Until you two are dating for real." Startled, I knock over a few bottles of dye at his statement. They roll off the table and tumble to the ground.

"Wha- What are you talking about?" I busy myself by picking up the bottles from the ground, not looking at him out of fear of giving anything away. We've been here two days, and my brothers are already suspicious of us. If Alex thinks we're lying, then Roman probably does too. If Roman thinks we're lying, there's no way either one of us will end up with a job by the end of this trip. That is, if Sienna doesn't get this other job offer first.

Alex chuckles. "Theo, come on, man, you two aren't fooling any of us. What I don't understand is why you told Roman you had a girlfriend in the first place." He gathers a few of the supplies from the tables, putting them in the bin we dragged out from the storage closet.

"Is it really that obvious?"

He answers my question with one look thrown my way. Sienna and I are screwed.

Having put all the supplies into the bin, I hear four distinctive clicks as Alex secures the lid. With only the tables left to fold up, we've cleaned up in half the time it would've taken me by myself, so I'm thankful for my brother's help.

"Look, it's obvious you two are faking to me because I don't buy for a second that you'd settle down so easily."

"Hey now." I point my finger at him as a warning. He laughs as we place one of the tables on its side and begin folding in the legs.

"Oh relax, I'm not calling you a slut. I'm just...Well, yeah, actually, you are a little bit of a man-whore." He says it as we fold the table in half. Now in closer proximity, I punch him in the shoulder at his insult, though it's not completely inaccurate.

Alex rubs his shoulder, feigning injury for my entertainment. I know for a fact it didn't hurt him because if any one of us knows how to fight *and* take a punch, it's him.

"I'm just saying, I know the two of you aren't dating, because I know you. But I think we can still convince Roman and Leo that the two of you are together."

After folding up the last of the three tables, we begin moving them toward the small storage room attached to the side of the house. The silence stretches between us as we finish cleaning. My brain is stuck on whether I should admit to Sienna's and my scheme.

"What gave us away?" I ask Alex, finally deciding there's no fooling him. When we place the last table in the storage room, Alex is sure to lock the door before shutting it. We're miles away from any other houses or public roads. Locking the doors always seemed pointless to me, but Alex says we can never be too careful.

"The two of you don't even look comfortable around one another, let alone the hesitation in the story of how you two met that you told at dinner last night." I wince at his words. Of all the things Sienna and I discussed on our drive here, the fake details of how we met one another really should've been one of them.

"We need jobs," I tell him, "Sienna and I. You know Roman's been an asshole about me working at Dad's company, and Sienna's been struggling to find a job in architecture. I thought we could help each other out."

"So you thought a fake-dating scheme was the way to do that?" He looks at me, confused.

I roll my eyes. "Yeah, it was my best idea at the time, alright? Roman put me on the spot, and I figured that if I could show him I'm responsible enough, he'd offer me a job. We were hoping Roman would use his connections to help Sienna schedule some interviews."

Alex chuckles, shaking his head. "There are better ways you could've gone about this. You're in deep shit now, considering you asked a woman like her to help you with your plan."

"What do you mean?"

He levels me with a look. "You should've picked

someone who was less your type. This is going to get messy and fast." He turns, rounding the corner toward the steps of the back deck to join the others inside.

Catching up to him, I speak in hushed tones, worried the others might hear us.

"It's not like that. We didn't even know each other before this, and now we're just friends. C'mon, man, just help us out with Roman."

"Alright. But I'm giving it a week until the two of you start dating for real." He opens the back door, and with others in earshot, the conversation is over.

Pushing him through the doorway, I laugh off his comment. Whatever he sees, he's seeing it incorrectly. Sienna and I might have a mutual attraction, but that's it. She and I are just two friends helping each other out. Besides, if she wanted something more with me, she wouldn't have applied for another job right under my nose. She'd be looking for an excuse to stay here. Then again, if she had any interest in me, she wouldn't have set so many rules.

Rules I promised her I wouldn't break, no matter how badly I might want to.

17

SIENNA

"When is your interview?" Beth asks me from the chair next to mine, where we are seated on the back deck.

"Tomorrow morning. I'm surprised they scheduled an interview with me so quickly," I tell her.

"I'm not. Didn't your dad say you've already got the job? So the interview is just a formality."

"Sure, but you can never be too cautious. I thought a few of the previous jobs I applied to would at least ask me in for an interview, and I didn't get a single one."

"Well, I'm sure you'll do great either way. This could be really good for you," she tells me as she takes a sip of her tea.

"Please, you just want an excuse for us to leave early so you don't have to be around Alex any longer." I copy her motions, raising my mug of coffee to my lips and taking a sip.

"I have no idea what you're talking about." She avoids eye contact with me when she says it.

We've been here for about five days now, and Beth has been getting along great with everyone, except Alex. I make a mental note to buy her a special edition of one of her favorite books as a thank-you for coming along on this trip.

The guys told us last night at dinner that we'd be going on a morning hike today. Another surprise that my coordination skills weren't too fond of. While the guys have been preoccupied with packing for the hike, Beth and I decided to take our second cups of coffee and tea outside. We've been ready to go for the past hour, but I'm in no rush to start trekking through the woods. Theo told me it was an easy trail, but something tells me his definition of "easy" is vastly different from mine.

"So it was Theo's idea for a wall of pillows between the two of you?" Beth asks, changing the subject from Alex.

"Yes, a full wall of pillows," I whisper, terrified Theo will overhear me even though he's still inside. "I mean, at least it's respectful. I just haven't gotten the best sleep the past few nights."

Beth nods her head slowly. "You don't seem too pleased with the arrangement."

Shrugging, I take a deep breath before confessing, "I'm not unhappy. I guess I feel a little bummed. I'm the one who insisted on having rules, so I don't know why I feel this way. I can't explain it, but every night I have to crawl into bed next to the pillows is another night I come closer to throwing each one on the floor."

Beth raises an eyebrow. Lacing sarcasm into her voice,

she asks, "And you have no idea what could be causing this feeling?"

"No..." When she doesn't say anything, I continue, "Okay, fine. I'm supposed to be focusing on my career, with no distractions, and now I'm sleeping next to a man who looks like he was carved from stone. I can't seem to get my mind to think about anything else. It's frustrating." I slump down into the cushions of my chair.

"Oh, honey," she says, patting my arm, "it wouldn't hurt if you gave in and had a little fun with him. Sometimes the only way to stop thinking about someone is to get under them."

I shoot her a glare. "I'm confident that wouldn't work. Especially not with my interview tomorrow morning. I need to stay focused."

"If getting under him won't work, then maybe you should get on top of him. Whatever works best for you." I nudge her shoulder as we burst into laughter over her joke.

"Seriously, though, I set rules for a reason. He's hot as hell, but I need to focus on my career. That's the only reason we're here. I don't have time for dating right now."

"So let's see if I understand this correctly. You suggested a specific set of rules to remain focused on your career goals. But now that you're here, sleeping next to 'the man carved from stone,' you're upset he's respecting the boundaries you put in place?" I stare at her, dumbfounded by her summary of what I've dumped on her this morning.

"Ugh." I throw my face into my hands. "I know, I

should be happy he's being respectful. I think I just wish he'd want to break the rules as much as I do. Not that I think we should. I just want him to want to. But the wall of pillows tells me otherwise."

"Well, I don't think it would hurt to have a *little* more fun with Theo while you're here." Turning my head, I cradle my cheek as I look at her. "You two aren't really selling the whole 'we're dating and in love' vibe. Maybe ease up on the rules a little bit. At least when you're around everyone else."

"Have we really been that bad?" I ask.

Beth winces as she nods. "You came here to get a job with the help of Theo's brother, right? And this other job isn't technically guaranteed yet?" I nod. "Then for the sake of your career, feel Theo up a bit. Use him to get close to his older brother and secure a job, interview, whatever it is that you need. Career is number one. You don't have anything to lose if you have a little fun along the way."

"I guess that makes sense, but—"

"Alright, ladies, ready to catch the best view of your lives?" Alex comes bursting through the door, and I don't miss the exaggerated eye roll Beth lets out in his presence.

"Bit of an overstatement, don't you think?" Beth stands, walking past Alex on the steps, but not before patting my hand in reassurance after our talk.

"Trust me, it's not," Leo says, following Alex down the steps after Beth. Roman follows shortly after with a backpack securely strapped to his shoulders that looks like it could burst open at any minute. I notice Leo has a backpack as well, a little less than bursting at the seams. Theo waits for me on the steps. Standing, I join him as we let the others get a head start.

"Beth has informed me that apparently, we aren't fooling anyone," I say.

He laughs. "Funny, I didn't think we were doing so bad until Alex told me the same thing the other night."

I look at him, surprised. "Seriously?" Looking down at my shoes in defeat, I continue, "We're so bad at this. I knew this would never work."

Theo grabs my chin between his thumb and forefinger, gently lifting it until my eyes meet his. "We're okay. I think we just need to sell it a little more. Will you be comfortable with that?"

My heart warms at the question, but the feeling quickly fades when I remember he's only doing this for his benefit. I nod.

"Good." He moves his hand from my chin and reaches down to interlock our fingers. "Let's start by holding hands for the hike. If at any point I make you feel uncomfortable, just tell me, and I'll back off."

"Okay. And you do the same. If there's anything—"

"Angel, you can do anything you want to me, and I'd have zero complaints." Theo smirks down at me, and my cheeks heat at the use of that nickname again. When his pupils widen, he gives a slight shake of his head before clarifying, "For the sake of selling our relationship to the others, of course."

"Right, of course," I say in response, disappointment fogging my brain.

Fingers locked together, we take off after the others as

I say a silent prayer that I don't fall face-first into the dirt, embarrassing myself. My failed tie-dyed shirt was embarrassing enough to last the remainder of my stay.

I was correct to assume that my definition of an easy trail and Theo's definition were wildly different.

By the fourth time that my toe catches on a rock and Theo has to balance me before falling, I'm ready to turn around and head back to the house. Thankfully, we're at the back of the group, but I can feel Theo holding in a laugh every time I trip and have to grab onto his bicep for balance.

"Stop it," I tell Theo, who could barely hold in his laugh when my shoe catches on another rock, not even a full two steps later.

He places a hand on his chest. "I didn't say anything." He insists on his innocence, but one look and I can still see the corners of his mouth turned up in a half smile.

His smile grows when I make eye contact with him, and I don't have to say anything further when he confesses.

"The way you keep grabbing onto me is cute. That's all." Great, I'm trying to resist making a fool of myself, and he thinks I'm "cute." Last I checked, women who men find "cute" aren't typically the ones they are willing to break a few rules for. Just another reminder that I need to stop thinking about the way his bicep flexes every time I grab on to him, or how his lips might feel on mine.

"We didn't do a lot of hiking growing up, so I'm not as accustomed to it like you clearly are," I say, trying to save face.

"How come? You grew up here, didn't you? Pretty rare to find a family in the Pacific Northwest that doesn't do a lot of hiking."

"Given that my mom and I share the same athletic abilities, hiking wasn't a popular family activity in my household. My dad tried to take us once when I was in middle school, and we made it about a quarter of the way down the trail before he picked us both up and carried us back to the car. We giggled the whole way back, but I think we were both grateful that we didn't have to endure another scrape on our knees."

"He carried both of you back?" Theo pulls at his shirt collar. "Remind me to get a workout session in when we get back to the house."

Laughing, I grab his bicep again, though not because I've tripped. "Oh please, with arms like these, I'm sure you'd have no problem doing the same."

His eyebrows tick up at my statement, and I look away from him, yanking my hand off his bicep. Not knowing what to say, I stay silent, worried I'll give my attraction away too easily if I keep talking.

Roman and Leo are far ahead, leading the way for the rest of us. They are framed by Alex and Beth, who are walking on opposite sides of the trail as if to avoid each other at all costs. Though I can't help but notice Alex keeps looking toward his right, where Beth continues on the trail. They are only a few steps ahead of us, but I'm worried that if I can't catch my footing, we'll never catch up.

"Here." Theo holds out his arm for me, as if reading my mind, and I place my palm in the crook of his elbow, ignoring how big his bicep is compared to my hand. The offer comes as a calming sentiment, assuring me I didn't make him too uncomfortable with my statement before.

"Where are we going anyway?" I ask Theo, trying and failing not to sound too out of breath.

"It's a surprise." When he looks down at me, the sun beams through the trees towering above us, shining down on Theo. He looks radiant, and I have to pull my eyes away before my thoughts drift to a place I've been working hard not to let them go.

"Alright, fine." I clutch his arm harder to avoid any more tripping incidents. "Did you hike this trail when you were kids?" I may be keeping my thoughts from drifting to speculation about what Theo looks like naked, but there's no harm in learning more about him. Especially if it'll help me sell this relationship to his brothers, particularly Roman.

"Oh yeah. Roman insisted on it every year. He said it's the one thing Dad would take us to do when we came up here. Mom wasn't much of a hiker either." He winks at me, and I shove his shoulder in response.

"Your parents took you here then?" I regret the question as soon as it leaves my mouth. It's not my place to ask about his deceased parents, considering he isn't my real boyfriend. The thought bothers me more than it should, but I brush it off as he responds.

"All the time. I don't remember much, but I've seen

photos of us all here. Mom and Dad bought the place when I was three, so we only had a short amount of time to enjoy it together before they passed." I squeeze gently on his arm when I hear his voice falter.

"I'm sorry. I shouldn't have asked. It seems like the four of you have built a nice tradition of coming out here, though." He chuckles, some of the tension easing from his shoulders, and in response, the tightness in my chest loosens a little.

"We have. It was Roman's idea, but he would never admit it. I swear there's a soft interior to his tough exterior. There just aren't a lot of people he lets see it."

I hum my agreement, not sure how to respond, but wanting to believe Theo for the sake of my career.

"I guess it doesn't really matter if you'll be getting a job offer any day now." He keeps his attention forward as he says the words.

"Well, no job offer is guaranteed. I still have to do well in the interview tomorrow. It's fine if I have your room to myself while I take the call, right?" I ask to check that he's still okay with the plan.

"Sure, and take however much time you need." He's still avoiding eye contact with me.

"Even if I accept the offer, I still plan on following through with my end of the deal. I'm not one to break a promise." I try to ease any discomfort he may be having over this.

"You wouldn't have to, I'd understand if you'd want to leave." He makes brief eye contact with me before continuing, "Although I am curious why you'd want this job. Didn't you say it was a receptionist position?"

"I did, but it's still a foot in the door into a construction company. It's one step closer to an architecture position."

I catch Theo nodding his head out of the corner of my eye, my grip on his bicep tightening as I avoid another rock with my foot.

"Is that what you want? Just a foot in the door?" Theo asks. "We can help you get a position at a top architecture firm in the city."

"I appreciate the offer, but I have to be realistic about this. You might be able to get me an interview, but most big architecture firms don't hire directly out of college. They look for experience, which comes from starting at places like JR Construction."

"I guess. But you strike me as the type of woman who would go after what she wants. I'm shocked you'd be okay with settling for a position you're overqualified for."

I'm quiet as I think through Theo's statement. It may not be the best job in the world, but it will pay the bills. One that will still help me achieve the future career goals I've planned out for myself.

"I am going after what I want." I try to bite back the irritation in my tone. "Not all of us have a multimillion-dollar company where we are guaranteed a job. Some of us have to start at the bottom and work our way to the top."

"Sienna...I wasn't trying to be rude," Theo says hesitantly.

Sighing, I say, "I'm sorry. I think the heat is getting to me. I know you weren't." I give him a small smile of reassurance.

"Send me your portfolio and let me take a look. It'll help me convince Roman to get you a few interviews. Even if you get this other job, it'd be nice if I could offer you some options."

"Thank you. That would be nice." When he flashes his smile at me, I can't help but return the favor.

"Does your brother always hike like this, or?" Beth asks from ahead of us, trying and failing to whisper. We've finally caught up to her now that I've gone the last ten minutes without stumbling. I still haven't let go of Theo's arm, though he doesn't seem in a rush to put distance between us despite our almost disagreement.

"No, he's definitely doing it to look at you," Theo responds from my left. The two of them are referring to the fact that Alex hasn't stopped looking to the right of the trail, rather than watching where he's going.

"I can hear you, you know," Alex says, only a few paces ahead of us. "And for your information, I'm only looking to make sure the women don't get hurt. I am a gentleman, after all."

"Oh, I'm sure you're such a gentleman," Beth responds, lacing her words with heavy sarcasm.

Alex stops in his tracks, letting us catch up to him. Once we do, we all come to a brief stop as Beth stands facing Alex, her arms crossed over her chest. Theo and I glance at each other. When our eyes meet, it becomes harder for both of us to hold in our smiles.

Alex takes a step toward Beth, causing her to strain her neck to look up at him as he towers over her short frame.

"Something tells me you don't care too much for 'gentlemen' anyway." He speaks quietly, but Theo and I over-hear, holding back a chuckle at his words.

Beth's only response is a scoff as she turns to continue up the trail. When Alex follows her, Theo and I bend over with laughter, holding on to each other for support, unable to hold it back any longer. I don't think Beth has ever met a match as equal as Alex.

I'm thankful for the laugh, as it helps break whatever icy tension was created between Theo and me during our prior conversation. He's looking to be made an equal partner in his family-owned company right out of college. I'm looking for any entry-level job remotely related to my field of study. Without building my career immediately, I fall behind on my life plan. Unfortunately, I'm not sure Theo will ever understand the pressure I'm under.

"I swear, you guys get slower every year!" Leo calls out to us. Alex lifts two middle fingers in response and runs to catch up to him and Roman. Beth and Theo continue to ensure that I'm not at risk of falling on my face, and we eventually catch up to the rest of the group as well.

Looking at the view at the end of the trail, I'm speechless.

"Surprise," Theo says to me. "Told you it was worth it."

"Absolutely." It's all I can manage as I look out at the expanse of the lake in front of us.

We've hiked to the top of a small cliffside. The lake is surrounded by more evergreen trees as the sun sits high in the sky, reflecting off the deep blue water.

Somewhere in the distance, a flock of birds flees from

one of the trees, and their caws punctuate the air. We've all fallen silent as we take in the view.

"It's beautiful," I whisper, more to myself than anyone else.

"Stunning," Theo agrees. When I glance at him, I notice he isn't looking out over the cliff. He's looking at me. The green of his emerald eyes is all-consuming. Theo is a sight to behold, framed by the trees behind him, the sun shining down on his lightly tanned skin. There's no question he belongs in a place like this. My eyes fall to his lips, forgetting we aren't alone until Leo interrupts the silence.

"Food is ready." I look past Theo to see that Leo has set up a large picnic blanket. A spread of snacks and sandwiches lay out across the plaid design.

Looking toward Theo again, I feel a sliver of hope that the previous moment isn't gone forever. But my stomach growls in protest, and when he notices, he grabs my hand, pulling me toward the blanket.

"C'mon." He chuckles.

Sitting on the blanket with the others, we're all enamored by the view as we indulge in the cold summer snacks. Finger sandwiches, bowls of fresh-cut watermelon, strawberries, grapes, and ice-cold lemonade are all enjoyed in complete silence. It's a type of peace I don't think I've ever had the chance to experience.

I'm overjoyed when we stay sitting there for a few more moments, no one moving to clean up the empty containers. When Theo leans back on his hands, placing one of them behind me, I lean my head on his shoulder, relishing in the added comfort he provides in this peaceful moment.

If this is what relaxation feels like, I've certainly been missing out. Theo breathes steadily beside me, and I watch as the breeze blows through the tops of the trees across the lake. I should be more concerned about bringing my plan to fruition, but I just can't seem to give a damn at this moment with Theo by my side.

18

SIENNA

When Theo explained the water balloon fight, I didn't think it would be so elaborate. Theo and his brothers have been setting up for it all morning. Beth and I have been watching them, sitting on the back porch steps. We offered to help, but they insisted we save our energy for the fight itself.

I guess I shouldn't be too surprised they've put so much thought into this game over the years. Watching Theo and his brothers the past few days, it's clear they've developed a smooth cadence with each other and their daily routines. One I'm sure they've been perfecting since they were kids.

Leo is the one to lead the charge when it comes to meals. Roman always plays the role of his sous chef. Alex and Theo have been given the responsibility of setting the table and cleaning up after a meal. Beth and I have taken it upon ourselves to help them with the latter.

In a strange way, their daily routine is beautiful to

watch. Seeing each of the men take on a role around the house without much communication among themselves speaks to how often they've done so over the years. My instincts tell me Roman is behind it. While he's a grump, I've come to learn he's an organized, methodical, rigid grump. I laugh to myself at the irony as I watch him set up for the water balloon fight.

The hike was only a couple of days ago, but the relaxation and calm I felt while taking in the view haven't gone away. The tiny voice in my head screaming "you're going to be murdered on this trip" has finally faded. The days are now filled with birds chirping, water splashing, or Theo laughing. I swear I could record Theo's laughter and listen to it on repeat. I'm starting to unravel, and it feels nice to take a small break.

I'd be lying if I said my relaxed state due to the lake house wasn't a big factor in acing my interview yesterday. As I watch Theo help his brothers, the email offer I received this morning burns a hole in my pocket. I haven't told Theo about the job yet, and I'm not sure why I've been so hesitant.

As the awkward tension between Theo and me has started to fade, I believe our fake relationship has become more convincing to the others. We've been sure to hold hands anytime we're near one another, and he's been performing basic chivalrous acts the past few days as well. Holding the door open for me, pulling out my chair, basic boyfriend tasks that have his brothers not looking twice in our direction out of suspicion. Behind closed doors, we keep the wall of pillows between us at night and have kept a comfortable emotional distance from one another. We've handled ourselves as the adults we are, and the others seem to be buying our ruse.

Whenever we are lounging by the water, Theo's arms are usually wrapped around my waist or thrown over my shoulders. We've been spoiled with delicious food, and Theo even fed me a strawberry at one point in the middle of a board game with Alex and Beth. Convincing the others has been successful, but sometimes when Theo looks at me, I forget that we aren't in a real relationship.

I'm happy to call Theo a friend, a fact I must remind myself every night as I crawl into bed next to the stack of pillows. Some nights we stay up, talking to get to know each other a bit better, in an effort to make our connection feel more real.

I've learned that his favorite color is blue, which wasn't hard to guess, given his Mustang's color. His favorite food is a cheeseburger, he definitely believes in aliens, and like me, he isn't much of a reader and prefers movies instead.

"I'm still struggling to picture it," Beth says, sitting beside me. "Grown men who look like them, having a water balloon fight." She turns to me with a smile that I return, still unable to believe it myself.

"Something tells me Roman isn't too fond of breaking tradition," I reply.

"It's impressive, considering his advanced age."

"Beth, he's only in his early thirties. I wouldn't really call that 'advanced age.'"

"Yeah, and I read the aging process starts at twenty-five, so he already has like, a decade's worth of aging under his belt. I'd consider that advanced compared to us."

"You read too much." I chuckle.

She lets out a gasp, clutching her invisible pearls. "There is no such thing!"

We're mid-laugh when Theo joins us on the porch steps. He stands in front of us, resting his right foot on one of the steps. The shorts he's wearing ride up slightly from the angle, revealing just how toned his thighs are. His knee is only inches from my face. It wouldn't take much for me to reach out and take a bite.

"What'd I miss?" I'm grateful when Theo's question pulls me from my inappropriate thoughts.

That's certainly no way to think about your friend, Sienna.

"Nothing," I respond. "Just discussing how seriously you guys take your water balloon fights."

Theo glances behind him, looking at the setup he and his brothers just completed. From the looks of the yard, I'd guess it was one of those training obstacle courses you'd find in boot camp or a mock war zone that they use for paintball fights. I'm starting to think the storage closet attached to the house is less a storage closet and more a Mary Poppins bag of never-ending supplies.

He turns back to us, rubbing the spot on the back of his neck, perfectly accentuating the vein running through his bicep as he flexes. My tongue darts out to wet my lips instinctively, and I mentally kick myself for it.

"I guess we go a little overboard, but it's worth it. We've added bits here and there every year, making the setup more challenging as we've gotten older."

"How exactly does scoring work?" Beth asks.

"We'll split into teams. Whichever team gets the most hits, each player on that team gets a point toward their final score." Beth and I stay silent, waiting for him to continue. "We figured you'd both be on a team with Alex and me. Roman and Leo seem to be pretty confident they can take all four of us." He rolls his eyes at the idea.

"I can join their team. I don't mind," Beth says with a little more enthusiasm than necessary.

"Are you sure? We figured you'd want to be on the same team as Sienna," Theo responds.

"Why, because girls always have to team up? We can be feminist and still enjoy a fun competition against each other, Theo. Besides, pelting Alex with a balloon sounds like fun." Theo laughs at her response. That's Beth for you. She's not afraid to speak her mind, and definitely not attracted to Alex.

As the laughter dies off, Theo looks at me. "Have you heard back about the job yet?"

I glance at Beth, who widens her eyes at me, in a nudge to tell him the truth. "Yeah, actually. They offered me the job," I say it with more hesitation than I mean to.

Leaning down, Theo moves to hug me. "That's great, Sienna. I'm so happy for you." Once he pulls back, he continues, "Are you going to accept?"

That's the one question I was hoping he wouldn't ask me. The one question I haven't been able to answer since I received the email.

"I'm not sure yet. They gave me a few days to decide."

He nods, his body shifting toward me more as though the next statement is only for my ears. "Well, I had a look at your portfolio. It's more than impressive to put it lightly. Any company would be lucky to have you."

"Thank you," I respond. My hand itches to reach out toward Theo, but he pulls back, the look shifting to something of concern on his face.

"We're filling up the balloons now. We usually wear swimsuits, and I think the guys mentioned we'll wear our tie-dyed shirts this year. Feel free to wear whatever you're most comfortable in," Theo says, changing the subject.

"We'll go get ready and be right down," I say as I stand and pull Beth with me.

Walking into the house, I can't help but be slightly frustrated by the mixed signals I'm getting from Theo. The hug was warm and congratulatory, but his tone and the shift in his face were enough to tell me he seemed almost disappointed that I'd received a job offer.

Most days, I think he's fine with our arrangement, and other days, he gives signals that he might want more. When we are together in front of his brothers, he can't keep his hands off me, but at night, he keeps that wall of pillows built between us.

Then there are small, private moments when he shows affection when no one is around. That first day we arrived, I thought he was going to kiss me, but maybe I misread the signal. He only uses the nickname Angel when it's just the two of us, but maybe he has a nickname for all his friends.

Theo strikes me as the type of man who would go after what he wants, despite some arbitrary rules I have in place. Yet he hasn't once broken a rule. That can only leave me to conclude that he has no interest beyond being friends who help each other.

But then why would he seem disappointed I've received an offer?

The mixed signals are maddening.

"Bikini, or shorts and a tank? What are you going to wear?" Beth asks, breaking me from my thoughts once we've reached her room.

Her question sparks an idea. I've been keeping Theo at a safe distance this whole trip. Not knowing if he feels the same attraction I do is plaguing my mind. Today gives me an opportunity to get some responses to my questions.

Not that we'd act on anything, but at least I'd have answers.

"Bikini. Definitely," I reply.

"Good answer." I meet her smile with one of my own as I head to Theo's room to change into the sexiest blue bikini I own.

19

THEO

It's official, Sienna is trying to kill me. The murder weapon? The blue-striped string bikini hugging her hips and the curves of her perky breasts.

"Oh fuck," Alex says on a breath from my right.

"I will *fucking* kill you," I say to him through clenched teeth, not able to take my eyes off Sienna.

"Wasn't talking 'bout your girl, bro. Relax," he whispers back.

I can only assume he was talking about Beth, given she is the textbook definition of his type, but I can't be bothered to look anywhere other than Sienna's direction as she slowly descends the steps of the back porch. She's moving in real time, but my mind must be playing tricks on me because I swear she's moving in slow motion.

When she reaches the bottom of the steps, the warm summer breeze blows her way. It picks her curly dark hair off her shoulders, bringing my attention from her body to her face. Something is almost flirtatious about her sly smile that makes me wonder if she chose this bikini specifically because it's my favorite color. Erasing the thought from my mind, I remind myself that we are only friends.

Friends don't get irritated when other friends receive job offers.

The thought floats through my mind against my will. It's true, I wasn't exactly ecstatic when Sienna told me she received the job offer earlier. We're only a week into our vacation, and I can't reasonably ask her to stay another week if she has a new job to prep for. Even if it does lessen my chances of getting a job myself.

Staring at her as she walks toward me, I get an idea. I'd hate for our agreement to be the only reason she stays if she accepts the job offer. If I can convince her how much fun we can have on this trip, maybe she'll decide to stay longer. Not because she feels obligated, but because she wants to.

My idea excites me as I let my eyes trail down her slender, toned frame. The dark and light blue stripes of her bikini perfectly complement the light brown of her skin. She's covered in gold accents from her earrings and the layered necklaces, down to the thin anklet she wears. The way her jewelry and soft, glowing skin hit the sunlight, I feel like a lost pirate at sea hearing a siren's call. I know that answering the call is only going to end in my demise, but I'm doing it anyway.

Shamelessly, as she gets closer, I take full advantage of her proximity and continue to blanket her body with my eyes. My eyes roam the expanse of her thin neck, wondering what she would taste like if I trailed my tongue from her collarbone to her ear. My eyes scan even farther down to her breasts, perky from afar, and even bigger up close. Her nipples are noticeably hard under the thin fabric covering them despite the warm weather outside. Her bikini top has me resisting the urge to reach out my hand to cup one breast and pinch her nipple through the fabric until she begs me to rip it off her.

I keep my hands clasped in front of me, hoping to hide the growing erection in my swim trunks. Thank God I had the foresight to wear underwear underneath them today, anticipating this. The guys and I took a more modest approach by wearing our tie-dyed shirts to avoid making the women uncomfortable. I guess the women had a different idea, but I'm certainly not complaining.

I'm not the only one with wandering eyes as I notice Sienna's gaze is locked on the small sliver of skin showing just above my swim trunks. She still has the original shirt I tie-dyed, leaving me with her smaller one that fits like a crop top. I've never been happier to have free access to my brother's gym than I am today.

"You guys ready to get your asses kicked?" Beth says, pulling my attention from Sienna. Though my eyes are still glued to her, only slightly turning my head toward Beth to acknowledge she's spoken.

Sienna and Beth burst out laughing, and I realize that neither Alex nor I has said a word, and I'm sure it's been longer than what would be socially acceptable for a response.

Beth links her arm in Sienna's, and they head toward the center of the water balloon field, surveying how many water balloons we've set up. Spoiler, it's a shit ton. When they walk away, I can't help but watch Sienna's hips move with each step. Perky tits *and* ass must mean she's either an angel or was sent by the devil to destroy me. I don't think I have a mind to care about which one it is right now if it means getting my hands and lips on that soft, glowy, tanned skin of hers.

"You're so fucked." I turn to Alex, who looks at me with one of those smug grins he loves so much.

I look from the women to my brother, and plaster on my own smug grin. "Bet you I'm not the only one who's fucked." His nostrils flare in response, and he walks away. I'd put money on the fact that he's going to be extra *Alex* today, just to show off for Beth.

I gather myself before joining the others in the middle of the yard, mentally preparing for being around Sienna in this temptation-filled state today.

"Nice of you to join us, Theo," Roman says. I throw a middle finger his way in response. I've taken up a spot next to Sienna, and as the breeze blows again, her strawberry summer scent wafts my way. I curse myself for taking such a deep inhale.

What is this woman doing to me?

"The only rule we have is anything above the neck is off-limits," Leo explains, pointedly looking at me.

I roll my eyes. "That was one time when I was *twelve*. Give me a break."

Beth starts a conversation with Leo and Roman about the strategy for their team. As they're talking, Sienna leans into my side, whispering, "I'm surprised to see you wearing the shirt. But I must admit, brown is a good color for you." Looking up at me, she smiles, and I swear I heard a hint of an innuendo in her tone.

Unable to help myself, I lean in to whisper in her ear, "And blue is a perfect color on you, Angel. But I must admit, that bikini would look better on the floor." I end my sentence by squeezing her hip lightly, allowing my thumb to travel beneath the string on her bikini bottoms. Her chest begins to rise and fall at a rapid pace from my touch. My erection threatens to spring to life again at the sight.

The high-pitched ring of a whistle yanks Sienna and me from our bubble, and the air around me chills from our lack of proximity as she pulls away.

"Fuck, I always forget he has that," Alex says, startled.

"Let's play! Get ready to lose, fuckers," Leo booms as he and Roman rush to their side of the yard. Alex and I follow, grabbing our bins and running to our side of the yard, tucking behind our barricade.

Dropping our bins, I realize Sienna isn't with us. One look back, and I see she's frozen in the middle of the yard, along with Beth. Muscle memory kicked in for the rest of us, but I realize now that we forgot to explain the initial rush to the two of them. Although they did have the right mind to grab a water balloon each. I laugh as they stand in the middle of the field, as if they are in an old western duel. They stare each other down, but neither one of them has thrown the first balloon.

"Go get your girl. I'll cover you," Alex says.

I do my best to ignore the warmth spreading in my chest at the thought of Sienna being "my girl" as I run to the center of the yard. Sweeping Sienna off her feet, literally, I throw her over my shoulder. She squeals, and I laugh as I feel the break of a water balloon on my back.

Turning around to face Beth, now balloon-less, I say, "You might want to run. I wouldn't want you left out in the open when Alex has perfect aim." Her eyes go wide for a second, and she books it to her side of the yard when a balloon breaks at her feet. Leo and Roman are already laughing behind their barricade when she joins them.

Setting Sienna down, we crouch behind our barricade, and she playfully slaps Alex and me on the arm.

"What's that for?" I ask as Alex and I continue to laugh.

"You guys didn't tell me you were just going to take off!"

"I'm very sorry." I gently place my hand on the side of her neck, cupping her jaw. "I'll be sure to remind you of that next time." I wink at her before handing her another water balloon.

I'm not thinking when I say the words, but I don't regret them. I haven't laughed this hard in a while, and it's nice to see my brothers having so much fun with Sienna and Beth around. Warmth overcomes me at the thought of Sienna joining us next summer.

It's just the heat. You couldn't possibly have real *feelings for this woman.*

As I say the words in my head, I watch Sienna enthusiastically listen to Alex as he explains the strategy we use every year to beat the other team, and I know I'm nothing but a liar.

20

SIENNA

Back in Theo's room after a long shower, I can't wipe the smile off my face. After winning the water balloon fight, no thanks to me, we had an early dinner, and I ran to the shower afterward. Okay, not exactly, but I did excuse myself politely. After today's events, a cold shower was needed.

Watching Theo run around in a soaked T-shirt that basically fit him like a crop top was enough to make me need a shower. Thinking about the way he effortlessly threw me over his shoulder and hauled me back to our barricade had me swooning. I shouldn't be surprised, given his muscle mass. I never thought of myself as the type of woman who would be turned on by a man doing something so barbaric as throwing me over his shoulder, but I feel a rush of heat between my legs at the thought of it happening again.

Theo's words replay in my mind. *I'll be sure to remind you of that next time*, he had said. The idea of there being a "next time" with Theo makes my stomach flutter.

The last time I had butterflies over a boy was in the sixth grade in English class when Jake Copperfield came to sit next to me. He was the one boy everyone had a crush on, and he chose to sit next to *me*. Obviously, I got butterflies.

What I felt for Theo today feels like more than just butterflies. Yes, my stomach flutters every time I see him, but Jake never haunted my mind the same way Theo does. His swim trunks barely hang off his hips. At one point, I was hoping they'd fall so my curious mind could finally get the answers it needed and move on.

Sadly, that didn't happen, and I'm still left wondering what he looks like under all the clothing he's been so insistent on wearing. After almost a full week at a lake house in the middle of summer, I have yet to see him without his shirt on.

There were no rules about looking at one another. I'm trying to find a middle ground here.

"You ready?" Beth's voice snaps me out of the mindless scrolling I was doing on my phone. I must be jumpier than I thought because she raises an eyebrow at me as though she caught me doing something I shouldn't have been doing.

Which is ridiculous, considering I've just been lying in bed, scrolling through social media...Okay, on Theo's social profiles. I guess internet-stalking your fake boyfriend isn't the most appropriate pastime.

The guys have planned a movie night for tonight, another tradition they do every year. They've been downstairs setting up the living room for the past few minutes.

The smell of buttery popcorn has wafted upstairs, and my stomach growls at the savory scent.

Dropping my phone on the side table, I join Beth at the doorway. We've opted for our usual movie-night outfits. I'm in a loose yellow tank and athletic shorts, and Beth is wearing the same loose tank in red and leggings. We bought the tanks on a buy-one-get-one sale a few years back at our favorite athletic-wear store. They are so comfortable that we declared them our official movie-watching attire.

Wrapping her arm around mine, Beth asks, "Thinking about Theo's abs?" She finishes her question by wiggling her eyebrows at me.

"Thinking about Alex's?" I counter as we begin our descent down the stairs.

"Fuck no. He's not even my type." She juts her nose up a little to make a point.

"We both know that's not true," I say, lowering my voice as we reach the bottom of the stairs.

"What's not true?" Theo asks. I hadn't noticed he was waiting at the bottom of the stairs, and I say a silent prayer he didn't overhear any other part of our conversation.

"Nothing to concern yourself with, Theo," Beth says over her shoulder as she makes her way to the living room.

Theo and I follow Beth into the living room and take up a spot on the far edge of the large sectional. The sectional is so large that Theo looks average-sized as he takes a seat next to me. Even with his legs stretched out on the chaise, his feet don't reach the end of it. I've ensured I'm sitting close enough to him to keep up our ruse but not close enough that I become tempted to act on my shower thoughts. My strategic distance is rendered useless when he throws a blanket over our laps and reclines back, swinging his arm around my waist. I lean in just a little to sell our relationship to the others.

No other reason, of course.

Roman has already taken up a spot in one of the two recliners near the fireplace. Beth is seated not far from Theo and me, with Leo on the other end of the sectional. Alex stands before all of us, holding a remote and a pillow in his hands.

Without warning, Alex launches the pillow toward Roman, who's been focused heavily on his phone screen for the last few minutes. His phone flies out of his hand, and his head shoots up to see who threw the pillow.

"Get off your phone, old man. Work will have to wait." Roman squints his eyes at Alex but doesn't respond. He does, however, toss his phone into his pocket after picking it up off the floor, then pull the lever on the recliner to lean back. Once comfortable, he motions to Alex to get on with whatever it is he is about to do.

Alex's comment reminds me that I still haven't responded to my job offer. It's not like me to wait so long to respond, but every time I open my phone to draft the email, I can't seem to find the words to accept the offer. Considering I still have a few days to respond, I'm hoping tonight's movie can help clear my thoughts.

"As winner of last year's Kane Family Games, and the year before that, and the year before that—"

"Get on with it already." Theo cuts him off, and I smile at Theo's little eye roll as he says it.

"I have the highest honor of selecting our annual Kane Brothers summer camp movie-night extravaganza, uh, movie." His hands are on his hips like he's Superman, and I let out a chuckle.

"Do you guys really call it that?" I whisper to Theo.

"Fuck no," he whispers back.

Alex clears his throat, leveling us with a look. "If you two are done. Drum roll, please."

Theo, Leo, and I start patting our legs. Beth, only a few cushions down from Theo and me, doesn't move an inch from her curled-up position under her blanket, and Roman lightly taps the armrest of his chair.

Alex points the remote at the TV, and on the screen, an old romantic adventure movie from the '80s flashes. Theo whoops and hollers next to me, impressed by Alex's choice of movie. I glance at Beth out of the corner of my eye, knowing the cult classic featuring a princess and a pirate is one of her favorites. It was a book first, after all.

I faintly hear Beth mutter, "Of course he'd pick this one," and have to suppress my giggle at her annoyance.

From the other side of Beth, Leo claps his hands as he says, "Great pick, Alex. This one has an excellent sound-track." Leo raises his beer glass, toasting to Alex's movie choice.

"Ladies, gentlemen," Alex says, motioning to each of us, "grab some snacks and settle in. We're about to go on a crazy, action-packed, romantic adventure for the next one and a half hours. The journey full of—"

"Alright, alright. Sit down and start the damn thing

already," Roman says, throwing a piece of popcorn at Alex. Alex catches it in his mouth and smiles as he sits down on the couch between Beth and Leo, reaching over Beth to grab a box of candy off the coffee table.

Theo leans as well, grabbing a bag of popcorn from the table. When he does, his hand slips lower, from my hip to my lower back, leaving me frozen as a chill runs up my spine. I'm still focused on where his hand touches my back, so I barely notice when he hands me a box of Milk Duds. My favorite movie candy.

I turn to him, about to ask if he knew this was my favorite, when he beats me to it.

"I got a little insider information," he whispers. His hand moves back to my hip as he leans back on the couch, getting comfortable for the start of the movie. When I don't settle in with him, he gently squeezes my hip, pulling me closer to him. Against my better judgment, I oblige. With my legs swung to my right side, I lean into Theo and open the box of Milk Duds.

When he whispers in my ear to ask me if his hand placement is okay, all I can do is nod as I remember how to breathe properly. A warning flashes through my mind that this situation might be on the verge of getting more complicated than either of us can handle. I let the thought pass when Theo's thumb lightly strokes my hip once, and I feel an ache low in my abdomen.

I imagine Theo isn't spiraling as much as I am, as I watch him pop a few pieces of popcorn in his mouth. For him, it's easy. We are two friends, pretending to be in a relationship to help each other get jobs. That's all this is. He's resting his hand on my hip to further convince his brothers we're together. Sure, his hand is hidden away under the blanket that lies over the two of us, but isn't that what a boyfriend would realistically do?

Popping a few Milk Duds into my mouth, I try to focus on the opening scene of the movie. Only an hour and a half of this movie and then we can retire to Theo's room with the safety of the pillow wall between us for the rest of the night. Right now, I'm hoping to get sucked into the movie, not having to think about my pending career decision or Theo's current hand placement.

My attention is pulled from the movie when Theo's hand moves under the blanket. His finger begins tracing small circles on my hip, just below the hem of my shorts. If focusing on the first thirty minutes of the movie was hard, I'm not sure how I'll get through this last hour.

As his hand trails higher, his fingers graze my thigh as he lifts the hem of my shorts, allowing his fingers to slip beneath. He moves his knuckles back and forth on my skin. Back and forth. Back and forth. Agonizingly slow, almost as if he's testing the waters, waiting for me to react. Or he just doesn't want his movements to be noticeable to the others under the blanket.

But wouldn't that mean he's doing this because he *wants* to and not to put on a show for the others?

I must not be thinking clearly. The heat that blooms from the spot he traces on my leg spreads to other areas of my body, making it hard to think through my reaction. I do my best to control my breathing, as it involuntarily grows heavier at his touch. It's an effort to do so as I am consumed by Theo at this moment.

All I can feel is Theo. All I can smell is Theo. All I can think about is Theo.

Wanting to feel more of him, I move my hand and greedily place it on his abdomen underneath the blanket. There's no harm in returning the favor. Maybe I'll get more answers about how he really feels.

Trailing my hand lower on his abdomen, I gently brush my fingers along his waistband before dipping them under the soft fabric of his shirt. His skin is softer than I expected, but his abs are as hard as I envisioned, whch has been more times than I care to admit since meeting him at the diner.

With my head still resting on his shoulder, I hear the moment his heartbeat increases as I mimic his hand motions. His fingers brush along the skin of my hips, the hemline of my shorts now pulled up farther than a few minutes ago. My fingers lightly touch the space above his belly button, dipping every so often to tease his waistband.

With each circular motion of Theo's fingers, he slides farther up my hip until he reaches the lace-lined fabric of my underwear. My hand on him stalls as he begins to toy with the lace, pulling slightly before tracing his fingers along the fabric backward toward my ass. Letting the lace go, he glides his fingertips back and forth on the bare skin of my ass, sending a shiver up my spine. When his hand flattens on my ass cheek, I can feel the growing heat between my thighs at the proximity of his fingertips to my already soaking wet core.

"You guys want more popcorn?" Leo's voice washes over me like a bucket full of ice water. I yank my hand from Theo's abs as he pulls the fabric of my shorts back over my hip. When he declines Leo's offer of popcorn, I glance at him. One look and he's staring straight at the TV screen, unbothered by the events that just transpired between us. I know he can see me looking at him out of the corner of his eye, but he won't look back at me. It feels like a slap straight to the face.

Adjusting his position, Theo pulls his arm from around me, grabs his water, and takes a sip. When he sits back, his arm doesn't return to its original position. Instead, he grabs a pillow and pulls it over his lap, resting both of his arms there. The pillow's position would make it impossible for me to return my hand to its original position, and the message is clear.

Embarrassed that I may have unintentionally made Theo feel uncomfortable, I excuse myself to go to the bathroom. Theo barely glances my way as I leave the living room.

Once I'm in the bathroom, I turn the faucet to cold. I cup my hands under the running water and begin splashing it on my face. The first wave stings, but it's nothing compared to the sudden lack of attention I'm getting from Theo. The cold water numbs as I continue splashing it on my face, hoping it will help clear my mind and distract me from the ache between my legs.

After what feels like a solid ten minutes in the bathroom, I still haven't cooled down. I'm not a virgin; it's not like a man has never touched me before. But something about *this* man makes the simplest touch feel earth-shattering in the best way possible.

I haven't been this worked up in a while. I curse

myself for not listening to Beth's advice about finding some random guy to sleep with the night of Theo's party. Then maybe I wouldn't be in this mess.

When I exit the restroom and look at the living room, I freeze. The thought of going back to sit with Theo feels suffocating. Everyone is still engrossed in the movie, so I turn the opposite way and head out the back door to the deck.

The summer night air cools my skin as I make my way across the deck, overlooking the lake. Gripping the railing as though I might fall off, I take a few deep breaths. As the cool breeze kisses my skin under the light of the moon, the sound of crickets surrounds me, and my body temperature begins to drop.

Inhale...Exhale...Inhale...Exhale...Inha-

The unmistakable sound of the back door sliding open breaks through the peaceful night air. I don't dare to look back as I wrap my arms around myself, wishing I had a shell to hide inside in the presence of the one person I didn't want to follow me out here. I don't need to look back to know it's him. Another breeze rolls through, and his scent invades my senses the moment he gets close.

Something soft brushes against my left arm, and I look down to find Theo holding out his sweatshirt to me.

"Let's talk," he says softly.

My stomach drops as he says the words. Tentatively, I take the sweatshirt from his hand, the heat between my legs returning in his presence. The night air continues to kiss my bare limbs, and when a chill runs through me, I put on the sweatshirt, leaving it unzipped.

My heart rate increases as I await his next words. I know where this is going. I've made him uncomfortable by crossing a boundary between the two of us. I got caught up in the moment, and I'm ashamed of my body's reaction. I should've known better.

He opens his mouth to say something, and I know only one thing for certain. I'll have no choice but to accept the offer sitting in my inbox, since I'll be kissing any job option I had with Theo goodbye.

21

THEO

I'm fucked. *So* fucked.

I wasn't thinking when I started to touch Sienna. Well, not with my brain anyway. I could feel the way her breath hitched under my arm as I moved my fingers higher up her thigh. Then she slipped her hand underneath my shirt, and I was done for. I thought she was finally making a move to act on our very obvious mutual attraction.

Each time her hand grazed over the waistband of my pants, my cock hardened further. By the time I was flattening my hand on her ass, my cock was so hard it ached, especially under the restriction of my sweatpants.

When Leo so rudely cockblocked me with his popcorn question, I realized I was taking things too far. I must've been misreading her signals by the way she pulled her hand away so quickly. The last thing I wanted was to push her into something she wasn't comfortable with.

I shamelessly used a pillow to hide my erection. My

stomach twisted further when Sienna excused herself to the restroom, and I couldn't follow her. Although getting up at that moment would've made the actions happening under the blanket painfully obvious. I wanted to sell this relationship to my brothers, but I wasn't desperate enough to expose myself like that.

In her absence, as I was forced to wait out my erection, I came to terms with the one thought I've been avoiding. I want Sienna. I think I've wanted her from the moment I spotted her sitting at that diner table, brows furrowed, staring at her laptop screen.

I've been treading lightly out of respect for her boundaries, but the urge I have to hold her against a wall and kiss her until both of our lips are raw has begun to consume me. When I first thought about showing Sienna how much fun she could have with me in an effort to get her to stay, I hadn't had this in mind. With every smile she throws my way, every laugh I hear come from her throat, every time we make eye contact, it has been slowly solidifying one fact.

I. Want. Her.

"Thought you might be a little cold out here," I say to Sienna, in an effort to break the tension.

"Thank you." She motions to my sweatshirt. The sight of her in my clothing has my cock springing back to life.

"It's beautiful out here at night," Sienna says, looking up at the night sky.

This far from the city, the pitch-black sky is dotted with tiny sparkling stars. Although I can't be bothered to look when an angel stands before me.

My eyes slowly cascade down her face to her lips,

then travel farther to her exposed collarbone. Taking in the way the moonlight glistens off her smooth, dark skin. What I wouldn't give to brush my lips across her neck right now.

"I'm starting to think this wasn't such a good idea," Sienna practically whispers. She's so quiet, I could barely hear her. Taking a step closer to her, I brush my arm against hers in the process as she goes back to watching the still waters of the lake. What I wouldn't give for her to glance in my direction right about now.

"What wasn't a good idea? The movie?" I play dumb, hoping she won't say the words I've been dreading since I came out here. She turns toward me then, finally giving me her attention.

"No, Theo. Us." She breaks eye contact, almost embarrassed, as if she said something wrong. "Not us, us. Because there is no 'us.' But this deal we made." She swings her finger between the two of us, but is restricted in her movement due to our proximity. When I smell summer strawberries and ocean waters, every nerve in my body screams that what she is saying is *wrong.*

"Look, this doesn't seem to be getting us anywhere. We've been here a week, Theo, and I haven't heard a word about either one of us getting a job at the end of this. I think I'm going to accept the other offer." She pauses and takes a breath. "Quite frankly, I think things between us are getting more complicated than either one of us wants to admit."

"Don't accept the other offer." Sienna's head turns toward me at my response, finally tearing her gaze from the lake. I continue when she doesn't respond, "I think you should stay. I'll talk to Roman, and I can get you a better offer than what you have now." I use every ounce of my strength to resist reaching out and tilting her face to meet mine.

When Sienna continues to stay silent, I say, "If you're upset because of the cuddling earlier...Sienna, I'm sorry if that crossed a line. I should've asked first." I pause. "Please, just stay."

"You don't have to apologize for that. It just makes things more confusing between us." My eyebrows pinch together as I watch her closely, waiting for her next words.

Her chest rises and falls before she admits, "I'm attracted to you, Theo. When we made this deal, I didn't think my attraction was going to get in the way of anything. I thought it was something I could compartmentalize and ignore." I stay silent, too afraid to respond incorrectly until I know for sure where this is going.

"The rules I put in place for us, they were more for me to ensure I didn't blur any lines, not you. I know you just want to be friends, but the bikini comment, and whatever that was on the couch...It's getting harder to compartmentalize my attraction to you and separate it from our agreement. I can never tell if the comments you make are genuine or part of the ruse. I think accepting the other job will just be easier." A slight shake of her head and she turns, moving past me to head back inside. I stop her by placing a hand gently on her arm.

"Did you want me to mean it?" I ask, leaning in close, our lips only inches apart. Sienna's eyes dart back and forth between mine, as though she is searching them for the correct answer.

"What?" She finally responds.

"The bikini comment. Did you want me to mean it? Because I meant it, Sienna. Every. Fucking. Word." We're both breathing heavier now. Neither of us moves, as if we are both afraid of scaring the other away.

When the silence stretches between us, I confess, "I can't stop thinking about you. Your smell, your laugh, those tight little shorts you wear before climbing into bed with me every night. It's intoxicating. *You're* intoxicating. I've been barely holding on, only following the boundaries you set out of respect for you. I'd be lying if I said I haven't thought about violating that respect every goddamn day since I drove you here." She's breathing hard now, the dramatic rise and fall of her chest accentuating her breasts in a way that makes my cock ache with need. Our lips, to my excruciating agony, are still not touching.

"Let me break one more rule, Sienna," I beg, my eyes still stuck on her full lips.

She nods her head so slightly that I barely catch it. My eyes dart back up to hers. "Words, Angel. I need words."

"Yes. Fuck the rul—"

Before she finishes her sentence, I crash my lips into hers.

22

SIENNA

I lose all thoughts as Theo crashes his lips into mine. I don't give him a chance to pull back as I turn into him, melting into the kiss.

He kisses me with an urgency that I feel deep in my bones. When he gently nudges my lips apart, I happily accept his invitation as I open and collide my tongue with his.

Theo's arm wraps around my waist. Slipping his hand beneath the sweatshirt, he presses on my lower back, pulling me even closer to him. The hand that rested on my cheek begins to travel lower. I pay it no mind until he grazes the side of my breast, the ache returning between my thighs.

His hand stalls on my ribs, cupping the side of my breast. I can feel his thumb only inches away from where I need him. My nipples harden at each brush against his chest as we continue to kiss. The thin fabric of my bralette and tank top does nothing to shield from the cool breeze, but it feels like the worst barrier possible between us, and I ache to take them off.

The hand wrapped around my waist drops lower, and his large hand cups my ass. With one tug, he's pulling me up and wrapping my legs around his hips. He does it as effortlessly as when he threw me over his shoulder, and the wetness between my legs grows.

He walks us over to the corner of the deck, a spot hidden just to the side of the house. The light doesn't quite reach this corner, and there's certainly no furniture over here, but I'm too distracted by his lips on my neck to pay attention to what he has planned. He leaves a trail of kisses from the corner of my mouth down my neck. When he reaches my collarbone, he licks the pathway he just carved, all the way up to my jaw. The little moan I let out when he does it prompts him to squeeze my ass harder, and the reaction tempts me to moan again.

When my ass comes into contact with a rough surface, Theo pulls back, hands braced on my waist.

I realize that he's set me down on the patio railing. Looking to the left, I can't help the smile that escapes me when I realize we are completely hidden from view. Theo wants this moment to be private. As if what he said before kissing me wasn't enough, this isn't to prove anything or a part of our fake-dating agreement. This is just us—Theo and I.

I reach out and take hold of his shirt, pulling him in toward me, kissing him again. His grip on my hips tightens as he pulls me toward the edge of the railing, pressing his cock against my core.

Theo's movements have caused my shorts to ride up

my thighs, almost exposing me completely to the natural elements that surround us. The fabric on his sweats is thin, allowing me to feel every inch of him against my center. The moment he presses against me, I let out a gasp, pulling away from our kiss to catch my breath.

I instantly regret pulling away. The moment my lips part from his skin, my mind starts to wander.

"We shouldn't," I tell Theo, more breathless than I intend.

"We should. We should've done this a long time ago." His husky, deep voice fogs my prefrontal cortex. He places a kiss on my cheek, then another on my jaw, then another on my neck, lingering there for just long enough that I start to lose myself again.

Before I give in to the temptation that is Theo Kane, I push him back, looking up at him again as I say, "Are you sure this is such a good idea? We may want this, but it doesn't make it the responsible choice." My mind continues to spiral as he puts a finger to my lips.

He moves a hand from my hip toward my bare thigh, dragging his fingers lightly, the sensation agonizing in the best way possible. I soften at his touch, my mind quieting as he begins to speak.

He lifts my chin with the finger that was pressed to my lips. "Are you telling me that if I were to touch you..." He grazes a knuckle along my inner thigh. "I wouldn't find you soaking wet for me right now?"

"That's not—" I'm at a loss for words. His grin in response to my speechlessness is mouth-watering.

"I'm tired of playing pretend, Sienna," he says, his hand on my inner thigh inching closer to my center. My hips have a mind of their own as they shift in a desperate attempt to coax his hand to where I need him most.

He lets out a low chuckle. "If I didn't know better, I'd say you're done pretending too." I ignore his words as I continue to chase the touch he is so rudely keeping from me. My hips still when he places a gentle kiss on my lips, stalling his hand.

"I'll make you a deal." Theo continues, "If I touch you, and you're not as wet as I think you are, then we'll go upstairs and fall asleep with the pillows between us like we've done every night since we got here, and we can forget this ever happened."

My heart drops the slightest bit at the thought of having any barriers between us any longer.

"But..." He places his forehead against mine, his fingers caressing the apex between my inner thigh and my core, just over the fabric of my shorts, not yet dipping beneath them. "If I touch you, and you're as wet as I think you are, then we stop pretending. We act on our impulses for the remainder of our time here. You forget about the other job and stay while we explore whatever this is. Let me convince you to stay."

He lifts my chin again so I'm looking up at him. "How are you going to do that?" I ask. He's smiling as he pulls me in for another kiss in response.

Maybe it is possible to explore our sexual connection while still focusing on our careers. It's not like we're going to fall in love. It's just sex, and I haven't been kissed like this in so long. If ever. A sense of relief washes over me at the thought of giving in to the distraction for once without worrying about the consequences that could follow.

Our kiss quickly escalates to something deep and passionate as our tongues collide. Theo has stepped in closer to me, pressing his length against my center once again, but he doesn't move his hand. He's still centimeters from where I need him.

"Theo, please," I whimper against his lips.

Theo bends as he leaves a trail of kisses down my neck, finally slipping his fingers beneath the fabric of my shorts. Wrapping one arm around me, he lifts me slightly off the railing to push the fabric aside. The cool breeze washes over my center, and I'm suddenly aware of just how wet I am.

"Fuck." His breath is hot against my neck, chilling the spot he just kissed. "You're fucking soaked for me."

He runs his fingers up and down my center a few times, sending a chill down my spine. I can already feel my core tightening at the slightest touch. The effect he has on me should be illegal.

As if to torture me more, Theo removes his hand from between my thighs. I look up, ready to beg him to touch me again, when he begins to lift his hand. He doesn't break eye contact as he slips the two fingers that he ran through my wetness into his mouth.

"You taste even better than I imagined," he moans, as he tastes me. I'm speechless as I watch him savor every last drop.

"Hold the railing," he commands as he pulls me in for another kiss. The cool summer night breeze hits my nipples as he pushes the sweatshirt aside, exposing me even further than I already am. One side of the sweatshirt falls off my shoulders. I feel like a mess, and I revel in every second of it.

The tank top I'm wearing is cut low on my chest, having shifted to expose more of my lace bralette underneath. My hardened nipples show through the fabric, and when Theo pulls back, he looks at me as though I'm something to be devoured.

Having his fill, he grabs my waist again, leaning down to kiss the spot below my collarbone.

My grip tightens on the railing as I lean back, granting him further access to my breasts.

Theo must notice the slight tension in my body at this angle because he whispers, "Relax, I got you."

I do just that as he holds me with one hand braced on my back, and one on my hip, trailing back to my core. Trailing kisses down my chest, Theo kisses all the way to my nipple over the fabric of my tank top. When he sucks my nipple into his mouth through the fabric, I lean back into his hand, letting go at the sensation coursing through my body. When his hand doesn't budge, I relax even further, knowing he won't let me fall.

Letting out a chuckle of approval, he switches to my other breast, kissing the nipple through the fabric before taking it into his mouth and sucking lightly.

Fed up with the teasing, I pull down my tank top, exposing my breasts to him.

"Fuck." His voice comes out breathless as he takes me in.

Leaning down, he leaves a trail of kisses on my sternum. I wiggle my hips in response, silently pleading for him to touch me exactly where he did before. I'm wound so tight, I feel like I'm going to snap in two if he doesn't provide me with any sort of relief.

He finally takes one of my nipples into his mouth, slowly sucking and licking at it. He continues until I'm throwing my head back in bliss at the feeling of his mouth on me. The cool breeze adds to the sensation, sending a chill through me each time he pulls away.

Reaching out, I grab a fistful of his shirt, pulling his mouth away from my breasts so I can plant another kiss on his lips. Our tongues collide, my bare breasts brushing against his shirt as my breath grows heavier and our kiss deepens. My other hand drops to his hip. If he insists on teasing me, I can do the same to him.

I begin sliding my hand down his chest, pulling on his waistband once I reach it. He lets out a groan at my touch, and it's all the motivation I need to dip my fingers beneath his sweatpants just to the right of his cock.

We kiss as we continue to play a game of chicken, seeing who will touch who first.

When he finally slides his fingers through my wetness again, my forehead drops to his chest, resting there as I try to regulate my erratic breathing. Regaining my senses, I brush my fingers along the side of his cock in his pants.

"Fuck." He lets out a breath. Grabbing his waistband, he pulls down his sweats just enough to let his cock spring free, and I gape at the size of it.

"And here I thought you couldn't get any wetter," he says, as he inserts two fingers inside me at once. I grab his cock at the same time, and we both let out a low moan.

I've never been happier to break a rule than in this exact moment.

I run my hand up and down the length of him, pumping his cock lightly at first, taking note of what he likes. He does the same as he inserts his fingers into me, then pulls out. In and out, in and out.

At the mention of how wet I am, I get an idea. I remove my hand from his cock and lightly nudge his from my core. Looking up at Theo, I run my hand down my center, then back up again, slowly. I watch him as he watches me and smile when his breathing increases to a pace as erratic as my own.

Maintaining eye contact, I use the same hand to grab his cock again, mixing my wetness with his precum and spreading it up and down his cock, my hand more easily gliding now.

"Jesus fucking Christ," he says before driving two fingers into me again and curling them, hitting me in a place no other man has been able to find.

As I begin to pump him faster, my hand circling the tip of his cock every now and then, his breathing becomes even more erratic. He presses his thumb to my clit, circling while still pumping his fingers in and out of me. The tightness building up in my lower spine is agonizing in the best way possible as I get closer to climax.

"Fuck, Theo, I think I might..." I'm barely able to get the words out through my heavy breathing.

Theo puts his forehead against mine, tightening his arm around my back as he brings me closer to the metaphorical edge. My grip on his cock tightens in tandem with the tightness inside me. If I'm going over the edge, I'm taking him with me.

"Come for me, Angel. I'm right behind you...fuck." Theo pulls me into a kiss as he continues to pump his fingers in and out of me, expertly circling my clit.

I pump him faster, he kisses me harder, and the moment he curls his fingers inside me again while nipping at my bottom lip, I lose all control.

"Fuck yes, just like that, Sienna," Theo breathes. We fall over the edge together. The tension in my lower spine finally explodes into a warmth of bliss, as he does the same into my hand. Theo holds me from falling over the railing as my back arches so far that I can almost see the trees behind me.

Catching me before I arch too far, Theo pulls me into his chest. We stay like that for a minute, listening to each other's breathing as we both come down from the high. He plants a few kisses on the top of my head, and I do the same to his bicep. Warmth overcomes all my senses as I listen to the beat of his heart, slowly coming down from its elevated state. It's a sound that could put me to sleep right here in Theo's arms.

When Theo finally moves, he fixes my shirt and shorts, zipping up the hoodie to properly cover me from the elements of the night. Wrapping an arm around me again, he gently lifts me from the railing, then looks us both over to ensure we are presentable enough to go back inside.

Peeking through the back door, we find the living room pitch black. We must've been out here so long that the movie ended and everyone headed upstairs for the night. That makes going back inside less nerve-racking at least.

I'm not looking forward to the many questions I'll be getting from Beth tomorrow.

Taking my hand, Theo leads me through the sliding glass door and up the back stairwell to his bedroom, both of us taking a turn in the bathroom on the way.

Once the bedroom door is closed behind us, Theo stands at the end of the bed, staring at the line of pillows down the center of the mattress. Moving to "his" side of the bed, he pulls all the pillows off, throwing them across the room to the seat at the bay window.

"I never want to see a pillow wall again." Pulling back the covers, he climbs into bed and pats the side next to him.

I smile at his distaste for the pillow wall, but stall when he invites me into bed. I still haven't spoken a word since we were downstairs, and I'm starting to feel over-whelmed that no pillow wall means yet another thing has changed between us.

"Hey, talk to me," Theo says softly as he props himself on one elbow on my side of the bed, leaving very little space for me to crawl in next to him.

"We just broke so many rules, Theo."

"I know. But I promise, this won't change anything. The goal is still for both of us to have jobs by the end of the summer. Don't you want to have a little fun in the process?" He reaches over to my nightstand to hand me my bonnet so I can begin prepping my hair for the night. The motion is so domestic, it sends a wave of butterflies through my stomach.

Beth has been telling me to have fun this summer. To let loose a little and give in to my urges. There's still plenty of time for us to secure our jobs. He'll talk to Roman, and I'll help him prove he's mature enough to work for his brother's company. Although I'm still not convinced taking this other job isn't the right choice.

This was by far the most fun I've had since I've been here. It was also the best orgasm I've ever had, and he only used his fingers. I can't imagine what sex with him is like. Maybe I am overcomplicating things.

Then again, I do like structure.

Finally climbing into bed next to him, I respond, "Of course I want to have fun. But if we're going to have a summer fling while still helping each other, then we need a new set of rules." This makes Theo smile.

"Are you sure that's a good idea? We clearly have a habit of breaking your rules." Theo winks and tosses an arm around my waist.

I give him a playful shove. "I'm serious, Theo. We can help each other and have fun in the process, but you can't fall in love with me." I cross my arms, hoping to convey my seriousness to him that this rule cannot be broken.

I was serious when I said I needed to focus on building my career. I can't be distracted by men. Especially not men like him. I simply don't have time for them until I've settled into my career path.

Theo raises an eyebrow at me. "Isn't there already a rule set. *You're* not supposed to fall in love with *me*."

"Trust me, that won't happen," I respond with an eye roll.

Theo falls to his back on the bed, making a hand

motion as though he just took a knife to the chest. I laugh off his dramatics while settling further into the covers myself. Theo's arm wraps around me again, flipping me to face away from him as he pulls my back into his chest.

"Okay, no falling in love. But please tell me you don't have a rule against cuddling?"

I look back at him over my shoulder. "No, I guess cuddling is fine," I say on a sarcastic sigh. Theo responds with a kiss to my cheek as he nuzzles into the back of my neck.

"Good night, Sienna."

"Good night, Theo."

I replay his comment in my head on repeat as I drift off to sleep.

We clearly have a habit of breaking rules.

Theo may be correct that we have a habit of breaking rules, but this is one rule we absolutely cannot break.

23

SIENNA

The past couple of days have been relaxing beyond relief. Filled with board games, dips in the lake during the hottest part of the day, and food made by Leo that should go down in history books as the most delicious food ever made. It also helps that without the pillow wall in the way, Theo and I have woken up tangled in each other's arms each morning. I hate to admit that it's the best sleep I've gotten in a while.

What's been most surprising is how much fun I've had hanging out with him and his brothers. Don't get me wrong, I'm still keeping my eye out for anything that points to there being bodies buried in this expansive land that they own. But I've been able to relax these past few days in a way that I haven't been able to for years.

Beth says it's because I finally got "laid," and no matter how much I insist that we didn't have sex, she's still skeptical.

"I swear, we only fooled around and did hand stuff when we were out on the porch. You know I don't jump into bed with men that quickly," I said to her when she didn't believe me.

"I still think you're hiding something. No man is that good with their hands," she said in response.

I was careful not to remind her that it's been a while since she was with a man, since she had taken an oath (self-imposed) to only date women, and she rarely brings a man home with her.

Beth and I are on the back porch, enjoying the lake view. It's warmer than usual today as a heat wave rolls through the area. Going into full effect tomorrow, we decided to spend some additional time outside. The remainder of our days will be spent inside, enjoying the air-conditioning or dunking ourselves in the lake if the heat lasts as long as our weather app says it will. It may rain here in the Pacific Northwest 90 percent of the year, but the other 10 percent can get so hot that sometimes it feels like your skin is going to melt off.

"I'm telling you, man, best buns I've seen in my life." Alex and Theo walk out onto the deck, mid-conversation.

"Ew! Alex, what the fuck?" Beth says, crinkling her nose. Beth grabs a pillow from the cushion next to her and chucks it at Alex.

"*Hamburger* buns, Beth. I'm talking about *hamburger* buns." Alex waves his arms at Beth in an effort to correct her. The look on her face tells me she's not convinced.

Theo follows Alex, wearing a T-shirt and shorts, showing off every toned muscle of his legs. A piece of his hair falls forward onto his forehead, and the combination of the two is enough to make a girl rethink her life choices.

Don't get me wrong, I'm still focused on deciding about this job offer. Just one more peek at those thighs, though...

No, Sienna. Obsessing over him is a slippery slope to breaking another rule.

"God, you're such a *man* sometimes." Beth gets up from the couch, walking past Alex to head back inside.

"Why, thank you," Alex responds, beating Beth to the door and sliding it open for her. He bows slightly as she walks past, and I fight to hold in my laugh. When she gives him the middle finger as she crosses the threshold, the laugh bursts out of me.

"You too?" Alex gasps. Looking at me, he places a hand on his chest as though he's been injured by my laugh at his expense. I ignore him, but the smile on my face doesn't fade as he follows Beth inside.

"This is a good look on you," Theo says from beside me, pulling my attention to him. Instinctively, I step closer to him, knowing we are alone on the patio. As I do, Theo pulls me toward him by my waist and plants a kiss on my lips. The action is similar to two magnets clicking together when they've been placed too close to one another.

"What's a good look on me?" I pull back slightly, looking down at my old band camp T-shirt, which I've had since the ninth grade. "This old thing?"

"No." Theo tugs at my waist as he huffs out a chuckle. Planting another kiss on one corner of my lips, he says, "This." Then he does the same to the other corner. "Smile."

I swat him away, and he continues, "I just like seeing

you happy. Although now I'm very curious about this band camp. What instrument did you play? Were you good? Do you still play?"

I laugh as it's my turn to pull him in for a kiss now, successfully shutting him down from asking more questions. "I played the flute. I was decent but not good enough to continue after high school. No, I do not still play. Now, no more questions."

Using his finger, he tilts my chin toward him. "I bet you were adorable. I'd love to see pictures of you from your childhood. Oh! I bet you had a stuffed bear that you tugged around with you everywhere, huh?"

Laughing, I move away to head inside. "It was a bunny, and I only had it until I was seven. Now leave me alone. Don't we have somewhere to be?" I swat his hand away as he attempts to grab at my waist playfully. He tries to ask me more embarrassing questions about my childhood, but I promptly ignore him.

My smile only falters when I realize his interest in my childhood is nothing more than a means of flirting. This is just a fun fling, no strings, no commitment. Hell, we haven't even had sex, so I highly doubt Theo has any actual interest in my past.

The idea of that makes my stomach twist into a knot.

When I catch up with the rest of the group in the kitchen, the conversation is a welcome break from my thoughts. The burger competition is tonight, and I find myself more excited than I expected. Although I credit that excitement to the prospect of tasting Leo's supposed "life-changing" burgers. Also, maybe because Theo and I are on the same team, we have a plan to give Leo a run for his money.

Beth opted out of this one but said she would help Theo and me pick out ingredients. Hence why all of us, except Roman, are currently in the kitchen deciding whose car we will take to the grocery store.

"Six people and we all drive Mustangs. Not something we really thought through here," Alex says to the group.

"So let's just take two cars then," Leo says as though the solution is obvious. Which, to be fair, it is, but then it poses another question.

"Who rides with who, then?" Theo asks from beside me, his hand wrapping around my waist again. I've learned it's his favorite spot to rest his arm.

"Well, you two should ride together, obviously." Alex motions toward Theo and me.

"Beth can ride with us, then," I add.

"And leave me with Mr. Grumpy? No thanks," Alex responds.

Leo rolls his eyes. "He's not that bad."

"Maybe not to you. But the drive to the grocery store is too long to be stuck in a two-door car with him. Theo, you take him, and we'll take Beth." Alex nods in Theo's direction.

"Not a chance if we're driving your car," she says to Alex with a scoff.

Roman finally joins us in the kitchen, having come from upstairs. He looks at all of us gathered around the kitchen island, his brows furrowed together.

"You ready?" he says to the group.

"Yeah, just trying to figure out the car situation," Leo says to Roman.

"It's a 'situation'?" He looks at his brother confused, and Leo grimaces as he shrugs. Roman pinches the bridge of his nose and sighs.

"Okay," Roman begins. "Theo, Sienna, you're with me." He points at Alex, Beth, and Leo. "The three of you can ride together."

Roman's confident tone leaves no room for debate. As we head toward the door, Beth stops me with a look. Staring at me with wide eyes, she mouths the words "kill me" before reluctantly taking off after Alex and Leo. I look after her with the best "I'm sorry" face I can muster, but I don't think it does much to set her at ease.

As everyone files out of the front door, I can't help but notice something peculiar that all the men do as they exit. I must have the question written all over my face because Theo leans down and speaks softly, just loud enough for only us to hear.

"You think it's weird, don't you?"

Looking up at him, I'm even more confused now. "Weird? No. Not at all. Just curious is all. She's a gorgeous woman, but I'm not sure...?" I'm not even sure how to finish the sentence. As each of the men exits the front door, they kiss the tips of their fingers and touch the picture frame. The photo is of a beautiful woman with wavy brown hair that falls to her shoulders and a smile that reminds me of Theo's. Taking a second look at the photo, I don't need Theo's explanation to know exactly who the woman is.

"That's my mom. We never fail to say goodbye to her

every time we leave the house. It started when we were younger, and the habit just grew with us as we got older. I can't imagine leaving now without doing it. Strange, I know." He shrugs one shoulder as though he's embarrassed by the habit.

Shaking my head, I turn to Theo in hopes of reassuring him. "Of course. I should have known. I'm so sorry. I don't think it's weird or strange at all. I think it's very sweet. My dumb summer brain just didn't put two and two together." That earns me a smile as he stands next to the photo of his mom. It's nice to see where he got his smile from.

"She was a beautiful woman," I say, looking back at the photo.

"Yeah, she was." I catch Theo smiling somberly at the photo of his mother before he kisses his fingertips, touches the frame, then exits through the front door.

I follow him, but not before lifting a timid hand, gesturing a small wave toward the photo. My own little "goodbye," mimicking theirs.

Theo and I laugh at Beth as she sits in the passenger seat of Alex's car. Alex and Leo made a show of getting her in the passenger seat as she was all but kicking and screaming. Not really; she's just occasionally dramatic, and they seem to get a kick out of messing with her. Knowing Beth, she hates that she loves every second of it.

As the Mustang takes off, she bangs her fists against the window, releasing a fake sob as the car whines upon acceleration. She may say she isn't having fun, but I know Beth, and she only gets this dramatic when she feels comfortable. So at the very least, she feels comfortable around these men, which says a lot more than you'd think, given her past.

It brings me some semblance of comfort knowing she's at least found a friend in Leo, and they've been able to get along during our time here. Especially while Theo and I...do whatever it is we're doing. Beth says we're "having fun," so I'm just going with that terminology for now. Although sometimes it feels like more than just "fun" between us.

Roman's Mustang is the newest of all the cars. Theo says it's a GT500, whatever that means. It's all blacked out, and I'm just thankful his car has working air-conditioning. There's an uncomfortable silence after we file into the sports car. Especially considering Theo insisted I sit in the front.

"What kind of gentleman would I be if I didn't take the back seat?" he asked.

"A shitty one," Roman responds, before settling himself in the driver's seat.

They left no room for argument, but the longer I sit in the front seat, the more I wish I'd fought back. Though it was entertaining to watch Theo squeeze his tall frame into the back seat of the Mustang.

Faint music plays; some R&B playlist streams through the music app on Roman's phone. I take the awkward silence as an opportunity to look out the window at the scenery as we drive by.

Where Theo is a warm summer day, Roman exudes

the energy of a cold winter's night. I've always preferred sunshine.

A small shiver runs through my body as the AC blasts through the vents in the car. I hope Theo talks to Roman soon, since I'm not quite sure how to bring up the idea of him helping me find a job.

"Hey, I know we've only just met, and you don't care to ever talk to me or look in my direction, but I was wondering... can you help me get a job?" Yeah, that's a great plan.

I have yet to respond to the job offer sitting in my inbox, and I only have one more day until they need an answer. I should probably respond, but something keeps me from hitting the Send button.

As if sensing my internal spiral, Theo leans forward in the back seat. He places his large hand on the side of my seat, and I get a momentary flashback to where his fingers have been.

"So, Roman, how's work? You've been on your phone a lot. Business must be good then?" he asks, looking at Roman, who doesn't take his eyes off the road.

Roman sighs, almost appearing to relax at the thought of work. "It's been fine. Business as usual," he responds, checking his rearview mirror briefly before snapping his eyes back to the road in front of him.

"Is your seat belt on?" he asks Theo. The leather on the steering wheel makes a cracking noise as he squeezes it tighter. The cobra engraved on the center of the steering wheel looks just as intimidating as Roman himself.

"Yeah, obviously," Theo responds by snapping his seat belt against his chest. Apparently, he snaps it too hard because he rubs the spot, mouthing the word "ow" to me, and I let out a giggle.

Theo turns his attention back to Roman. "Did I tell you that Sienna graduated with her degree in architecture?" Theo winks at me, and I draw my brows together in confusion.

He can't possibly be bringing this up *now* when I'm in the car with them. I thought he was going to talk to Roman alone. I shake my head slightly, begging Theo not to have this conversation in front of me.

A muffled "hmm" is all the response Roman bothers to give.

To my dismay, Theo continues, "Yep, that's right. Architecture. With my business degree, we might as well start our own construction company." He smiles at Roman.

"Very funny," Roman responds, looking at Theo through the rearview mirror briefly before snapping his eyes back to the road.

"You're not amused by that idea? Is that because you have a job already waiting for me at Dad's company?" Theo pokes Roman in the shoulder.

Roman scoffs. "*If* I give you a job at *my* company, it'll be when you've proven yourself worthy of working at *my* company. We've already been over this, Theo, and I won't discuss this further when we have a guest."

A final statement by Roman, but Theo pushes on anyway.

"Okay, fine. But Sienna's been looking for a job too. You know how it is nowadays. Every company wants ten years of experience for 'entry-level' positions." Theo makes air quotes with his fingers.

"We don't have in-house architects. You know we hire out for all of that," Roman responds.

"Yeah but maybe you could pull some strings, set her up with an interview over at Rose City Designs. I'm sure Graham would be more than willing to lend us a favor." Theo turns to me. "Graham is Roman's best friend. They work together a lot." My heart rate picks up at Theo's words.

"Wait, Graham Emerson is your best friend?" I say, joining in on the conversation. Theo mentioned that Roman had connections to Rose City Designs, but he never mentioned he was *best friends* with the owner and CEO.

Even though they are my dream company, I didn't apply with them because I never thought I'd have a shot right out of college. Working for them wasn't written into my plan until I was in my late twenties, after I had gained enough experience to have a shot at an interview. Getting an interview now could fast-track my career. The thought makes the offer from JR Construction look entirely unappealing.

I get a curt nod from Roman, who seems entirely unamused by this conversation.

"I absolutely love their designs. I attend the Parade of Homes every year and always fall in love with their homes. There's a sophistication but practicality to their designs that really brings character to the modern-day home." I fade out my sentence when I realize that I'm explaining Graham's company practices to his best friend as if he doesn't already know.

My cheeks heat from embarrassment at my sudden rambling. I notice Roman's shoulders shake for a split second, mirroring a slight chuckle, though it's gone in a flash.

"I'll let Graham know you're a fan of his work. That fucker loves hearing anything that inflates his ego."

"Great, it's settled then. You'll talk to Graham about a job for Sienna, and you'll continue to consider letting me work at Dad's company," Theo chimes in from the back seat.

Roman puts his hand up. "I said I'd pass along Sienna's comments to Graham. I'm not sure he has any openings right now." He shrugs and turns his head toward me, though he keeps his eyes on the road, when he says, "Sorry."

"Roman, c'mon. Just send him her portfolio. It couldn't hurt. I've already looked through it, and I think Graham would be very impressed," Theo all but begs his brother to help me. The words make me sound more desperate than I'd like to appear, and I suddenly wish the seat would open up around me so I could disappear into the leather.

Roman thinks over Theo's words for a few moments and finally nods. He directs his next words toward me. "Email it to me."

Shocked, I respond, "Yes, of course. I'll send it tonight. Thank you." Looking back at Theo, I smile, my excitement overcoming any previous embarrassment.

For the remainder of the drive, I think about Theo's

words. If I'm being honest with myself, this other job offer isn't what I want, not even close. The prospect of an interview with Graham is more than enough to make me realize the real reason I haven't accepted the job offer.

I don't want to settle.

That's the whole point of my ten-year plan anyway, so I never have to settle. If I start my career by doing just that, I'm afraid it will begin a pattern of settling that I'll never be able to escape from.

Before I can talk myself out of it, I open the email app on my phone and send a quick message in response, declining the job offer. After texting my dad to let him know, I put my phone back in my pocket and keep watching the road as a nearby city comes into view.

I don't like the idea of my plan shifting, and not accepting this offer is taking a bigger risk than I normally would. But the potential to work at Rose City Designs earlier than I planned would put me years ahead of my schedule.

Maybe then, I'd have more room for things like dating early on. When I look back at Theo, he flashes his sunshine smile at me once again, and at that moment, the risk I'm taking doesn't seem so scary.

24
SIENNA

I'm losing a fight with the comforter as I've woken up in a pool of my own sweat. The added heat of the blankets feels suffocating, and I kick them off me, just as I notice Theo isn't in bed. When the heat doesn't let up, despite lying in bed in only shorts and my bralette, I know the heat wave has finally hit us. Although I thought the house had air-conditioning, so I'm not exactly sure why it's so hot inside.

I don't bother to remove my bonnet, since it's currently keeping the hair off my sweaty neck, as I throw on the oversized heart-shaped tie-dyed T-shirt. Heading out of the bedroom, I run into an annoyed Beth standing in the hallway.

"Well, we've officially made it to hell." She throws her hands up, the motion causing a strand of hair to fall out of her messy top bun and into her face.

Beth and I make our way downstairs when we hear a chorus of voices coming from the living room.

"We can fix it ourselves. It'll be fine," Leo says.

"You can't fix shit, Leo. We should just call a guy and float in the lake the rest of the day," Alex says as we descend the stairs.

"You're still upset you lost the burger contest, aren't you?" Leo responds.

It's true. Leo won, and Alex was upset because, apparently, he "always wins," but how could he not? The burgers everyone made last night were great, but once again, no one's cooking could compare to Leo's. Seriously, his kitchen skills need to be studied.

Alex tried to get some cooking tips from him as they were cooking, but Leo wasn't interested. He said normally he would be honored to teach his brothers some tricks in the kitchen, but there was no way he was going to give Alex tips that could help him win. Seems like Alex isn't the only one hell-bent on winning this year.

"I was wrong, we aren't in hell. We've died and gone to heaven," Beth says in front of me, only loud enough for the two of us to hear. When I catch up to her at the bottom of the stairs, I turn my attention toward what she's looking at.

In the living room, all four brothers have gathered. Shirtless. In shorts. With a faint sheen of sweat glistening on their chests.

"Oh my God, do they all *live* at the gym?" I whisper-scream to Beth.

The living room is currently a sea of muscle. A mix of toned, lean abs and bulky, built biceps. Not to mention, V-lines for days. It's all noise to me until my eyes lock onto Theo's body. I caught a glimpse of his abs the other night, but something is different about him this morning.

His hair is disheveled as if he woke up in a sweat like the rest of us. A few pieces fall into his face, making his already perfectly chiseled jawline and beautifully carved smile even more deadly. My eyes greedily take in the curves of his chest and abs. The defined V-line points directly to the very generous length I had my hands all over just the other night. The early morning sun streams through the windows and hits his body, highlighting the peaks and valleys of his muscles perfectly. His shorts hang low on his waist, and I have to cross my arms over my chest in an effort to hide my hardening nipples at the sight of him. The man looks like Michelangelo himself carved him.

Beth takes a deep breath. "Why did I swear off dating men again?"

We're interrupted before I have a chance to respond. "You ladies want to take a picture? We make for a nice screen saver." Alex raises his fists to flex his biceps. My cheeks heat when I realize they've all just caught us gawking at them.

"And once again, a nice moment is ruined by a man opening his mouth," Beth says as she passes the living room, making her way toward the kitchen.

Stealing one more glance at Theo's V-line, I follow Beth to the kitchen. With the open-concept layout, I'm sure to keep my back toward the living room as I make a breakfast plate. Busying my hands until the nerves of just being caught subsides. That plan is thrown out the window when the men join us in the kitchen.

"Sorry for the cold breakfast spread today. With the AC dying on us, we couldn't risk turning the oven on this morning." Leo says, grabbing a bagel off the breakfast he put together. I've appreciated his dedication to having breakfast ready for us each morning.

I load my plate up with fruit, hoping the cold food will help me cool down from the inside out. Especially if Theo doesn't plan to put his shirt back on anytime soon.

"The AC is out? It's only seven in the morning, and it's already ninety degrees out," Beth complains from beside me before viciously tearing into a bagel.

"Don't worry, we've got a guy on the way," Alex reassures us.

"No, we're going to fix it ourselves. It'll go faster, and we only have until about ten o'clock until the heat really gets bad." Roman heads toward the back deck, motioning the guys to follow. "C'mon, we don't have all day."

Leo grabs four waters from the fridge before following Roman out back. Alex grunts in irritation but follows anyway. I barely catch any of it because I'm too distracted by Theo's body to notice anything happening around me.

I'm watching a drop of sweat make its way from his collarbone down to the waistline of his shorts when he interrupts me by grabbing a piece of pineapple from the plate I forgot I was holding.

My eyes dart up to his, and without saying a word, he pops the piece of pineapple inside his mouth, smiling at me as he follows his brothers out back.

I was hoping to catch Roman this morning to see if he had any thoughts on my portfolio that I sent him last night. Given the urgency with which he books it outside, I decide to hold off until the air conditioner is fixed.

"Why does part of me think they did that to us on purpose?" I snap out of whatever trance Theo put me in when Beth asks me a question.

"Did what on purpose? Make the AC go out?" I take a seat at the counter after grabbing a couple of cold waters for the two of us.

Beth comes to sit beside me. "I just meant making sure they were shirtless, looking their best, when they knew we would come down here having just gotten out of bed. But I like where your head is at too." She has that look on her face. The one that says *I'm developing one of my evil plans, and you're going to be dragged into it.*

"Beth, no. They didn't do any of this on purpose," I say as I dig into my plate, relishing the chill of the fruit as it slides down my throat.

"Even if they didn't do it on purpose, I say we get them back later." She nudges me with her elbow.

"Get them back?"

"Yeah. By the time we're done, he'll be the one wanting to take a fucking photo."

And suddenly, it becomes clear. This isn't about *them;* it's about *him.* I chuckle, biting into a piece of fruit, nodding along to the "plan" Beth has for later.

It's innocent enough, and honestly, I wouldn't mind seeing Theo squirm a little.

"Game on, boys. Game fucking on." Beth raises her water to me, and I properly clink my plastic bottle to hers.

25

THEO

How many Kane men does it take to fix an air-conditioning unit? Apparently four.

By the time we finish, we're all dripping in sweat from the heat outside. I'm in desperate need of a cold shower and a break from being around my brothers. I love them, but whenever we have to fix something, Roman thinks he knows best, Leo sides with him, and Alex just wants to fight everyone on everything.

"Prince Charmings have come to the rescue!" Alex says as we head back inside. It's just as hot inside the house as outside, but at least we have some shade. With the air-conditioning fixed, it should cool down by tonight as well.

Heading toward the kitchen, I'm stopped dead in my tracks at the sight laid out before me.

Beth and Sienna stand near the kitchen island, fussing over something on the counter. I don't bother to look because I can't pull my eyes away from Sienna.

Her thick curls are tied up on top of her head,

exposing her slender neck and kissable collarbones. She's wearing that goddamn blue-striped bikini top again that perfectly supports and barely covers her perky breasts. I have flashbacks of taking one of her brown nipples into my mouth. The thought sends a wave of pleasure through my body and straight to my cock.

Her shorts hang low on her hips, exposing the ties of her bikini bottoms just above her waistline. I take a few deep breaths to get control of the growing erection in my shorts, but all hope is lost once she picks up an ice cube.

Torturously slow, she drags the ice cube up and down her neck, across her collarbones, and then over her chest. Seemingly to cool herself down in the presence of this heat. I want nothing more than to lick the cool, melted liquid off her.

"You fellas want to take a picture? We make for a nice screen saver." Beth's comment pulls me out of the spell Sienna has cast on me.

I hear the click of a phone camera next to me. One sharp turn of my head and I see Alex standing next to me, with his phone out as though he's just taken a photo. One glance at the phone screen shows only Beth in the frame. Lucky for him because if so much as one curl on Sienna's head was in that photo, he would've been dead.

Making my way over to Sienna, I wrap my arm around her waist, still enamored by the melted water that has pooled on her chest.

"Oh my God, you fucking creep. Delete that right now," Beth all but squeals at Alex.

"No. You told me you made a nice screen saver, and you were right." Alex shows us his phone, which shows that he did, in fact, make Beth in her red bikini his new screen saver.

Beth and Alex continue fighting as she chases him into the living room. Finally getting hold of his phone, she continues yelling at him to give her his password. I know he'll eventually give it to her. He just really gets a kick out of messing with her.

When Sienna reaches for another ice cube, I gently grab Sienna's wrist, stopping her before she can torture me again. Whispering in her ear, I say, "No more. I'm begging you. Not in front of everyone."

"Jealous?" She smirks up at me.

"Jealousy doesn't begin to explain what I'm feeling right now." I plant a kiss on her cheek, whispering again, "Be a good girl and drop the ice cube, or you won't get your present later."

Her pupils dilate, and her lips part slightly at my words. Now it's my turn to smirk, proud that I got the results I wanted from her.

"Where did you find this?" Leo asks from the other side of the counter, holding a small laminated piece of paper. Roman clenches his jaw, looking down at the plate on the counter. That's when I notice what, exactly, Sienna and Beth were fussing over when we came inside.

Mom's no-bake cookies. The ones we haven't had since she died, given that we haven't been able to find any of her recipes. Leo remembers a few, but there are so many my brothers talk about that I never had a proper chance to try.

"I found it in a small box tucked away on the bottom shelf of the pantry," Sienna responds, then moves to grab a box on the counter. "Here, there's a whole bunch of recipes. We were looking for ingredients to make something when we found these." She hands the box to Leo, who accepts with a shaky hand.

"These were our mom's recipes. I thought these were lost forever," Leo responds.

"Oh, I'm so sorry, I had no idea. We were just looking for something to make that didn't require turning on the oven, as a thank you for the work you guys put in today." Sienna wrings her hands together as though she's nervous about how we're going to react.

I place a hand on hers, hoping to provide comfort. Her hands still, and she relaxes into me a little.

Without saying a word, Roman reaches for one of the cookies. When he takes a bite, the corners of his mouth tick up just enough to be considered a smile.

"They're perfect," Roman says more to himself than anyone else. Grabbing a handful of them, he takes off upstairs without saying another word.

Leo's halfway through his second one when he says, "Thank you for finding these." Lightly hitting me on the shoulder, he says, "You brought home a good woman, Theo." Leo then makes his way over to the dining table, sitting down with the box of Mom's recipes to look through them.

"Yeah, I really did," I say, looking down at Sienna. She looks up at me briefly before avoiding eye contact.

"I really hope I didn't overstep. I didn't even think about the fact that they could be your mom's recipes," She looks at me again, turning toward me. "Theo, I'm so sorry if I crossed a line."

"Sienna, you didn't." I place my hand on her cheek, speaking so only the two of us can hear. "You gave us a piece of our mom back. I speak for all of us when I say we are immensely grateful for what you've done today."

Leaning down, I place a gentle kiss on her lips, still aware that we aren't completely alone, whispering, "Thank you," into the kiss. Before I can pull back, she places her hand on the back of my neck, tugging me in for a deeper kiss this time.

"You're welcome," she says, then lifts a cookie to my mouth, urging me to take a bite.

My eyes roll to the back of my head as the chocolatey flavors hit my taste buds. I don't remember these much, considering I was so young when Mom died. It's one of the many things my brothers have the pleasure of remembering vividly that I don't. Now I see why they were always so obsessed over these. They are perfect little mounds of heaven. I've never been more sure of the nickname I've given Sienna until today.

"They're perfect. Just like you, Angel." That earns me a smile just as priceless as what she's done for my brothers and me today.

26

SIENNA

After scarfing down a few of the no-bake cookies with the guys while cooling down as the AC finally started to kick in, Beth and I retired to our respective rooms.

I was hesitant about Beth's idea to surprise the guys, but I'm glad I let her talk me into it. The look on Theo's face when I dragged the ice cube across my chest was amusing to say the least. The look on his face when he tried the no-bakes for the first time was priceless. All I've been able to think about since then is how to make him that happy again.

The men are currently occupied downstairs, doing the dishes from our kitchen adventures. Leo commented on how messy we were and followed up by giving Beth and me tips for cleaning as we go. We listened intently but ended up laughing with him as he said, "A towel must always go over your shoulder when you cook."

I may not be anywhere near as good as Leo, but years of baking with my mom have given me the skills to at least follow a recipe. Leo and I spent a short time going through the recipes together. He let me photograph some of the pastries I wanted to try baking with my mom back home. The thought that he would let me take part in something so personal to them instilled a warmth in my chest that doesn't seem to want to go away. Another ache rolls through me when I think about leaving this place at the end of the week.

I grew up an only child and enjoyed every second of it. I never felt alone because I always had Beth. But when Leo was giving us tips in the kitchen and sharing his mother's recipes, I felt a brief longing for an older brother I could share moments like these with. Much in the same way that Theo has his brothers.

I'm lying on Theo's bed when the longing for siblings flashes through my mind. A longing I've never experienced until I met Theo. Until I met his brothers.

Shaking off the feeling, I make my way toward the bathroom down the hall, deciding I'm in desperate need of a shower. Making sure to grab my bag of toiletries on my way out of Theo's bedroom.

Theo said he wanted to have fun with me, not add me to the Kane family. Thinking about his brothers in a familial sense means I'm teetering dangerously close to breaking that last rule. The one we swore we wouldn't break.

I throw my hair up on top of my head, deciding I need more of a rinse-off than a full hair-wash shower. Turning on the showerhead, I step in and let the lukewarm water wash over my body. I begin to feel lighter as the water washes away the sweat that's been pooling on my skin all day. Sweat, combined with melted ice cubes (Beth's idea, not mine), created a wet yet sticky combination that I'm grateful to finally be washing off. I would've hopped in sooner, but Beth won rock paper scissors. I should know by now she always chooses scissors.

I splash enough water on my face to probably constitute waterboarding, trying to clear my thoughts. With the AC on full blast now, I turn the dial in the shower a little warmer, standing under the stream of water, as I let the sound wash away any unwanted thoughts I'm having.

"Room for one more?" Two strong arms wrap around my bare waist and pull me back from the shower stream. I jump slightly at his touch but calm the instant my brain recognizes the voice and who it belongs to.

As if on cue, the universe has delivered my *favorite* distraction.

"Hmm..." I turn around in Theo's arms to face him, surprised at how hard he is already, as his cock presses against my stomach. "I'm not sure. You're so big you take up too much space already."

I reach up and rest my arms on his shoulders, smirking up at him. The thought of him being too big for this shower is laughable. The walk-in shower is big enough for four people, complete with two showerheads and an entire bench along the tiled wall. He'd have to be a literal giant to be too big for this shower.

"I'm too big, huh?" He leans down to kiss me, but stops just before his mouth reaches mine. "Don't worry, Angel, I'm sure it'll fit." Then he presses his lips against mine.

I burst out laughing mid-kiss and squeeze his

shoulder in response to his innuendo. We separate for a second, only for him to grab my waist again and pull me back, this time pulling me in for a deeper kiss. When his tongue teases my lips, I open my mouth at the silent request, and our tongues collide.

I feel the cold sting of the tile on my ass and spine when Theo presses me into one of the walls of the shower. Breaking the rhythm of our kiss, he places one hand on the side of my neck, his thumb lightly pressing on the bottom of my chin so I can look up at him. With his other hand placed on the wall next to my head, his presence is all-consuming, and I'm pleasantly over-whelmed by his size.

"Leo said dinner will be ready in a couple of hours." He slides the hand that was on my neck down the front of my chest, between my breasts, and he flattens it across my stomach just before reaching the place throbbing for his touch.

"What will we do with the time?" I reach up on my tiptoes in hopes that his hand will move lower, but he doesn't budge.

"I have a few ideas," Theo looks at me through his lashes, and my center floods with arousal as he finally lowers his hand.

Theo slides his fingers along my center, his other hand wrapping around my waist as my knees start to give out at the slightest touch of my clit. He leans down, pressing his forehead against mine, a welcoming invasion of my space. He continues his slow, languid draws of fingers back and forth through my now dripping wetness.

"Always so wet for me," he all but growls. He trails

kisses from my jaw down to my collarbone. I tilt my head back against the shower wall, allowing him better access and letting a moan slip free.

"Shh." Theo places his large hand over my mouth, pulling back to look at me. "You need to be quiet, Angel." He slides one finger inside me, keeping his hand over my mouth, and the combination of the two sensations floods my core.

"We can't let anyone hear how good I'm making you feel, now can we?" he says, sliding a second finger inside me, punctuating his last word by curling his fingers. Another moan escapes my throat, the sound muffled by his hand.

"Think you can be quiet for me?" Theo slowly lifts his hand, his fingers still inside me but not moving an inch.

"Yes...I'll be quiet...Please, Theo..." I say breathlessly, trying to move my hips in a desperate need to get movement from his fingers. But he's too good at withholding what I need.

Theo smiles at my promise to be quiet and leans down, giving me the faintest of kisses to my lips before barely pulling away to say, "Good girl."

I don't have time to process the hottest two words a man can ever say to a woman, before he begins driving his fingers in and out of me. His arm supports me when my knees give out.

Theo's cock presses up against the side of my stomach, and I'm reminded of just how big he is, which only adds to my building orgasm. While his fingers continue to pump in and out of me with so much urgency, I grab his shoulder in an attempt to regain some sense of reality.

"Theo...I'm close...I need..." I can't find the words to finish my sentence when Theo begins to curl his fingers inside me again.

Without missing a beat, Theo's mouth drags from my collarbone down to my sternum, leaving a trail of kisses, licks, and bites in its path. I watch as he lowers to his knees in front of me, my heart skipping a beat at the sight. When he looks up at me, my eyes lock onto his forest-green swirls when he adds his thumb to the mix, slowly circling my clit.

A low moan escapes me as my orgasm continues to build at the base of my spine. Theo sucks one of my nipples into his mouth, letting it go with a pop before moving onto the other one to do the same. He continues to tease my nipples, just barely circling my clit, giving me exactly 90 percent of what I need.

For a few minutes, he continues bringing me to the edge, just to move his thumb for a few seconds before returning it to its original rhythm. I've never stayed so close to the edge of an orgasm for this long, and I'm loving every second of it.

A cool wave rushes over my body when Theo removes his fingers from my core. Mimicking what he did on the patio, he brings his fingers to his mouth, sucking every last drop of me off them. I watch in awe, convinced I'm going to come just at the sight of Theo on his knees in front of me.

"Fuck," he says when he removes his fingers from his mouth. "Tasting this good should be a crime." When he looks back at me, something darker is in his eyes. His pupils dilate so much they're almost completely black, leaving only a sliver of green left.

Placing a strong hand on the back of my left thigh, just below my ass, Theo lifts one of my legs over his shoulder. He begins kissing my stomach, and as he trails his kisses lower, it doesn't take much for the orgasm inside me to start building again.

Before fully reaching my core, Theo glances up at me, just long enough for me to respond. "Yes," before he grabs my other leg and throws it over his other shoulder.

Fully suspended in the air, only held up by my legs on Theo's shoulders, his hand on my ass, and the shower wall, I am once again entranced by Theo's strength.

Every nerve in my body comes to life as he gives one long sweep of his tongue along my core. I reach up my hand, grabbing onto the built-in shelf above my head, in an effort to ground myself when he circles my clit with his tongue in one slow motion.

Using his free hand, he thrusts two fingers inside me again, continuing that torturously pleasurable curl motion as he sucks my clit into his mouth. *Thrust. Curl. Suck.* Over and over again until I'm bursting at the seams with arousal.

I grab Theo's hair as I feel the peak of my orgasm on the horizon. "Theo...fuck..." That's all I get out before I explode. My back arches as I'm thrown over the edge by his tongue, and Theo does what he can to hold me in place between his shoulders and the tile wall. My orgasm rushes through me with the same passion and urgency as the night Theo first kissed me. The orgasm wipes my mind blank. I can't remember what I was so worried about before walking into this bathroom.

He brings me down from the high by placing gentle kisses on my clit as the aftershocks of my orgasm pass. Setting me on my feet, he stands and plants a kiss to my lips, still holding me where he can as I catch my breath.

I can feel his hard length pressed against me again, and I decide I still need more of him. Sometimes I worry my need for him is insatiable.

In an effort to calm my worries again, I pull his lips to mine, kissing him with a passion that screams "stop being so gentle with me."

Getting the message, Theo pulls me into him, his hard cock pressing against my stomach further. A strong reminder that he still needs a release.

Placing my hands on Theo's broad chest, I push him up against the shower wall. Kissing his neck, I take his cock in my hands, stroking up and down, spreading the bit of precum accumulated at the tip, along the length.

Theo lets out a little moan that brings my arousal to life again. Reaching up, I gently kiss him on the mouth, as he did to me. "I thought we had to be quiet?" I ask against his lips.

"The only thing I care about right now is seeing you on your knees." A smile spreads across my face that I couldn't hide even if I tried.

Holding on to Theo's waist, I gently lower to my knees, the tile biting into my kneecaps when I do. I pay it no mind as I'm too distracted by what's standing at attention in front of me to care.

Keeping a hand on the base of his cock, I swirl my tongue around the tip ever so lightly to get back at him for edging me the way he did. I glance up, smiling at Theo around the tip of my tongue on his cock. When I do, his expression changes from awe into something animalistic. As if I thought he couldn't get any more beautiful.

"You have about ten seconds before I lose control." Theo fists his hand in the hair at the back of my neck. "And then I'm afraid you won't like me very much."

His deep, raspy voice is all the motivation I need to suck the head of his cock into my mouth. I hear Theo breathe out "fuck" before I take him deeper, still not quite reaching my hand that's wrapped around the base of his cock.

Pulling him out, I lick the underside of his cock, glancing up again at him as I do. He still hasn't taken his eyes off me. I've never felt hotter than at this moment. I've never felt so in control.

Relishing in that fact, I stop teasing him and take him into my mouth as deep as I can. Theo's other hand grabs the back of my head, meeting the other one that was already there. Pulling my lips back to just the tip, I look up at him, patiently waiting for him to lose control. After all, he did promise, and I can't think of anything hotter at this moment.

I tap Theo's hip lightly, and that's all the signal he needs before he starts fucking my mouth. My hands grip his hips as I feel his hard cock slide across my tongue as he thrusts in and out.

"Fuck, Sienna, I'm gonna..." Theo is breathless as he reaches his climax. He tries to pull away, but I grab the base of his cock again, keeping him in my mouth. I continue to suck as he finishes down my throat, only letting up when the aftershocks become too much for him.

Theo helps me to my feet and pulls me in for another kiss. As our tongues collide, this one feels deeper than the others. Heavier.

"You really are an angel sent from heaven, aren't you?" I respond to Theo's question with another kiss, this time, laughing at his ridiculous question.

"I don't think angels do what we just did." He kisses me again, as though he can't get enough of his lips on mine.

Theo helps me clean up in the shower, the water now cold, being the only thing that stops us from going for round two. Throwing on my robe, I gather my things as Theo stays behind to clean himself off.

Cracking the bathroom door open, I check that no one is in the hallway before stepping out. Quietly sneaking down the hall, I head back to Theo's room.

"Have a nice shower?" I jump at the sound of Beth's voice from beside me.

Turning, I point my finger at her. "You saw nothing." Beth smiles like I just let her in on a secret, and I continue down the hallway to Theo's room.

"Letting go looks good on you," Beth says before heading back to her room. I catch a glimpse of myself in the mirror that hangs on the back of the door once I'm in Theo's room. I hate to admit it, but Beth is right.

The permanent smile on my face speaks a thousand words as I realize this is the most carefree I've been in a long time.

27

SIENNA

"As your team captains, Leo and I will pick our teams." Alex stands before us in the grass by the lake, with Leo at his side. "Leo, you know the drill," Alex says, turning toward Leo, holding his hands in a starting position for a game of rock paper scissors.

"Damn, he is competitive," I whisper to Theo, and it gets a chuckle out of him. I turn my head to catch a glimpse of his smile. I find myself doing that a lot lately.

"And why do you two get to be team captains?" Beth asks from beside me.

"Team captains are chosen as follows," Theo says in a surprisingly good announcer voice, which causes a giggle to well up in the back of my throat. "Last year's winner will lead one team, and the person currently in first place will lead the other."

"I'd be happy to give up my spot for you, if you think you can handle the responsibility." Alex winks at Beth, which prompts her to roll her eyes so hard I'm surprised she didn't hurt herself.

Alex and Leo bang their fists against their palms; Leo picks rock, and Alex picks paper. Alex turns to the rest of us with a huge grin on his face. "As the winner of rock paper scissors, shocker." He throws a look Leo's way on the last word.

Leo interrupts Alex. "Might I remind you, I'm still winning the bigger competition here. Don't get cocky."

Alex places his hand on Leo's shoulder. "Too late, buddy. As I was saying, as the winner, I get first pick. Roman, congrats on being the first drafted."

"What an honor," Roman responds flatly, grabbing a red belt from the bin set out in front of us.

Leo picks Theo, leaving Beth and me as the last picks. Beth mutters something along the lines of "typical" under her breath, but I focus more on the fact that I'm about to make a complete fool of myself.

If you had told me a couple of weeks ago that I was going to be running around the backyard of a lake house with four giant men playing flag football this summer, I would've called you a liar.

"I pick Sienna," Alex's words prompt Beth and me to say "huh" at the same time.

"Just thought I'd mix things up a little." Alex shrugs and claps his hands, sending us to break off into our teams.

While I don't love the idea of not being on the same team as Theo, I do find a little hope in joining forces with Roman. It's been a few days since I emailed him my portfolio, and I haven't received an update yet. My patience is wearing thin, and I'm starting to think it wasn't such a great idea to turn down the other job offer. Granted, he never said exactly when he'd send it over to Graham, but I was hoping to have gotten an update by now. I'm hopeful this will be an opportunity to open up communication between Roman and me, giving me a chance to speak with him later about my portfolio.

Theo grabs a red belt for me and a blue belt for himself. As he moves to help me put my belt on, my heart begins to beat faster as our bodies inch closer together. His generous, skilled hands at my waist do wonders to distract from the anxiety riling up inside me at the potential of falling on my face in front of everyone.

"And instead of tackling someone, you just pull one of these flags off, like this." Theo yanks one of the flags off my belt. The harsh movement throws me off balance, making me fall forward into Theo's arms. He catches me with ease, and I straighten, turning my face away so he can't see my embarrassment.

"I might be a little too uncoordinated for this. I'm not sure you really want to put a football in my hands."

"I'm sure you'll be great." He lifts my chin with his knuckle. "It'll be fun. Trust me."

An odd feeling rushes over me at his last words. I nod my head the slightest at Theo, trusting him more than I care to acknowledge.

"Hey, no fraternizing with the enemy." Alex pushes Theo away from me and motions for me to huddle up with him and Roman.

"Okay, Roman and I will focus on getting the touchdowns and grabbing most of the flags. Sienna, I need you to do your best to distract Theo. If you can do that, that brings their team down to just Leo, meaning we got this win in the bag." Alex barely gets the end of his plan out before he notices I'm holding back a laugh.

"What's so funny? Do you want the football? I just overheard part of your conversation with Theo earlier and thought..."

"God no, please don't pass it to me unless you have to. I'll probably drop it."

"Then why are you laughing?"

"No reason. I'll distract Theo. Got it."

We put our hands in at Alex's command, raising them to break, getting ready to start the game. I keep quiet since I don't have the heart to tell Alex there's no way in hell we're winning this game, even if I distract Theo as we planned.

The other team has a secret weapon, Beth. She's the most coordinated person I know. The coordinated Yin to my uncoordinated Yang. She grew up dabbling in basically every sport known to man, so with Alex on the opposing team, I have a feeling she won't hold back.

Roman and Leo are opposite each other on the right side of the yard, farthest from me. I take up a position on the left side of the yard, in front of Theo, smiling sweetly at him in an effort to make Alex's plan work. I figure that at least trying to win the game might get me some brownie points with Roman. Alex takes up a position in the center of the yard, his eyes locked on Beth, who, by no surprise, has convinced Theo and Leo to let her start with the ball.

Beth smirks at me as she's getting in position for her

play. I mouth the words, "Be nice." Theo scrunches his eyebrows, looking back at Beth as I do.

When Leo blows his whistle, Beth takes off down the yard, heading directly toward Alex, who looks determined not to let her pass. Theo tries to make his way toward me, and I take off in a jog with him. I raise my arms slightly as I do, as though I'm trying to block Theo from getting a pass. In actuality, I'm trying to make sure my blue crop top rides up the slightest bit, exposing a sliver of skin between my shirt and shorts. I know it's working when Theo's eyes dart to my stomach, losing focus on the game.

It doesn't matter because Beth wasn't going to pass him the ball anyway. As she takes off toward Alex, he charges her. His hands are out and ready to grab one of the flags on her belt. They are only inches apart from each other when she fakes going left, then turns sharply to go around Alex on his right. Alex's momentum is thrown off, sending him forward, face-first into the grass as he just barely misses grabbing one of her flags.

Beth laughs as she continues to run, shouting Leo's name from across the yard. Leo is already three-quarters of the way toward the end zone markers, Roman lagging behind. I guess that's one downside to being as big as Roman is, you can't move as fast as someone like Leo. Beth's speed stalls as she throws the perfect spiral toward Leo. He catches the ball, then takes off, scoring the first touchdown.

I run to Beth, as we both bend over with laughter, holding on to each other for balance. When we catch our breath and look at the men, a second wave of laughter rolls through us at their reactions to what just happened. They stand there shocked, presumably at Beth's evident athleticism.

After a few moments, Theo and Leo begin whooping and hollering, approaching Beth for high fives. Alex comes rushing toward Roman and me with a giant smile and a little dirt on his face. "*Now* it's a game!" he says excitedly.

I glance at Theo, who I find is already looking at me from the other side of the field. When our eyes meet, a fleeting thought crosses my mind. This is the most fun I've had in a while. This is something I could get used to.

Roman catches me looking at Theo, and almost to his own surprise, he asks, "You really like him, don't you?" His eyebrows are scrunched together when I pull my attention away from Theo.

"Of course I do." The words roll off my tongue easier than I expected them to. With one nod, and a clap from Alex, we're back into football mode before I have a moment to contemplate the implications of Roman's question.

After completing a few rounds, each team is tied at a score of four to four. I haven't touched the football once, but I've successfully distracted Theo a few times. I'm feeling a sense of pride in the way I've been helping until Alex decides to change the strategy on Roman and me.

"First team to score five points wins. I know we can win this." Alex tries his best to motivate Roman and me, but to be fair, most of our touchdowns have been pure luck. The other team is playing better than us, and Alex knows it.

"Instead of throwing the ball to me," Alex says to Roman, "throw it to Sienna."

"What?" Roman and I say at the same time.

"They won't expect it. Theo and Leo have been covering my ass like a motherfucker. If you throw it to her, she'll be wide open."

"Yeah, but that means she has to actually catch it," Roman responds. "No offense," he says to me with a grimace.

"None taken. I'm with you on this one."

"Just trust me, it's the only way we'll win. High risk, high reward."

Roman and I exchange a glance, both clearly unsure about this plan, "I can adjust my throw, and if you stay close, you won't have to catch it from a far distance. All you'd have to do is run."

Taking a second to contemplate that, I worry my lack of coordination could cost Alex his win. I've never been a competitive person, but I think Alex is rubbing off on me. For some reason, I want to win this. Not just to help Alex, because apparently that's something I care about now, but I can't imagine the look on Theo's face if I scored the final touchdown. Seeing his smile would surely be a high reward.

"Okay, let's do it," I say in the most confident voice I can muster up.

Alex claps his hands in excitement, clearly eager to win the game. A pit forms in my stomach at the thought of letting him down.

The play starts, and just as expected, Leo and Theo rush to cover Alex as Roman fakes a throw his way, then switches at the last minute to toss the ball toward me. When I actually catch the football, I'm so stunned that I forget to move.

Beth, who isn't far from Roman, excitedly yells, "Run!" I immediately begin moving my feet at the sound of her words.

As I approach the endzone, I pass where Alex had been positioned, Theo gaining on me as he goes to grab one of my flags. When he gets close, I hold a singular finger out at him. He comes to a stop, that beautiful smile spreading across his face, once again. I feel spoiled to get my reward before I've officially made the touchdown.

By another miracle, I reach the end zone, throwing the ball down to the ground as the other guys have been doing all day. I barely get the chance to celebrate before Theo wraps his arms around me and lifts me into the air. My legs instinctively wrap around his waist as the world around us falls away, and we celebrate together.

Spinning me around, he whispers in my ear, "That's my girl."

I'm so overwhelmed with joy at my accomplishment and hearing him call me "his girl" that I pull him in for a kiss.

We stay like that for a moment before we remember where we are, and Theo sets me back down. He looks at me curiously when he does. We've been affectionate in front of his brothers before but this felt…different. I can tell by the slight sparkle in Theo's eyes that he feels it too.

Out of the corner of my eye, I see Roman standing beside us. Turning toward him, he seems to be studying Theo before shaking away the expression on his face and raising his hand to give me a high-five. The others all follow, and my hand is raw by the end of the celebration.

As Alex heads inside with the others, he continues to rattle off the current score of the games. This win officially made him and Leo tied for the belt. A warm feeling spreads through my bones at the accomplishment of being able to help Alex secure a win today.

"I have an idea." Theo pulls me into him by my waist, keeping us outside for a moment longer.

"Oh please, no more football. That was a miracle. I don't think I can recreate it."

Theo chuckles. "No, no more football." He lowers his head to touch his forehead to mine. "Go on a date with me."

"What?" My chest tightens.

"Sorry, will you go on a date with me?"

Before thinking and without hesitation, I respond with a smile. "Okay, but where?"

"I told you, I have an idea. But it's a surprise. Just be ready tomorrow night." He kisses me on the forehead, and my smile doesn't fade as I follow Theo inside for dinner.

Upon waking up the following morning, I find a tray with a covered plate and a note stuck to the lid lying in bed next to me. I'm intrigued by this surprise, but my heart falls the slightest bit when Theo is nowhere to be found.

After giving my eyes a moment to adjust to the morning summer sun shining into the room, I sit up, setting the tray on my lap. A whiff of fluffy, buttermilk pancakes, maple syrup, and bacon wafts through the air, and my stomach growls.

Tearing into the note, I read:

> Good morning, Angel. Here's a pancake breakfast from me to you. (Don't worry, Leo helped me make them so they're edible). Be ready tonight by 5 p.m.
>
> P.S. Do you like me? [ ] Yes [ ] No

Pulling off the lid from the tray, I find the source of the delicious breakfast aroma. A stack of pancakes, complete with bacon and a side of strawberries, is arranged on a plate. I dig in, the buttermilk and maple flavors mixing in my mouth, causing a moan to escape my throat as the flavors hit my taste buds.

A few minutes later, I realize I've cleared the plate in front of me. Setting the tray aside, I cozy back in Theo's bed for a few more minutes, rereading his note.

Going into this trip, I was focused solely on my career. Theo and I have been having fun as friends with benefits, but something changed between us yesterday. I don't think I can deny my feelings for him much longer.

I was worried that jumping into a relationship too soon would throw off the trajectory of my career. I've yet to hear from Roman. Theo kept me occupied last night, and I didn't get a chance to talk to him before he went to bed. But I still have a chance at getting five years ahead of my plan if Graham likes my portfolio. I'm starting to wonder whether I should rethink other parts of my plan.

Grabbing a pen on the nightstand, I mark the box that says "yes" before setting the note on his pillow. I pull the covers off and stretch my arms over my head, looking out the window at the lake. Moving closer to the window, I watch as the sun sparkles off the water. Cracking the window, I cozy into the bay window seat, listening to the high-pitched song of the early morning birds as I make peace with my feelings.

I wouldn't mind spending my summers here. If Theo will have me.

28
THEO

I may not have known it at the time, but when I told Sienna I'd take an axe through the heart for her, I wasn't kidding. I'm not sure where these strong feelings come from, but the more time I spend with her, the more these thoughts keep going through my head.

I've spent all day setting up the perfect date night for Sienna. Or at least, what I hope she'll find to be the perfect date night.

"Thanks again for making a trip to the store for me, Leo," I say as I finish packaging the sandwiches I made into the cooler.

When I approached Leo to help me make dinner, he said, "Even the most un-edible of foods made by you would be more romantic than any dinner I could whip up for her. Looks like I still have a few things to teach you, little bro." I rolled my eyes, annoyed that he still saw me as a kid at times.

Nevertheless, he was probably right. I've packed Sienna and me a nice dinner of sandwiches, fresh-cut fruit, a couple of chocolate cupcakes, and a bottle of champagne to take with us tonight.

Leo throws his arm over my shoulders, squeezing me in a side hug as I pack up the last of the items into the cooler. "Not bad. I would've cut the fruit into little hearts, but it's a good start."

"Oh fuck off," I say through a laugh, shrugging him off me.

"Where's my sandwich?" Alex says, joining us in the kitchen.

"In the fridge." I tilt my head toward the fridge behind me.

Alex goes to open the fridge, and at the same time, Leo looks at me with a question written on his face.

"All I see is lunch meat, sliced cheese, and half a loaf of bread."

"Exactly. Make your own damn sandwich." My response makes Leo erupt with laughter, while Alex launches toward me to get me into a headlock.

"Alright, I think I'm in the mood for a knuckle sandwich." Alex tousles my hair as I struggle to get out of the headlock he has me in. Damn him and his fighter strength. At least I have better abs.

"Knock it off, you two, before you break something," Roman's voice booms as he enters the kitchen from the back porch, where he had been lounging for the day.

Alex and I separate but not before I give him a little shove. Turning toward the mirror that hangs just between the living room and the kitchen, I straighten out my rumpled clothes and hair. I catch Roman approaching me through the mirror.

"Surprised to see you actually planned something," Roman says with a smirk on his face, indicating that he's joking. Regardless, the comment still irks me.

"Ha ha," I say as I continue fixing my hair.

"You going to be safe tonight?" Roman crosses his arms, asking me a question he doesn't usually ask my brothers. I clench my molars at his question.

"Yes, *Dad*, I have condoms if that's what you're asking." I finish running my fingers through my hair and turn toward him.

"Don't call me that, Theo. You know that's not what I meant." His eyes squint slightly, the muscles in his jaw mirroring mine as they tick.

"We'll be fine. You do realize I'm a fucking adult, right? I know how to take care of myself. You don't have to baby me all the time." *And if you hate being called dad so much, then stop acting like one and just be my fucking* brother *for once.* Once again, I'm too much of a coward to say the words I've thought for years.

Roman has always treated Alex and Leo as his brothers. A luxury I have never been awarded. For some reason, Roman can't seem to get it through his head that I'm an adult and should be treated as his equal. While I appreciate everything he's done for me, I don't need the parent angle from him anymore. I just need a brother.

"Theo." He drops his arms, and his mouth opens like he's going to continue, but he shuts it, a wave of anger crossing his face before he continues. "Just fucking be careful." Then he storms upstairs to his bedroom, ending the conversation.

I look toward my brothers, both of them doing a

terrible job of pretending they weren't listening in on the conversation.

"He needs to get laid," I say.

My brothers don't get a response in before we are all interrupted by a voice at the bottom of the stairs.

"Gentlemen, the moment you've been waiting for..." Beth announces, motioning her hands upward toward where Sienna descends.

The moment my eyes land on Sienna, something in my chest tightens, as though it can only be relieved by being closer to her. Listening to the feeling in my chest without hesitation, I walk toward Sienna, meeting her at the bottom of the stairs.

Sienna's warm brown skin is radiant and glowing, as the sunset light shines on her from the windows. Her pinned-back curls showcase her slender neck and collarbones that I'm compelled to kiss and nip at every time they are exposed. Two small braids frame her face, decorated in small gold accents.

The real killer? The fucking sundress. The shade of yellow perfectly accents the gold she's adorned her body with and complements her skin tone. The dress drapes over her, hugging her breasts, caressing her waist, hanging off her hips, and stopping just short of her midcalf. I'm afraid her overwhelming beauty will send me to an early death if I don't touch her soon.

Someone clears their throat next to me, and I see the bouquet I picked up for Sienna out of the corner of my eye. I know it's one of my brothers, but I don't care to see which one before taking the bouquet and shoving them away.

Handing the flowers to Sienna, I say, "You look stunning. As always."

She hesitantly takes the bouquet from me. "Thank you," she says softly. "These are gorgeous. Are these—"

I interrupt her with my response, too excited for tonight. "Angelica, yes. And the other ones are roses, but I'm sure you already knew that." My tone comes out shakier than I intend, but the sight of her smile instantly calms my racing heart.

She raises a brow at me. "I didn't know you knew so much about flowers."

"I don't. But I saw the name at the flower shop and thought they were perfect." Breaking a small piece of white angelica flower off its stem, I tuck it behind her ear.

I can't hold back at the sight of Sienna's smile. Pulling her in by the waist, I'm barely able to suppress my moan at the softness of the sundress fabric at my fingertips as I press my mouth into hers. She kisses me back with a passion that I feel deep within my bones.

A whooping and hollering starts in the kitchen. Sienna tries to pull away from the kiss, but I keep her close, only removing a hand from her waist to flip off our audience.

After a few moments have passed, I pull away. "Ready to go?"

Sienna nods her head, a moment of hesitation crossing her face that contradicts the passion I felt come from her during our kiss.

"You okay?" I ask, checking to make sure I haven't done anything to make her uncomfortable. We're in uncharted territory, after all.

"Yeah, but"—she lowers her voice—"Roman looked upset when he passed me on the stairs. Is he okay?"

"He's fine. Just being a grumpy asshole as usual." I wave off her concern about my brother.

As she nods her agreement, I grab the cooler from my brothers. We head out the front door, and I make sure I leave a kiss for Mom on the way out.

I pause when I notice Sienna gives a small wave to the photo before closing the door behind her. I'm at a loss for words on how perfectly she fits in with us. Even joining in on the strange habits we've developed over the years.

I think, in many ways, Sienna is a breath of fresh air I've needed for a long time. I might've lied when I told Roman I met a woman who was helping me be more responsible, but it wouldn't be a lie now.

I'd do anything to be worked into Sienna's plan. That is, if she'll have me.

After a short drive, we arrive at our destination. A secluded opening among the trees, just uphill a little way from the lake house. With no houses for miles around, my brothers and I claimed this spot the moment we found it years ago.

In the middle of the opening, I set up a picnic blanket with a pile of pillows and blankets. I've downloaded a few movies on my tablet to ensure Sienna can have her pick.

As we approach the blanket, Sienna is quiet. She doesn't seem eager to sit yet, so I remain standing with her. She's been quiet since we arrived, and a wave of doubt rushes through me as I worry this doesn't meet her standards.

"This was my brothers' and my hideaway growing up. We would hike up here, sometimes racing to this spot, and hang out for hours." I take a few steps toward a nearby tree. "We carved our initials into this tree, officially marking our territory...and when I put it like that, it sounds so ridiculous." I laugh. Sienna stays quiet.

"I figured we could eat the delicious, two-star meal I've prepared for us." Opening the cooler, I show off the mediocre sandwiches I've prepared. "We could throw on a movie, and once the sun sets a bit more, the opening provides the best view of the stars."

Sitting down on the picnic blanket, I motion my hand up toward her. She tentatively grabs it, sitting down next to me. A wave of relief washes over me when the breeze sends her strawberry scent my way.

Not letting go of my hand, Sienna looks up at the sky. "It's perfect. Thank you, Theo." Placing a hand on my cheek, she pulls me in for a kiss.

The sky has changed from the purple-orange hue it had when we first arrived to pitch black, with only the moon and stars lighting the area around us. We've been here just long enough to watch a movie and let the food settle in our stomachs.

In my head, I pat myself on the back for making it through the movie without making a move on Sienna. I've kept a respectable distance, only holding her hand or putting my arm around her. But I'd be lying through my teeth if I said I haven't wanted more.

The way she sits sideways on her hip causes her dress to ride up slightly, revealing her leg through the slit. I can almost see the lace of her underwear, and it's been driving me mad. I missed half of the movie staring at her thigh.

"You were right," Sienna says after a few moments of silence following the end of the movie. She's looking up at the opening in the trees.

"Gorgeous, isn't it?" I stare at her, watching the star's reflection in her irises.

"Stunning. I've never seen so many stars in the sky before." She looks almost pained when she peels her eyes away from the night sky and looks in my direction. The moment her eyes land on my lips, her pupils dilate, and that pained look disappears. It's immediately replaced by one of hunger.

"I'll have to remember to bring you back next summer so you can see the stars again," I say presumptuously.

"Next summer?" Her brows cinch together slightly. I resist the urge to run my thumb between them to smooth the skin.

Taking her hand, I respond, "Yes. Next summer. If you want to come back, that is."

Her eyebrows squeeze together even more, and she looks away. But I take note of the fact that her hand is still in mine. When I notice she starts to spiral, I try to ease any discomfort I might've caused.

Placing my hand under her chin, I lift it so she's

looking at me again. "Hey, you don't have to answer that. I'm sorry if it puts you in a weird position. I've had a lot of fun with you, Sienna. I'd like to keep having fun if you'll let me."

"Fun, right." She gives a small smile, and mine falters at the sight. Did I say something wrong?

"Did I tell you how gorgeous you look tonight?" I inch closer, pleased when a larger smile takes the place of the small one.

She plants a gentle kiss on my lips. I move my hand to her cheek, but when I try to deepen the kiss, she pulls back. Once again, I'm left wondering if I did something wrong.

"You know, Beth pushed me to accept your offer. She always says that I need to loosen up and not be so focused on my future all the time. It seems like everyone in my life thinks I shouldn't have such a meticulous ten-year plan." She speaks almost hesitantly.

"That's funny. I've heard the opposite from Roman. All he wants me to do is plan and be more responsible. Never mind the fact that I have great ideas, but he refuses to listen to them just because they aren't packed into a pretty presentation for him."

"Well, it might not hurt your chances at getting a job if you made a small presentation for him," she says with a grimace.

I laugh at her response. "I suppose I could. It'd be easy now that I have an expert planner by my side."

She waves off my joke. "I think maybe I've done a little too much planning lately."

Testing the waters, I ask, "And this plan of yours, is it flexible in any way?" In a way that could account for *me*?

Her eyes widen at my question, but she avoids giving an answer. "Let's just enjoy our time together. This trip has been a nice break for me, and I'd rather not think about my plan or even my career for our final days here. Can we do that? Just enjoy our time together without worrying about what comes after this?"

"Deal." Placing my hand on Sienna's cheek again, I pull her in for a kiss. When I lick her lips, she opens up at my invitation, and our tongues collide, deepening the kiss.

There's a slight pain in my chest at her dismissal of my question. If she wants to live in the moment, then I'll give her a moment to remember. I'm not sure our partnership was ever fake for me. As she kisses me with more passion, I realize that somewhere along the way, this stopped being fake for her too.

But I can respect if she isn't ready to confront that yet. I'll take whatever she is willing to give me tonight.

Sliding my hand to the back of her neck, I tilt her head to deepen the kiss. She tastes like a mix of the strawberries and champagne we had with dinner, and I savor her sweet taste.

Finally having a chance to do what I've wanted all night, I drop my hand to her bare thigh, through the slit of her dress. Playfully teasing her skin, I slide my hand up and down her leg but never quite reach the lace of her underwear.

The teasing must pain her as much as it pains me because, to my surprise, she lifts that leg over me and straddles my lap. Breaking our kiss for a moment, I greedily take her in.

The yellow dress, which perfectly contrasts her smooth brown skin, splits at the slit. It rides up so high that I can see where she is pressed against my cock, a thin layer of lace and denim the only thing separating us.

Sliding my hands up her thighs, we fall back into a kiss. My cock twitches at the taste of her again. When Sienna runs her hand through my hair and gently tugs, I can't help but grip her hips in response.

She lets out a small moan when my grip causes her hips to rock on my cock. Her wetness seeps through the fabric of my pants as she continues to grind down on my cock. A groan slips free from my throat at the rock of her hips.

Kissing a trail from the corner of her lips, across her jaw, and down her neck, I stop just short of her chest. Taking her in again, I watch as my hands slide up her body, snagging on her dress as I skate my hand across her toned stomach to cup her breasts through the fabric.

Biting down on the fabric just above her breasts, I pull down, scraping my teeth across her nipple as I do so. Her body shivers against mine at the touch. I do the same to the other breast, leaving them both exposed as I plant a few kisses on her sternum. My cock throbs when she grinds down harder on me at my touch, her bare breasts now fully exposed.

Licking up her sternum, I massage her breasts, lightly brushing my thumb over her nipples, teasing them as I go. The slight sting to my scalp as her grip tightens in my hair in response to the teasing is all the motivation I need to keep her on the edge.

Fed up with my teasing, she pulls me in for another kiss. "Fuck me," she says, her lips still touching mine. I nip at her bottom lip with my teeth, enjoying the moans I pull out of her as I do.

"Please, Theo." I marvel at the sight of her grinding on my lap, begging me to fuck her. She tugs at the bottom of my T-shirt, pulling it off over my head. Her eyes follow her hand as she drags it down my chest to my abs. Reaching up, I brush my thumb across her bottom lip.

Sienna has her life planned out down to the last second. Her ambition is unmatched, and her determination is unlike anything I've seen. She was compassionate with my brothers and me, and sensitive to our reactions when she found Mom's recipes. She entertains Alex's dramatic behavior. I even think she's warmed up to Roman. Without a doubt, she's the most gorgeous woman I've ever laid eyes on.

I think the most attractive thing about her is the grace, ambition, and determination with which she's set out to reach her goals. It's motivating and sexy as hell, to say the least. I've never been a "plan" man myself, but something about her makes me want to beg to be worked into her plan in any way she'll have me. I'd just be happy to be included.

But she's not ready to hear all of that. So instead, I live in the moment with her, at her request.

"Patience, Sienna..." I plant another kiss between her breasts and place my hands under her thighs. "But first..." In one swift motion, I flip us over so she's lying on her back on the blanket. I wiggle against her as I settle between her thighs.

"I never got my dessert." I punctuate my sentence with a thrust of my hips against her core. I smile when she lets out a small squeal in response.

Kissing down her neck, I take one of her breasts in my hand again, this time, massaging her nipple as I take the other into my mouth.

Her moans are a sweet symphony in my ears as I continue to suck, pinch, and nip at her nipples. But it isn't enough. I wasn't lying when I said I was still waiting on dessert.

As I move down her body, I take note of how she reacts to my touch. I burn every movement into my brain in case I'm ever lucky enough to get this opportunity again. Or more likely, in case this is the only time I'll get the opportunity to be this close to Sienna.

The way she lets out the smallest of giggles when I kiss her sides. The way she moans anytime I kiss near her breasts. And the way her back arches when I kiss just below her belly button.

With my hands on her hips, I slide my thumbs underneath the lace of her underwear as I continue to kiss her just below the belly button. Sliding my thumbs back and forth, I get closer to her center as I do, but never quite reach it. The smell of her arousal is intoxicating, but it isn't until she slides a hand through my hair and moans my name that I lose all patience and control.

Grabbing the lace of her underwear, I rip a hole straight down the center. Exposing her to me, I'm pleased with her gasp. She glistens under the moonlight, and my cock strains painfully in my jeans at the sight. A moan escapes my throat as I lick up her center, finally getting to taste her again.

"Fuck," I moan against her thigh, and Sienna's grip tightens in my hair.

As I continue to lick and kiss her core, I slowly slide my index finger inside her. When she tightens around my finger, I have to reach down to unbutton my pants, providing some relief for my aching cock.

Fuck. If she's already this close, she must be as affected by this connection as I am. The thought only makes me harder. I could come just from the taste of her.

I enter a second finger into her at the same time as I begin to suck on her clit, her moans and grip on my hair doing nothing to tame my hunger.

I continue to suck and lick at her clit as my fingers thrust in and out of her as she continues to tighten around me. Knowing that she's close, I curl my fingers, causing her to instantly arch her back.

I continue my steady rhythm of thrust, curl, suck. After a few moments, she's arched so high I have to place my other hand on her lower stomach, pressing ever so slightly. The added pressure undoes her. Her release comes fast as she convulses under my tongue. I greedily lap up the mess she makes, adding in a few kisses when the sensations become too much for her.

Rubbing her thighs as she comes down from the high, I sit up on the back of my heels. Looking down at Sienna lying before me, I work hard to commit the vision to memory.

My cock has sprung free of my jeans but is still

contained by my underwear. Only inches from Sienna's wet core, revealed by a hole in her lace underwear. Her dress is now bunched at her core, only covering the smallest section of her waist. Her deep brown curls are fanned out around her, framing her face almost as if she had a halo. The moonlight shines off her skin, creating an aura of light around her, making it look as though she's glowing with starlight.

The reality hits me like a freight train when she smiles up at me. "What?" she asks.

"You truly are a fucking angel." It comes out more breathless than I intended. I'm shocked that I can get any words out at all, considering I'm caught speechless at the beauty of the woman who lies before me.

There's no question about it. I'd do anything to make her happy. Anything to be worthy of her attention. Sienna is mine, and I'm never letting her go.

29

SIENNA

If I'm an angel, then Theo is a god.

After giving me one of the best orgasms of my life again, Theo sits between my legs, staring down at me as though he hasn't had enough. Bathed in the moonlight, I can see every rippled, toned inch of his muscle. A small bead of sweat pools on his chest, and I can still see remnants of me on his chin.

The sight of him towering over me has my core rushing with arousal again.

Leaning down, he rests his elbow beside my head. His presence becomes all-consuming when his scent overwhelms me.

His hand finds its home back on my hip. I'm quickly realizing it's one of his favorite places to touch me, and instinctively, my hands go to his chest.

When he kisses me, I decide I'm not done with him yet. Gliding my hands down his abs to his waistband, I slide my hand beneath the waistband of his boxers and grip his cock.

When I start moving my hand along his length, he grabs my wrist, stopping me. My brows furrow in confusion. Does he not want this?

"Fuck." He puts his forehead to mine. "I won't last long if you do that."

"Fuck me already then," I respond, sounding more desperate than I intend.

Theo pulls back, his eyes sparkling, seemingly pleased by my request. The corners of his mouth turn up in excitement, my own mouth mirroring his.

Sitting up on my elbows, I watch as he pulls down his pants, taking his boxers with them. When his cock springs free, I can't help but stare. I could barely fit him in my mouth. I have no idea how he'll be able to—

"You can take it," he says, a slow smile spreading across his face as he leans down to plant another kiss on my lips as I hear the unmistakable sound of foil ripping.

A slight sting hits the sides of my hips as the fabric of my underwear cuts into me. The sound of lace tearing echoes through the night, and I watch as Theo throws aside my underwear.

"Those were my favorite pair." I look at him in shock.

"I'll buy you a million more, and this time, I'll make sure they're in my favorite color."

I laugh at the thought of Theo hating my underwear just because they weren't blue. But I'm quickly pulled back to the sensations flooding my core when the head of his cock brushes against my clit.

With one hand on my thigh and the other on his cock, he lines himself up, and I watch as he slides into me—inch by painfully pleasurable inch.

I'm not convinced I can't take it anymore as I continue to stretch around him. Dropping my head back, I listen to his reassuring words. "You're doing so good, Angel."

He lets out a grunt when he's seated inside me fully. The noise causes me to clench tighter around his cock that's already stretching me to the max.

Any pain I was feeling before turns into overwhelming pleasure when he slowly starts to move. Both hands now on my hips, I notice his grip tighten at the slow pace. He's holding back.

"Stop holding back, Theo," I say on a breath. "As you said, I can take it."

That devastatingly gorgeous smile spreads across his face once again. "That's my girl."

Almost immediately, he starts thrusting into me harder. Each thrust hits a spot inside me that I never knew existed, bringing me closer to a climax that I always thought was a myth.

Watching his muscles flex under the moonlight, his body framed in the stars of the night sky, brings me close to the edge.

"Fuck, Sienna." He moves one of his hands to my breast, pulling and pinching at the nipple, causing me to arch my back and grab onto the blanket beneath me, looking for something to ground me at this moment.

"You're so fucking tight," he all but growls at me, thrusting into me even harder when I let out a moan.

Theo is so sweet and gentle, but this is a side of him I can't get enough of. The animal that's brought out of him when he's bringing me to orgasm.

"Theo," I moan his name.

His hand moves from my nipple to my clit, rubbing his thumb in pleasurable circle motions with enough pressure to send me over the edge.

"Come for me, Sienna," he says, shifting the angle of my hips, thrusting as deep as he can. "I want to see you unravel again."

The change in position, combined with his words, sends me hurdling over the edge. Stars flood my vision as my back arches, my mouth releasing a chain of expletives I'm not even sure are real words.

Theo follows after me, my climax rolling into his, his grip bruising my hips, leaving his mark on me as he seats himself fully inside me and unloads.

We stay there for a moment, the aftershocks flooding through us both, before he removes himself and lies down beside me.

Theo is already looking at me when I turn my head toward his.

We stare at each other for a minute in silence. I'm not sure if he feels it too, but something has shifted between us. I know I said I was just having fun, but I'm not so sure that's quite what this is anymore.

For the first time in forever, I'm starting to think I actually can have it all. Roman will talk to Graham about my portfolio, guaranteeing me an interview, and I've finally been able to relax these past couple of weeks with Theo. It's been one of the best summers I've ever had the pleasure of experiencing.

Maybe I don't have to sacrifice relationships to have a successful career. Maybe I can have both.

Leaning over, I kiss Theo through the smile I can't

seem to wipe from my face. His smile matches my own when he kisses me back.

It may not be going according to plan, but everything is falling perfectly into place.

248

30
THEO

I don't think I've ever been happier than right now. With Sienna in the seat next to me, windows rolled down, the summer night breeze rolling through the car. Soft R&B music plays through the speakers, and I can feel the bass reverberate against Sienna's thigh where my hand rests.

Thank God this car is an automatic, because I can't imagine not touching her right now.

The image of her looking up at me from where her head rested on my chest, underneath the night sky, will forever be burned into my memories.

Looking over at Sienna, I find that she's already looking at me, smiling.

"What?" I smile back.

"I had a lot of fun with you tonight," she said, putting her hand on top of mine.

"Well, the fun doesn't have to be over," I say. As we get closer to the lake house, her comment gives me an idea.

She looks at me, a silent question written on her face.

"Do you trust me?" Sienna nods, a glimmer of wonder in her eyes. I love seeing her relaxed like this.

As we approach the turn into the driveway of the lake house, I hit the gas. The Mustang roars beneath my feet as Sienna's hand grips mine. One quick look and the smile on her face tells me she's game for what I have planned.

Keeping weight on the gas pedal, I turn the wheel sharply. Hitting the brake as we reach the beginning of the turn, I lock my back tires while turning the wheel as we drift around the corner.

Sienna lets out a laugh in tandem with the screech of the tires scraping against the asphalt. I laugh with her as we slide along the road, the breeze kissing our faces once again.

I know I shouldn't, but I look over at Sienna, wanting to cement this moment and her beauty to my memory forever.

As we approach midnight, the roads are blanketed in darkness. My headlights are the only objects lighting the way back to the lake house.

That's why I don't notice the pothole until we hit it halfway through the turn.

When I hear the scrape of my bumper against the asphalt, my attention snaps back to the road. Sliding sideways around the corner, I grip the steering wheel tight as I struggle to gain control of the car again. Adrenaline pumps through my veins as the car spins out of control, taking us off the road as I fail to straighten out the wheel.

At the sound of metal crunching against something hard and unmoving, we finally come to a stop. The seat belt digs into my chest as my body is thrown sideways by the force of the hit. No airbags deploy, giving me a sliver of hope that the crash isn't as bad as it felt.

Heart racing, I try to catch my breath as I process what just happened.

"Shit. Shit. Shit." I look over at Sienna in a panic, ripping my seat belt off so I can take a closer look, immediately checking her for any signs of blood. She's conscious, and there's not a drop of red in sight, but when my eyes meet hers, I see a hint of water pooling at the bottom of her irises. The sight is like a knife through my chest as I realize I'm the cause of those tears.

"Sienna, I—" Before I can finish the sentence, the driver's door is flung open, and my body is being hauled out of the driver's seat. Two rough hands grab at the sides of my face.

The lake house stands tall behind Roman as he holds on to me. The light from the back deck lights the area around us. We must've spun out of control and hit one of the trees on the side of the house.

Roman's eyes are frantically scanning my body the same way mine did Sienna's just seconds ago. Although his eyes are filled with something much darker than fear.

"I'm okay," I say through the shock of the moment. The seat belt did its job, and I'm confident I didn't hit my head on anything. The crash was more of a shock than it did any actual damage to me, from what I can tell. But even if it did, all I care about is checking that Sienna is okay.

Pushing Roman off, I turn around toward my car. Upon first glance, I see that the tail end of the Mustang hit a tree, the front three-quarters still intact. That explains why the airbags didn't deploy.

Beth rushes toward the passenger side door, pulling it open with such force it looks as though she might yank it off its hinges. I see Sienna's arms reach up to hers as Beth helps her out of the car. Again, she doesn't look hurt, but I need to get my hands on her to make sure.

"Sienna, are you—"

At the sound of my words, Roman turns me around. He fists my shirt in his hands and slams me against the side of the Mustang.

"What the *fuck* were you thinking? In Dad's fucking car!" His voice booms through the night air as his fists shake against my chest. We're eye to eye, Roman only an inch shorter than me, but I've never felt smaller than I do at this moment. I need to make sure Sienna is okay.

"I just have to check on her," I say, my voice coming out more pained than I intend. Looking to my right, I see Beth and Sienna standing near the front of the car. When I try to escape Roman's hold, his grip on my shirt tightens.

"Don't go near her," he all but growls at me. "I told you to be fucking careful, Theo! What the fuck were you thinking, drifting around the corner like that at night?"

I'm too distracted by Alex and Leo joining the chaos to answer Roman. Seconds later, Alex stands within eyesight a few paces back from Roman, arms crossed, staring me down as though I'm the last person he wants to be looking at right now.

Leo has rushed to Roman's side with a first-aid kit in his hands. He sets the first-aid kit on top of the car, right next to me, and that's when I notice how much he's shaking. He doesn't look at me as he's trying to open the kit, his hands unable to steady themselves long enough to unlatch the box.

Roman lets me go to place his hand on Leo's shoulder in an effort to calm him. I can't remember the last time Leo had a panic attack. The clear signs that I've triggered his anxiety send a wave of nausea through my stomach.

Placing my hands on Leo's, I speak softly, "I'm okay. No one's hurt. We're okay." When he finally looks at me, he crashes into me, wrapping his arms around me and hugging me so tight, as if he lessens his grip, I'll disappear on him.

We stay there for a moment as Leo's breathing starts to steady. Roman's breathing becomes more erratic by the second, but we've all learned to stay calm when Leo needs it. When Leo has finally calmed down, he pulls away, moving to check on Beth and Sienna. A sigh of relief rolls through me that someone is at least checking on her.

Looking back at Roman, he stares at me, still seething with rage. Slowly, I raise my hands, keeping my voice calm.

"I was just trying to have fun," I say.

"Fun?" Roman's eyes squint, his eyebrows pulling together. I place my hands at my sides, in an effort to control the shaking.

Roman takes a step back, creating a fraction of distance between us. "You're just like him! You have no responsibility, no respect for others, and after pulling a move like this tonight, you have no future at Kane Construction."

My anger boils up quicker than I expect, fueled by the adrenaline coursing through my veins. "We had a deal! Just because I fucked up one night doesn't mean it erases everything else. And what do you mean I'm just like him? Like who?"

"Dad!" Roman throws his arms out, his voice booming as he points at me, continuing, "You're just like Dad. You may have been too young to remember, but I do. I remember getting the call that Dad had wrapped his car around a tree in the *exact same fucking Mustang,* killing both himself and Mom in the process." Roman takes a breath, trying but failing to regulate his temper at this moment. "You're selfish and irresponsible just like he was. You almost took this young woman's life just like Dad took Mom's."

I open my mouth to say something, but realize I have nothing to say. I know better than to argue with Roman when Mom and Dad are brought up. At this moment in particular, I'm not sure I have anything to combat what he's just said.

"This little stunt you two are pulling is over."

"What are you talking about?" I ask.

"Whatever this thing is between the two of you"— Roman gestures back and forth between Sienna and me —"it's over. There's no place for you at my company, Theo. The deal is off." Turning toward Sienna, he continues, "Sienna, I was impressed by your portfolio, but I'm not impressed by the lies you've been telling in an effort to get a job. I wouldn't hire you based on that one character trait alone, and I know Graham won't either. I think it's time that you and Beth leave. I can give you both a ride home in the morning."

Sienna looks as though she was just struck across the face, and a pain spreads through my chest at the sight.

"Roman. They're not your guests, they're mine. I say when they go," I say, adding a bite to my tone. Stepping away from the car, I block his eyesight to Sienna, stopping him from saying anything else that might cause her further pain.

I continue, "It might've started out as a lie, but it's not anymore. I—"

Roman cuts me off with a raised hand. "Stop lying, Theo. I entertained this for too long. It's time you grow the fuck up. Bringing a fake girlfriend on our family trip was a stupid, immature idea, and tonight, you put her life in danger."

I open my mouth to speak, but he continues, "This is final, Theo. We can talk more in the morning, but this shit ends tonight."

With that, he turns his back and heads inside.

"Can you believe him?" I try breaking the ice with Leo, but his expression doesn't change at my quip.

"In Dad's fucking car," Leo mumbles, shaking his head as he walks off, fists clenching and unclenching at his sides.

I turn toward Alex, but he puts his hand up to stop me when I take a step toward him. "No, Theo. You can't charm your way out of this one. You're not six anymore." He turns his back to me as he follows Leo inside.

Watching my brothers turn their backs on me as they

walk inside the lake house is the cherry on top of seeing the look on Sienna's face when we hit the tree. It makes me want to crawl out of my own skin. Adrenaline still pumping through my veins, I'm overcome with a need to be anywhere but here.

Turning back toward Sienna and Beth, I ask, "Are you okay?" I have to force myself to look her in the eye as I push past the shame of my mistake tonight.

When she doesn't answer, I take a tentative step toward her. When I do, Beth puts her arm around Sienna's shoulders and holds out a hand to me, indicating that I shouldn't come any closer.

"I'm not physically hurt," Sienna finally says, avoiding eye contact with me.

I try getting closer, ignoring Beth's warning, but Beth puts her hand up again. "No, Theo. You've done enough." At her statement, they move to head inside, following the others.

As I stand outside alone in the darkness, next to my wrecked car, Roman's words replay in my head. He wasn't wrong. I'm irresponsible and shouldn't be wasting my time on stupid fake-dating schemes. Even if my feelings for Sienna are real, I've proven tonight that I'm not worthy of being with her.

Not able to join the others inside, I head down the hiking path on foot. I'm not sure where I'm going, but I need to clear my head. I'm not far down the path when I break out into a full jog, forcing the adrenaline out of my body. When I finally tire, I reach an old bench on the path about a mile from the house.

Sitting there, I catch my breath as my heart rate

finally starts to come down. Though the anger and disgust I feel toward myself lingers. I put Sienna's life in danger tonight. Her carefully thought-out plan could've been destroyed because of one stupid moment of fun. I almost robbed the world of seeing Sienna Parker's beautiful architectural designs. Beth could've been leaving here without her best friend, her sister. I almost took away her father's little "pumpkin." Her mother's baking partner. The look of fear in her eyes flashes before mine again, and I know what I have to do.

I refuse to repeat history. I refuse to be my father.

31

SIENNA

I'm not sure if it was the shock of getting into a car wreck, the adrenaline coursing through my body, the mixed look of fear and anger on Beth's face when she helped me out of the car, or the embarrassment from what Roman had said to me, but the moment we were back inside the lake house, I broke down into tears.

Beth took me up to her room to help me calm down. Thankfully, she knows exactly what I need. Silence as she sits there with me, her hand on mine, while I let out the many emotions I'm feeling at this moment.

When I finally stop crying, I look at Beth, conveying to her what I can't bring myself to say out loud.

"I'll pack my bag and call a car to pick us up. You focus on getting your things from Theo's room, and we'll be out of here soon." She gives a small, reassuring pat on the back of my hand, and I nod, moving to go get my things. I appreciate her understanding, as I don't think either of us wants to ride in a car for two hours with Roman in the morning.

It's amazing how much can change in an hour. I was naive to think I could have it all. To think this plan was actually working. Roman's words and Theo's recklessness put things into perspective for me tonight. I've been wasting my time.

Roman was right. This isn't the respectable way to get a job. I knew I made a mistake turning down the other offer. This opportunity was too shiny to ignore, but I see now that I've made the wrong decision. I should've never agreed to this deal in the first place.

Theo is nowhere to be found. He never joined us inside when Beth and I walked away from him. Despite my mixed emotions right now, I still find myself hoping he's okay. Then again, if he truly cared about me, wouldn't he have followed me inside?

I've just finished packing up my things when Theo walks in the room. I look toward the doorframe, aiming my eyes at the floor as I'm too embarrassed to look him in the eye.

"You're leaving already?" There's a slight crack to his voice I try to ignore.

"I am," I respond.

When Theo stays silent, I finally make eye contact with him. "Roman was right. We never should've tried to deceive our way into a job. We had fun, but it's time we get back to reality."

Why didn't you follow me? Are you okay?

The questions cross my mind but get caught in my throat when I try to speak them out loud.

"Right. Well, at least we had fun." The bite in his voice is like a slap across the face.

No. It was more than that. I feel more than that.

Again, words I can't bring myself to say out loud.

"Right." I nod my head, like this is the business transaction I originally wanted it to be. "This had to come to an end eventually."

The truth of my words hits me harder than expected. Summer flings are named for a reason. They don't exist outside of the summer. I was beginning to think I could make room in my plan for Theo, but the bite in his voice tells me he would have no interest in such a thing. It's time to take the rose-colored glasses off.

Theo is a distraction. Tonight reminded me that I have no time for distractions.

Seeing Beth in the hallway out of the corner of my eye, she holds up her phone, signaling to me that our ride is here.

I hold out my hand in a gesture to shake Theo's. "Thank you for having me, Theo. I appreciate the hospitality. Fake dating was worth a shot, but it's time to cut our losses."

His lip curls up slightly at the sight of my hand. "Right well, good luck with your job search then." Ignoring my hand, Theo turns to exit the room, passing Beth as he heads down the stairs. Beth and I wait a moment to give him space before following, with our bags in hand. When we reach the front door, I catch a glimpse of Theo exiting onto the back patio.

Alex waits for us at the bottom of the stairs, but Leo and Roman are nowhere to be found. Leo seemed to take the crash pretty hard, his hands shaking when he tried to check me for any signs of injury. Thankfully, I didn't get a scratch on me. The whole crash looked worse than it actually was. I was hoping to see him before I left, to make sure he was okay and to thank him for checking on me.

Unable to help myself, I ask Alex, "Is Leo okay?"

He nods. "He'll be fine. He hasn't had an anxiety attack this bad for a while, but we know how to handle it. One day of rest and he should be much better tomorrow."

"I'm so sorry, we didn't mean to trigger anythi—"

"It's okay, Sienna. I know this wasn't your fault. Come on, I'll take your bags. We should get you guys in the car before the driver accepts another ride." Alex gives us a smile, but it's dimmed compared to the others I've seen from him. His voice carries less enthusiasm than usual.

As we head outside toward the car waiting for us in the driveway, Alex takes our bags. As he's loading them into the trunk, I watch as the sun just barely begins to rise, painting the sky the faintest tint of blue from its previous black shade.

"Thank you," Beth says to Alex, and I quickly follow suit.

"No problem." Alex looks as though he wants to say more but shakes his head. "Have a safe trip." It's all he says before heading back inside. Beth and I cozy into the back seat of our ride, our driver taking off shortly after.

I shut my eyes until Theo's Mustang is out of view. They start to blur as I watch the trees go by outside the car window.

This is the last time I'll see Theo, and he couldn't even shake my hand. An ache settles in my chest. One that I'm not sure will ever go away.

32
THEO

Cursing under my breath, I watch as the rock I just threw skips across the lake.

She's only been gone an hour, and every second has felt like torture. My plan when I got back to the house was to let her go tonight. To tell her to leave me and that I didn't deserve her. I could never put her life at risk again.

What I wasn't prepared for was her willingness to go. Her comments that this thing between us was just "fun." It was so much more than that to me.

I might've agreed with her in an effort to create distance between us, but I didn't believe a word I said. It wasn't until she tried to shake my hand that I knew she was being serious. I shouldn't be so hurt. After all, distance between us means I can never hurt her again.

But something about the distance feels wrong.

I throw another rock and watch as it bounces across the lake. As the sun begins to rise, I'm shocked I'm still standing, having not slept in almost twenty-four straight hours.

Another rock flies across the lake, this one not coming from me, but from my right. I look over to find Roman standing next to me. He stares out at the expanse of the lake, coffee mug in hand. The sunrise casts a warm orange glow just behind the tip of Mount Hood, high-lighting its snowy peak.

"What do you want?" I don't hold back the bite in my voice.

"Wanted to see if you were okay."

I scoff at his response. "Oh, now you want to check on me? Not even a couple of hours ago, you were berating me in front of my girlfriend!" I motion toward my Mustang near the side of the house, doing my best to hide the wince on my face when I catch a glimpse of the back bumper. Yet the cost of the repairs is the least of my worries right now.

"*Fake* girlfriend," he corrects.

Realizing this is a losing battle, I give up, "How'd you know about that anyway? Did Alex tell you?"

"No one had to tell me. You've always been the worst liar. Ever since you were seven and told me the monster under your bed stole my keys so I conveniently couldn't go to work on a Saturday." He levels me with a look.

"Yeah well, I wouldn't mind if your ass was at work right about now."

"I'd gladly rather be there than here, dealing with your bullshit," Roman snaps.

"What do you fucking want from me, Roman? I've tried everything to convince you that I'm responsible."

Despite my exhaustion, my voice rises, and my limbs begin to shake as adrenaline flows through my body once again. "Now you've taken the job offer off the table and sent Sienna home. She could barely even look at me when she left because of what you said."

"Because of what I said? Or because of what you did?"

Both. Neither. She left because she realized she deserves better.

"You put a woman's life in danger, Theo. After everything we've been through, how could you have possibly made the same mistakes Dad made sixteen years ago? Do you even remember Mom? What she looked like? Sounded like? Smelled like? No. Because Dad took her from us. He left and took her with him, out of his own selfishness. Tonight, you showed me you're more like him than I thought, and I didn't raise you to be this irresponsible."

My anger comes out more forcefully than expected. "Shut up, I get it! Dad was a piece of shit and you think the same of me. If you knew it was fake, why didn't you just say something? If you didn't want me to buy a Mustang like the rest of you, why even give me access to my nest egg money? Maybe if you had been there for me as a brother like you were for Alex and Leo, instead of a dad, you wouldn't find yourself so disappointed in me right now." I shove my forefinger into his shoulder for good measure. To my displeasure, he barely budges an inch.

"You were six, Theo. Someone had to step in and raise you. Alex and Leo were older. Things were just different with them. If you want to be ungrateful, do it somewhere other than *my* fucking house." Roman turns, walking back toward the house.

His back is to me when I yell after him, "Mom and Dad left everything to all four of us! You don't just get to claim ownership because you're the oldest, asshole!" Roman continues to ignore me as he shuts the sliding glass door. Not looking back once.

Annoyed, exhausted, and still disgusted with myself, I head toward my wrecked car. Climbing into the driver's seat, I look for the keys, only to find a small note on the steering wheel.

I'll tell you where your keys are once I know you've gotten some sleep. - Leo

It's just one fucking thing after another today.

Deciding I'm too tired to fight two out of three of my brothers, I pull the seat lever and recline the driver's seat as far as it'll go.

Settling in, I close my eyes. Lying there for a few moments, I replay the events of tonight. If I'm so irresponsible and only good for "fun," then fuck them all.

I don't need Roman, and I certainly don't need Sienna. If she doesn't care, then neither do I.

Eventually, I fall asleep to the thoughts of my own lies.

33

SIENNA

I scrape the edge of my spoon along the bottom of the ice cream container as tears stream down my face. Wiping them away, I eat one last bite of cookie dough bliss before setting the empty container down on my parents' living room table.

The television screen in front of me is the only light in the room despite it being two o'clock on an August Wednesday afternoon. I've closed all the curtains, not wanting any reminders of summer anymore. Not wanting anything to trigger thoughts of *him* anymore.

It's been a couple of weeks since Beth and I left Theo's lake house. Despite my best efforts, I haven't been able to get him off my mind. His scent, the feeling of his skin on mine, the way he chuckled every time one of his brothers amused him.

I tried to go back to business as usual, but my apartment felt suffocating. Job applications became muddled, and I lost the energy to fill them out. My "regularly scheduled program" only lasted about a day before I broke down. The breakdown happened after I tried to return to my barista position, and they informed me that due to my long vacation, which they initially approved, they removed me from the schedule after some further thought.

Beth was the one who suggested a change of pace, a change of location. Knowing that my parents are currently on vacation at the beach, I decided to stay at their place for a few days. Before I knew it, a few days turned into a couple of weeks.

Lying down on the couch, I wrap one of my mom's quilts around me, mindlessly watching the movie I put on the screen. Taking a deep breath, I wipe away my tears with a corner of the blanket, the smell of home calming my senses. A mix of eucalyptus, soil, and oak.

My parents moved us into this house when I was only eight years old. I remember my mom being so happy we had a backyard, albeit a small one, but it was somewhere for her to finally start a garden. My excitement came from seeing my room, much larger than the one we had in the apartment. The kitchen was larger, the bathroom larger, and even the living room felt grand.

Now lying on the couch, I realize how small the place is. A realization I've slowly come to as I've gotten older. Only a one-story house, the kitchen sits to the right of the front door, the living room immediately to the left. I stare at the small dining room table pushed up against the wall of the kitchen, opposite the sink. I remember many nights spent staring at the wall while I ate my dinner, trying to find shapes in the drywall texture as my parents discussed the events of the day.

When I was younger, I didn't mind much. But as I grew older, I started to yearn for a view. I quickly outgrew the space I had once been so excited about.

My phone buzzes on the coffee table. Hitting the red button on the screen, I decline another call from Beth. I've texted her enough to let her know I'm alive, but don't particularly enjoy the thought of anyone ruining my pity party right now.

Thud. Thud. Thud.

The noise at the front door makes me jump. My shocked heart rate steadies at the voice that follows.

"Sienna! If you don't open this door right now, I'm breaking in." The thick front door muffles Beth's familiar voice.

I continue to ignore her when I hear the click of the lock and the squeak of the door opening. It only takes a few moments before Beth lifts my legs and places them on her lap when she sits next to me on the couch.

"So what're we watching?"

I smile at her obvious attempt to make small talk when she clearly knows what movie I've put on.

"Do you want to talk about it?" she asks, her tone turning serious.

The space behind my eyes tingles as tears threaten to spring free. I think I've cried out all the water in my body because no more tears fall as I shake my head.

With that, the issue at hand is taken off the table, and we don't discuss it. I'm thankful for my friend who sits with me for the rest of the night as we watch movies from our childhood.

Nostalgia rushes over me the next few days as Beth continues to visit. Her visits throw me back to when we were kids, having sleepovers in this very same house.

Although, unlike when we were kids, I'm now the one who desperately needs the sleepovers, not her.

It's been a relief having her around. I don't realize how much weight she lifts off my shoulders when she's here until she leaves for work and I'm left alone in this empty house.

Relaxing in one of my mom's lounge chairs in our small backyard, near her garden, I run my bare feet through the thick, lush grass. The midafternoon sun beams down on me and warms my skin as the grass blades tickle and prick my feet. Finally able to enjoy the sunshine again, I inhale and exhale as I make an effort to ground myself.

For a fleeting moment, I forget all about my troubles. I forget I don't have a job lined up. I forget that my degree was more than likely a waste of time. I forget about my carefully constructed ten-year plan. I forget about Theo too.

Opening my eyes, I curse at how fleeting that moment of ignorance was before slinking back into the lounge chair.

The sun, high in the sky, blinds me as I look toward the clouds. Closing my eyes, I do the one thing that I've always refused to add into my plans.

I fall straight into a midday nap.

"This isn't like her, John. I'm very worried."

"Sara, our daughter is simply taking a nap in our garden. There is no need to worry."

Familiar faint voices speak in the distance. They sound muddled, as though I'm underwater. Still being half asleep, I can't place who they are, and I can't find the will to care.

"She does look peaceful, doesn't she?"

A low chuckle pulls me further out of my sleep. "Yes, she does. And beautiful, just like her mother."

"Oh, John." That's all I hear before the smacking sound of kissing begins, and I'm sprung awake out of disgust.

"Ugh, ew. You guys know I'm awake, right?" I sit up in the lounge chair, stretching out the kink in my neck. "Go get a room or something. You know I hate it when you do that."

I look up at my parents, who have now burst into a fit of laughter, something they did quite often with each other. The action reminds me of the many times Theo and I laughed in the same way, igniting the pain in my chest once again at the memory.

Having just driven back from the beach, my father stands before me in a lightweight sweatshirt and shorts. The sun was good to him over the past couple of weeks, and he's relaxed, a state I rarely see him in.

My mother stands next to him, radiant as ever, surrounded by the colorful flowers of her garden, which she tirelessly maintains. They definitely spent a lot of time in the sun, her usually pale skin donning a slight tan, complementing the dark brown curls that frame her face.

Usually, I'd laugh with them, but watching them laugh together, lit up by the setting sun, I have a hard time connecting with their happiness today.

My parents' laughter dies down, and their once-happy faces now bear the classic parental concern. My mom leans down and gives me a gentle pat on the knee as my dad takes a seat in the lounge chair next to mine.

"I'll go get us some lemonade," my mother says, heading into the house.

I mirror my father by swinging my legs over the side of the chair to face him. He stares at me and patiently waits for me to say something.

When I say nothing, he caves, "So, Pumpkin, how was the trip?"

I stare at him, trying to discern his ulterior motive by asking me about the trip. I already know Beth called my parents and told them I have been staying here. She didn't tell me that directly, of course, but I saw the text message come through on her phone when my parents told her they'd be cutting their trip short by a few days. Thankfully, she didn't tell them about the car wreck. Otherwise, I would've gotten a very stern call from my father days ago. From my father's question, I'd assume Beth kept things fairly vague when she spoke with them.

I wasn't expecting them to arrive this soon. Certainly not while I was taking a nap, of all things. It's ignorant to think that I can keep anything from them when they've caught me in this state.

Letting out a sigh, I finally speak, "I don't know..." I pause, trying to find the words. "Fine, I guess." *Wow, descriptive, Sienna.*

"Well, your mother and I had a great time at the beach. We were sad you couldn't go with us this year, but I'm happy you've been getting some rest." My dad gives me a soft smile.

"Rest, right." I scoff at the idea. I might be getting some physical rest lying around my childhood home all day, but I've been lacking emotional rest.

"Do you not feel rested?" my mother asks, bringing out a pitcher of lemonade and three glasses. She pours us each a glass, and I take a sip before answering.

"I wasn't entirely truthful about Beth's and my trip this summer." I wince at the admission to my parents.

My mother's brows furrow with concern. "What do you mean, sweetie?"

"Well..." I take the time to explain to them what Beth and I actually did this summer. I explain that we did not rent a lake house ourselves and instead went to the Kane family's lake house with four men. That got a grunt from my dad, but he remained quiet as I explained further.

I explained the entire fake-dating scheme and the goal of ending the summer by securing a job in line with my ten-year plan. Leaving out all the dirty pieces one does not tell her parents, of course. I also left out the car wreck. My dad would kill Theo if he knew, and while he's not my favorite person right now, I'd rather not see him dead.

"With all that said, I'm falling behind on my life plan, and I don't know what to do. I came here to clear my head, but I haven't submitted a single application since being here. I just can't find the motivation. I should've never turned down that job offer with JR Construction." I finish my long-winded story with a sigh, grateful to finally get that off my chest.

My parents share a look. I'm not sure what passes between them, but when they turn back to me, my father asks me one question. "What exactly do you gain from accomplishing this life plan?"

"Everything. The whole point of the plan is to finally live my dream life. I'll be able to travel the world and buy clothes off the new racks instead of the sales racks. I'll be able to afford my dream wedding, have as many kids as I want, and take them on extravagant vacations." I take a breath. "I won't be able to do any of that if I don't climb the corporate ladder first, which I can't do if I don't get a job and start building experience now. My career has to be my number-one focus right now."

"Does it?" my father asks.

"Yes, it does. If I don't put everything I have into building my career and I let distractions get in the way, I'll never be successful. I'll never be a top-earning architect."

"Hmm..." My father continues after a moment. "You know, I had a plan very similar to yours."

"You did?" He's never told me this before.

"I did." He places a hand over my mom's. "I was going to be the CEO of my own accounting firm. I wanted to help small businesses hit the ground running. I wanted to travel and make the Forbes thirty under thirty list."

"What happened?" My dad has become a successful accountant, but he's nowhere close to being the CEO.

"I met your mother." He turns to look at her then, and she smiles, a glint of reminiscing in her eyes as she looks at my father. "And we had you." He turns to me then.

Is he blaming the two of us for not being successful right now?

The confusion and anger must be written on my face because my father chuckles. "Let me be clear, Sienna, there is no amount of money or success that could replace the life I have built with the two of you."

When I relax a little, he continues, "What I'm trying to say is that plans change. Meeting your mom was the best thing that ever happened to me. I had plans to build my accounting firm from the ground up, but when your mother came to me and told me she was pregnant with you, everything changed."

I think about the stories they've told me before, trying to fit this new information in. My parents met shortly after my father graduated from college. My mother was a barista at a local coffee shop, and she had accidentally spilled his coffee all over him. He's always described it as the moment he felt his life click into place.

They were married within a year of dating. Then seven months later, my mom gave birth to me. So I'm having a hard time connecting the dots with what he's telling me now.

"The plan needed to change to account for you and your mother. I *wanted* the plan to change to account for you and your mother," he continues. "Stability was not something I grew up with, Sienna. So it was nonnegotiable when I found out we were going to have you. I found a job with an accounting firm and worked hard to earn a steady paycheck that would pay the bills and provide a stable, happy life for all three of us."

"And what an amazing job you did providing a wonderful life for us both." My mom interlaces her fingers with my dad's.

"But didn't you two always wish we had more?" I ask, confused.

"What more is there to ask for in life than a beautiful family, a roof over our heads, and dinner on the table every night?" My father's statement makes me think.

"Sienna," my mother says when I don't respond, "you've always been ambitious. It's one of the many traits we love about you. But you shouldn't let that ambition get in the way of your happiness."

"But the success I'll achieve as a result of my ambition is what will make me happy."

"That's what I always thought, until I met your mother." My father speaks again. "Besides, success can take many forms, Sienna. It isn't always presented by the physical things we own or what people on social media portray they have."

"I know that, but I feel like there has to be more to life than just this." I gesture around to the small backyard where we sit.

Both my parents level me with a look that has me immediately apologizing. "I'm sorry. I don't mean it like that. I'm very grateful for the life you've both provided me. I just mean...I want to travel and see the world, and I want to own a car straight off the lot that's less than ten years old. I want nice things, and while I appreciate the life you've given me, I don't think it's unreasonable for me to ask for these things from the life I'm going to give myself."

"That's fair," my father responds, "but you do realize there is more than one way to spend one's money, right?" My brows furrow when he says that.

"Maybe this is on us, darling. We really haven't talked to her much about finances," my mother says to my father. She turns to me. "I'm sorry, Sienna. We should've explained."

"Explained what?"

My father starts, "True success is usually quieter than you would suspect. Yes, we do have outdated cars, but you also don't have a single student loan. We may have a smaller house, but we are only three years away from paying off the mortgage. Our retirement accounts have been so successful that I'm only five years away from retiring. The early retirement allows me more freedom than buying a car right off the lot would."

"I guess I never thought about it that way. So this whole time, you've been—"

"Living way below our means?" My mother finishes my sentence. "Yes, and now in only five years or so, we will have the freedom to spend our days together, something we always dreamed of."

"The true purpose of my specific plan was to allow myself that kind of freedom," my father explains. "I may have gotten there a little differently than I originally thought I would, but the result was better than I planned because I now have you and your mother. After all, success means nothing if you have no one to share it with."

"And it sounds like this Theo might be someone who is making you second-guess your plan?" my mother asks with a mischievous smile.

I put a hand over my face. "Ugh, Beth told you, didn't she?"

"Well, she knew you certainly wouldn't tell us." My mother laughs.

"Theo was just a friend. I don't feel that way about him," I lie. "Besides, my plan doesn't allow for dating until three years in anyway, so this whole summer was a waste."

My mother sighs. "Oh, sweetie, that's not true." She moves to brush a curl behind my ear and places a soft hand on the side of my face. "You don't always get to decide when you fall in love, Sienna, or who you fall in love with. It's not something that can be planned, only something that can be felt when the time comes."

Her words stick with me through our dinner. I couldn't possibly love Theo. I've only known him for a few months.

My brain continues to battle my heart as I toss and turn all night in my childhood bedroom. The restless night has become my new normal since leaving the lake house weeks ago.

34
THEO

A sense of relief washes over me each time my fist collides with the punching bag hanging in front of me. I punch in a basic one-two rhythm. It's unlike any of the combos I've seen Alex perform, but it gets the job done.

"Your form is shit," Alex says behind me, but I don't so much as glance at him as my attention stays focused on the bag in front of me.

One, two. One, two. One, two.

"You're going to hurt yourself if you keep hitting that way." Alex is in front of me now, holding the bag in place as I continue to punch. My hits grow more aggressive and erratic as visions of my own stupidity flash through my mind.

You almost fucking killed her.

Hitting as hard as I can, I curse, as Alex was right. My shitty form causes a pain to shoot up through my shoulder on my last punch. A disgruntled noise leaves my throat at the feeling.

Stomping away from the punching bag, I take a seat on a nearby bench, ripping my gloves off.

"Told you," Alex says smugly.

"Shut up."

"Feel better?"

"Not even a little." I run my hands through my hair, wiping the sweat from my brow. Alex moves to sit next to me, handing me my water bottle as I take a moment to catch my breath.

I think I speak for all of my brothers when I say we're thankful that Alex chose this line of work. When he opened his boxing gym a few years ago, he gave all of us a key and told us we could come here whenever we needed to, no questions asked. I would guess that Roman uses his key most often, but I have no evidence to back it up.

I've never felt I had a reason to use my key until a few weeks ago. I've spent every day here for the past two weeks trying to get Sienna out of my head. To my agony, I've been unsuccessful.

Alex lives in the apartment above his gym, so he knows how frequently I've visited over the past few weeks, but this is the first time he's joined me. I'm thankful he opens later on Sundays so I could sneak in this morning and have the place to myself. Before Alex came downstairs, that is.

Looking around the empty gym, I take note of the high-end equipment. The ambient lighting is set to the lowest setting, as I didn't think anything else would be fitting for my current mood. Alex's gym is another reminder of how I've only failed where my brothers have succeeded.

"You want to talk about it?" Alex finally asks after a few moments of silence.

"Not particularly, no." I hesitate before continuing, "I fucked up. There's no fixing it, so I'm trying to figure out how to live with it."

"The 'it' being..." He waits for me to finish his sentence.

"Losing Sienna, disappointing Roman, once again failing to help him see that I'd make Dad's company more successful, although at this point, I'm even starting to doubt that."

"Hmm..." When that's all Alex responds with, I look at him to find him staring at me with a concerned look I rarely ever see from him.

"What?"

"Why do you insist on calling it 'Dad's company'?" he finally asks.

"Because that's what it is. Kane Construction is Dad's company. Roman always says it's his, but it isn't. He's always trying to erase Dad." The question brings me back to my conversation with Roman, anger boiling my blood once again. "We didn't just lose Mom. We lost Dad too. Roman never wants to acknowledge that. If it weren't for Dad, none of us would even have the money we do for you to open this gym, or Leo to go to culinary school, or me to go to college or buy the Mustang. Roman takes the credit for everything, and I just don't understand why."

"Theo, that's because *Roman* is the reason we have the lives we do. Not because of Dad."

"What are you talking about?"

"Sure, Dad started Kane Construction, but he was

only building a few houses a year. His 'company' consisted of a truck with some tools thrown in the back. Any money he made, he spent immediately. It was enough for us, but not enough to build the business properly. Dad didn't leave us enough money when he and Mom passed. That money ran out in a year."

"No, we all have inheritances, nest eggs, or whatever you want to call them. You got yours when you were twenty-one, just like me," I correct my brother.

"No, that's what Roman wanted us to think. Listen, I've gone along with it because you know how Roman is. He doesn't like the attention. But I overheard him and Leo talking about the finances when I was a teenager. Roman took a small portion of the life insurance money and invested it in funds for us, not Dad. It was Roman who built the company up to what it is today. He's the reason you went to college, the reason I own this gym, the reason Leo is as great of a chef as he is today."

I'm too busy trying to process the information to respond, so Alex continues, "He made a lot of sacrifices to get us here, but he did it. Look, I love Dad just as much as you, but he made a stupid decision that led to Mom's and his death. Even dumber ones led to us not being properly set up for their early departure in life. It was hard on all of us, but I think it was toughest on Roman. That's why he's been so hard on you lately. He was scared you're turning out like Dad. The incident with Sienna didn't help."

My mind is blank as I can't find the words to say. Why wouldn't Roman tell me all of this? Why wouldn't he be honest with me? Why continue to let me think it was Dad who had set us up for success despite his early death? Roman let me say such awful things to him, and he didn't correct me once.

"I had no idea," I say as I weed through the many questions plaguing my mind.

"I know. I'm not even sure Roman knows that I know. He'd probably kill me if he knew I was letting you in on his little secret. But I'm telling you because you've got to make shit right with him."

"I've been a complete asshole, haven't I?"

He nudges my shoulder. "You said it, not me."

A hint of a smile spreads across my lips at that, the first time in weeks that I've come close to actually smiling.

"Come on, I'll make us breakfast while you shower. You're stinking up my gym, and I have good-paying customers coming in a few hours."

Following Alex up to his apartment, I say, "I don't smell that bad." Taking a whiff of my shirt, I'm proven wrong instantly, and Alex laughs when he catches the grimace on my face.

The thought of a shower brings back memories, and I'm thrown back to the lake house. A blue bikini, my hand weaving through deep brown curls, and the smell of summer strawberries. Despite my many attempts this morning to forget Sienna, I'm still reminded of her at every corner.

35
THEO

It's been a week since my talk with Alex, and I've been working nonstop. I'm tired, but working has been rewarding in a way I wasn't expecting. At times, it even keeps my thoughts occupied long enough that I forget all about Sienna. Those moments are fleeting, though.

The day I joined Alex for breakfast, he helped me plan the next couple of weeks. I mentioned to him what Sienna had said to me about making a presentation for Roman, and Alex agreed. He said that while I might have great ideas for the company, they usually don't mean shit in business unless I can back them up with a detailed plan.

I realize now that I need to show Roman I'll be a great business partner, not just a great brother. Unfortunately, I haven't been either lately.

I've been working the front desk at Alex's gym every day since our talk. Any downtime I've had between shifts has been spent working on my business proposal for Roman, finally putting my degree to good use.

Matt and Jessie have been up my ass about not attending their various "end of the summer" parties. I don't care, as the sense of accomplishment I feel over my proposal is worth it. Locking myself in my room every night, instead of partying, this is the most effort I've ever put into anything.

I'd be lying if Sienna hasn't been the driving force behind my recently increased work ethic. I'm not sure I'll ever have another chance with her, but if I do, I need to make sure I'm someone she can easily fit into her plans. Not someone she just wants to have fun with.

Checking the recently downloaded calendar app on my phone, I stand outside the building, with my family's name displayed on the front in letters several feet tall—the Kane Construction building. I'm fifteen minutes early, which means I'm right on time per Roman's standards. Donning my nicest black slacks, button-down shirt, tucked in of course, and blazer, I open the front doors, stepping inside the lobby.

I've been here plenty of times over the years. I practically grew up here with Roman putting in late hours while I did my homework in a small corner of his office or in one of the conference rooms. I feel like an idiot for not realizing how much work he's put into this company.

Shaking off the nerves, I approach Sharon at the front desk. Her short gray hair is pinned back perfectly as usual, and I take note of the new baby photo sitting on her desk.

"Theo! What a pleasant surprise." She takes note of my outfit. "Don't you clean up nice." Seeing as how I usually visit in a sweatshirt and sneakers, I register how shocking my outfit must be. I try to push past the feelings of impostor syndrome creeping into my bones as I make small talk.

"Hi Sharon, how are you?" I adjust the three-inch binder, filled to the brim, in my hands. "Rebecca had her baby, I see. How does it feel to finally be a grandma?" I flash her my most charming smile that she's loved since I was little.

"Oh, it's everything I thought it would be and more. You're so sweet to ask." She waves me off, pointing toward the elevator. "Roman is in his office. You can just go right on up."

"Actually, this is more of an official visit today. If you wouldn't mind telling him that I'm here, I'd like to keep things professional."

"Oh, I see." She picks up the phone, winking at me as she talks into it. "Roman, your one o'clock is here."

I hear his muffled response on the other line and straighten my blazer in anticipation of his arrival. Sharon reaches up to tuck a strand of hair out of my face. At the same time, I hear the elevator, and Roman steps out, wearing a suit that costs three times as much as mine.

As he looks me up and down, I hear him mumble, "Let's get this over with," motioning for me to follow him.

I take one last look at Sharon before following Roman, and she waves me off, giving me a thumbs-up while mouthing, "Good luck." I thank her as I follow Roman to the conference room on the first floor. The one he usually uses for salespeople he has no interest in doing business with.

I could use all the good luck I can get right now.

Roman takes a seat at the head of the conference room table, opposite the large TV screen hanging on the wall.

I set the binder down in front of him, having already memorized the entire thing. After getting my presentation set up on the screen, I begin, "Thank you for the opportunity to present my business proposal today. I know you are very busy..."

I proceed with my business proposal to expand Kane Construction into the commercial sector. Not moving away from residential but instead creating a whole new branch of the company that I would help oversee.

Throughout the entire presentation, Roman doesn't move once. He listens diligently but the only movement he gives me is the slight tap of his finger against the table every so often.

"Thank you for your time." I finish my presentation, the nerves washing away now that it's over, with a sense of pride.

Not only is this a great idea, but I have the stats to back it up, too. All of which I presented to Roman today. Only an unskilled businessman would say no to a proposal like this.

"No." I wait for Roman to say more, but he doesn't.

"No? That's it? No?"

Roman stands from his chair. "I appreciate the proposal, but I'm not interested."

As Roman heads for the door, I look at the binder he

left on the table. The binder containing the research, statistics, graphs, charts, and budgets I spent two weeks putting together. Hours of sleep missed, and fun times with friends sacrificed. All for him to say no.

That's when it hits me. Over the past two weeks, I've experienced a fraction of the sacrifices Roman spent years making. The smallest look into what he must've gone through so many years ago. Sienna's words echo in my ears. She had said some people have to start at the bottom and work their way up. Something that takes hard work, grit, and determination. I now see that both she and Roman have it, and I've barely scratched the surface of earning the position here.

Before he can open the door, desperation seeps into my voice, and I say, "I'm sorry."

He stops just moments before his hand reaches the doorknob.

"You were right about everything. I'm sorry I wasn't listening, but I'm ready to make a change." That gets his attention long enough for him to actually turn toward me.

"Go on," he says as he crosses his arms over his chest.

"I've been an entitled asshole who thought I was deserving of a position here because I believed it was Dad's company. I know now that it's not. Kane Construction wouldn't exist if it weren't for you. I know about all of it. The money you put away for us, the endless nights you spent working to build this company into what it is today. I've been an ungrateful asshole about all of it."

"You weren't supposed to know about any of that. Did Leo talk to you?" he grits out through his teeth.

"No, Alex did. He overheard you and Leo talking about everything when we were kids. I had no idea about any of it until now. Why didn't you say anything?"

He runs his hand across his face, his posture loosening. "You were only six when Mom and Dad died. You saw them in a light that the rest of us weren't able to. Especially Dad. I couldn't ruin the image you had of them."

"So instead you ruined yours?"

He puffs out a semi-laugh. "Yeah, I guess I did."

I round the table to meet Roman where he is, grabbing the binder in the process.

Handing the proposal over to him, I say, "I want to work with my brother. You might not see it, but I think we could be a really good team." I let out a sheepish laugh. "I hate to admit it, but you're the one I've always looked up to. The only reason I got a degree in business was so I could work here with you."

He takes the binder from me. "I'll think about it. I still don't like what you pulled at the lake house."

A sense of relief washes over me at his first words. "Yeah, I know I fucked up. Big time." He nods in approval of my admission. "If it helps, Sienna and I haven't spoken since that night. I'm pretty sure she wants nothing to do with me, and I don't blame her. She deserves better." I pause before continuing, "And...I've listed the Mustang for sale."

"Mmm." He looks at me carefully, as though he's thinking through what to say next. "That's a shame on both accounts, considering you love that car, and you love Sienna even more."

My eyebrows shoot up. *"Love?* Who said anything about love? She hates me. She said everything was a mistake, and practically agreed with everything you had said that night."

"If you honestly think she hates you, you're not as smart as I thought you were."

"Smart, huh?" I adjust my jacket, standing a little taller, trying to change the subject from the one person I've been failing to avoid thinking about for weeks now.

"Don't change the subject." He points a finger at me, and I swat it away.

Continuing, I offer him a new deal. "Don't make me your partner. At least, not at first. Think about the proposal and have me shadow one of the project managers. I want to earn my position here, like you did."

He looks as though he's contemplating my offer for a moment before speaking. "Okay, you have the job. You can work your way up under my mentorship, and we'll put your proposal into place once you're ready. But I'll only agree to this on two conditions."

"Anything, what is it?" I'm embarrassed at how eager I am, but I can't help my excitement at the chance to prove to my brothers I'm not a kid anymore. That I can work just as hard as they have.

"When I was your age, I spent countless nights building this company. To help take care of you and your brothers. I don't regret a single moment doing that after seeing where you've all ended up today." Roman sighs. "But it didn't leave much room for personal endeavors. Needless to say, I want you to promise not to make the same mistake I did."

Roman puts a hand on my shoulder. "If you love Sienna, go after her. You have plenty of time to build a career here, but the right woman only comes around once. If you let her go now, you'll regret it for the rest of your life."

He speaks as though he has experience with this regret, but when I catch the look in his eyes, I decide against asking him about it.

"I don't think she wants to see me again, even if I do love her." Shit, do I? "I'm not sure I could get her back."

"I might have an idea." Roman throws his arm around my shoulders as he pulls us out of the conference room. "Let's discuss it over lunch in my office. I have a few questions about this proposal we can discuss as well."

I nod my agreement, and we head toward the elevator. As we ride the elevator to the top of the building, I realize I've only agreed to one of his conditions.

"Hey, what was the second condition?"

"Oh, right. Don't sell your Mustang," He pulls on my shoulder, whacking me lightly with the binder. "Dad always did have good taste in cars."

By the time we reach his office, Roman and I are both laughing. For the first time in weeks, I don't feel like a complete fuckup.

36
SIENNA

After spending a few more days with my parents, I finally decided to go back home to my own apartment. Talking with them lifted my spirits but also gave me a lot to think about. I didn't want them to give me any other ideas if I stayed for too long.

The conversation gave me a lot to think about, and I'm not sure which part freaked me out more. The concept that my plan has officially fallen apart, or the much more terrifying concept that I've fallen for Theo without realizing it.

I've scaled back on job applications for now. Between the money I have saved up and my parents' offer to cover my share of the rent if needed, I'm able to take a much-needed break. This will give me a chance to look for jobs that actually interest me. Not just places I think would hire me.

I hate that my dad was right about burnout, but I

appreciate him being there for me when it happened. I've needed a reset, and with this reset, I'm learning to be comfortable with the unknown. This new non-plan might set me back a bit in experience, but finding a job I'm passionate about will be much more rewarding.

I think back to Theo's words on the hike. He was right, I don't want to settle. That was the point of my plan from the beginning. Things might be messier without a carefully constructed plan, but I need to do what will actually make me happy.

You were happy with Theo.

I curse my brain for the thought that floats through my mind.

Currently unemployed and scaling back on my job search, I usually spend my days doing nothing, trying to find what brings true happiness in my life. Although after two days of doing nothing, I felt too pent-up. No one said learning to be comfortable with the unknown would be easy. Eventually, I went to Beth for some help.

With her bookstore search, she had plenty to keep her busy, and I asked to tag along. If not to help, then something to take my mind off my unproductive days. Something to take my mind off Theo, who I'm still not sure whether or not I love.

Beth and I have spent the last week searching for the perfect place to open her bookstore. She seems to enjoy having me part of the process, claiming that I have an unmatched eye for design and that I'll find her the perfect place. I think she's just happy I have a reason to put on something other than yoga pants.

Either way, this plan is working. Helping her design her bookstore and find the perfect place to host it is bringing back the creative spark I hadn't realized I'd lost.

The one thing this plan hasn't helped with is taking my mind off Theo. I'm still struggling with my parents' words about not being able to plan for love. Sometimes, I don't think they realize that the type of love they found with each other is one in a million.

Then again, it doesn't matter what I do. I can't get Theo off my mind. I wake up thinking I'll find him in bed next to me, my heart sinking when I find my bed cold and empty. The trees outside remind me of his emerald-green eyes. The smell of grass brings me back to our night together under the stars. Any cheeseburger I see reminds me of the fun I had with the brothers, watching Alex and Leo fight over the best way to cook a burger patty. I don't just miss Theo, I miss the feeling of being part of a larger family.

As if that's not bad enough, I still haven't been able to bring myself to unpack my suitcase. It's only been a few weeks since I left the lake house. I'm still in the throes of summer, and reality just hasn't hit yet. That's all this is. That's all it can be.

Theo himself agreed with me that what we had was all in good fun. He agreed that it was all a mistake. He let me go.

"You ready to go?" Beth stands in the doorway of my bedroom, bag in hand. We have another full day of real estate hunting, and I'm grateful for the reprieve from my room as I started to feel the walls closing in on me.

Grabbing my bag, I head out the door with Beth, excited to spend another day helping my friend. Besides, even if I did love Theo, and I'm not saying I do, but even if I did, he made it clear that he certainly does not love me back.

37

SIENNA

Beth and I arrive at what looks to be an old coffee shop. Standing by her car, we take in the building. It's empty now, the windows covered so we can't see inside, but the exterior has a certain charm that perfectly suits Beth. The detailed trim around the grand windows that stand tall on either side of the doorway is already painted in Beth's favorite shade of green. Not to mention, since it's just outside of downtown, there's a full parking lot. Upon finding a spot, we immediately added it to our pros list for this location.

The only con is that it shares walls with two other buildings. The one to the right, I'm not sure houses an operating business, as it looks just as run-down as the one standing before us. To the left is some sort of gym. It's hard to say what kind, considering it isn't open yet.

"Oh, this place is actually super cute," Beth says beside me.

"I agree, but I thought that's why you wanted to check this place out, because it had the exterior you were looking for." I'm a bit confused by her comment. She had originally told me she drove by this place randomly one day. After getting in touch with the owner, she set up this meeting. So I'm not sure why she's speaking as though she's seeing this for the first time.

"Right. Well, shall we?" I respond to her question with a gesture to the front door, prompting her to lead the way.

I'm too busy admiring the trim work around the front door up close to notice a man stands just inside the empty building. When my eyes lock onto pools of forest green, illuminated by the light filtering through the open front door, my heart stops.

"Theo…" His name leaves my lips in a gasp.

"Sienna." My name on his lips sounds like a beautiful melody has touched my ears. I want to run to him, to hug him, to feel his lips on mine again. But my feet don't move an inch.

Seeing him again throws me back to this summer and the words he spoke to me.

…blue is a perfect color on you, Angel. But I must admit, that bikini would look better on the floor.

You gave us a piece of our mom back…They're perfect. Just like you, Angel.

Well, at least we had fun…good luck with your job search, then.

"What is he doing here?" I snap at Beth, putting my guard back in its rightful place. She stares at me, guilt written on her face. I can't help but steal a glance at Theo as I wait for her response. Damn, he looks better than I remember.

Another reminder that he's not taking this separation between the two of you as hard as you're taking it, Sienna.

"Just hear him out, please. I think he can help," Beth says in a hushed tone that only I can hear. Louder, she says, "I'll wait outside while you two talk."

Beth exits, and I contemplate the ways to get back at her for this. I was beginning to make progress on getting Theo off my mind. Then she tricks me into coming here. Unbelievable. Now I'll have to start the process of forgetting those forest-green eyes all over again.

"Don't blame her." Reluctantly, I make eye contact with Theo, who now stands in front of me, closer than he was before. When his familiar scent overshadows the stale, musty smell of our surroundings, I take a small step back, inching closer to the front door.

"Then who should I blame for this meetup?" I brush a stray curl out of my eye. The least Beth could've done is ensure I wasn't wearing a sweatshirt, with my hair loosely tossed on top of my head. My look is reminiscent of the time we met in the diner before he came crashing into my life, tearing apart my plan.

"Blame me, this was my idea. I reached out to Beth and convinced her to set up a meeting with us." He hesitates, and I wait for him to continue. "I didn't think you'd exactly be up for the idea of meeting with me."

"Mmm..." I sigh, my guard slipping the slightest. "What did she mean when she said you wanted to help?"

Theo pulls out a piece of paper from his pocket and hands it to me, "I've set up interviews for you all over town. They all take place next week."

"You what?" I do what I can to tamp the shock in my voice.

"Roman still had the link to your portfolio. We worked together to send it out to various architecture and design companies in the area. A few of them got back to us and were open to meeting with you." He rubs the back of his neck, my guard slipping a little more at the grimace on his face.

"Who says I still need help finding a job?" I jut my nose up, and the motion causes another curl to fall onto my forehead, making my confidence waver slightly.

Theo smiles. "I don't doubt that you can find a job on your own. I went through your portfolio myself and was impressed by your work. You combine modern lines with vintage details so perfectly. It's truly astonishing and I—" He stops himself. "I'm getting carried away. I was impressed to say the least, and everyone on that list was as well. You may not need a job anymore, but I figured I'd give you options. It's the least I could do." His eye contact tapers off at the end of his last sentence.

Theo holds the piece of paper out to me, and I take it, making sure my fingers don't brush his accidentally, as I'm not sure I could handle the feel of his skin against mine. Looking down at the list, I read a list of companies, names, addresses, dates, and times. Half of the list are companies I've already applied for. The ones that turned me down for an interview. The other half are companies I didn't bother applying to because I didn't meet their application requirements.

At the bottom of the list, Rose City Designs is

scrawled out in Theo's sharp, slanted handwriting. Next to it is Graham Emerson's name.

"How'd you get me an interview with Graham?" I ask Theo, still staring at the piece of paper in my hand. I'm afraid if I look away, the name will disappear.

"I guess the Kane name means something in this town, thanks to Roman. He put in a good word with Graham after I talked to him." When I look up at Theo, he takes a tentative step closer to me. "Roman isn't as scary as he looks. He was also impressed by your portfolio. Despite what he said, he thinks you'd be a great fit at Rose City Designs, so he texted Graham and set up an interview for you."

"You didn't have to do all of this," I finally say. "I'm sure this took away time from trying to get a job with Roman."

Theo waves me off. "Who said you can't have both? Roman is giving me a chance. All I did was ask that he give you one too."

I sigh. "Thank you."

Theo reaches up and brushes the stray curl that's fallen into my face again, behind my ear. "Anything for you, Angel," he all but whispers.

He inches closer by the second. So close that it wouldn't take much for me to lean forward and touch my lips to his.

I stop myself before giving in to my urges. That's what got me into this mess in the first place. But I don't stop myself when one question crosses my mind. "Why do you call me that? Angel?"

Theo flashes me his heart-melting smile. "When I

first saw you in that diner, you were hunched over your laptop, wearing an annoyed look because of my shitty friends, and I thought it was quite endearing. Your focus was admirable. But what caught my attention was when you finally looked up from the screen in front of you. The light above the table illuminated you just right, framing the top of your head as though it were a halo. Then I saw your face, those gorgeous brown eyes." He brushes a knuckle across the side of my face. "Those tempting lips." His thumb brushes across my bottom lip. "And the luscious curls that shaped your face perfectly." His knuckle rests under my chin now. "And I knew you must be an angel because a beauty this grand would be wasted on a human."

I hold back tears as he continues, "Then I took you to the lake house. Where you so effortlessly fit in with my occasionally off-putting family." I can't help the small uptick of the corners of my mouth at his words. "You're the most determined, hard-working, strong woman I've ever met. To say your grit is inspiring would be an understatement. Sienna, you gave us a piece of our mom back. That's something only a true angel could do."

Our lips, his even closer to mine now, are almost touching. I feel a pull in my chest as though the forces of the universe scream at me to move closer, to seal my lips to his, to touch him again. Instead, I pull back, a sob trapped in the back of my throat at the absence of his touch under my chin when I do.

"Thank you for the explanation." I clear my throat. "And thank you for the interviews. This at least gives me options with the ones I already have lined up. I appreciate it." I catch myself in another lie.

Regardless of what he calls me, regardless of whether he wants to kiss me back, it doesn't change anything between us. He agreed that we took things too far. He left me when I needed him. He almost got in the way of my future that I've been working toward for the past four years.

Theo clears his throat, taking a step back from me, our distance growing once again. "Of course. Well, I'm happy you have options." He motions to the piece of paper I still hold in my hand.

Unsure of what to say next, I move to leave, turning my back toward Theo. He stops me with a hand on my elbow. "Wait, I don't want things to be awkward between us." Turning my head, I'm intrigued by what he has to say next. "I want to officially apologize for what happened at the lake house. I never meant to put your life in danger. I just wanted to have some fun with you, and I see now that I made a lot of bad decisions that night."

A lot of bad decisions.

The words echo in my mind as I think of the events before our drive back to the lake house. Any sliver of hope I might've felt at his explanation of calling me Angel is washed away by those five words. Clearly, I see now that any feelings I have toward Theo will never be reciprocated in the same magnitude.

I pull my elbow away from his hand. "It's okay, Theo. I agree, a lot of bad decisions were made that night. I think it's best if we just move forward as friends." His head reels back slightly, as though I've said something wrong, even as I agree with his recount of events that night.

"Right, friends." Theo holds out his hand, prompting me to shake it.

I tentatively reach my hand out and interlock it with his. The slight squeeze he gives reminds me of his grip on my hips, my thighs, my hand warming at the touch of his. Hands interlocked, we stand there for a moment, the dusty coffee shop fading away as his eyes lock onto mine.

My mind screams at me to say something, screams at me to fix what's been broken between us, but my mouth doesn't move.

Eventually, I pull my hand from his, raising it in a goodbye wave before turning my back on him again. This time, Theo doesn't stop me. As I head out the door, reconnecting with Beth in the parking lot, I don't dare to look back. Leaving him behind as he once left me.

As Beth and I shuffle into her car, I look at the piece of paper I hold in my hand again. The list is a physical representation of everything I've wanted. It's the starting point to the life I've been planning for years.

Beth drives off to our next location as I fold the list and tuck it into my bag. The pit in my stomach grows larger the longer I look at it.

38

SIENNA

The last week has been a welcome change of pace from my days of doing nothing. I've been to every interview Theo had set up for me, and they've all gone surprisingly well. Really well. Which is shocking, considering I'm fighting through thoughts of Theo as I answer questions.

My plan is back on track, but something feels off about it this time. I'm not as excited about the prospect of working in the architecture field as I was before. Something's missing. My heart seems to think it knows the answer, but I continue to ignore it as I stare up at the building towering above me.

I'm standing in the heart of downtown Portland as cars drive past on the street behind me. The coffee shop on the first floor of the building I stand in front of is buzzing with people. I assume they are trying their best to get their caffeine fix before starting their workday.

My gaze travels up the building, and I cover my eyes

when I stare up at the twelfth floor. Counting the windows as I go. The September sun shines bright. I squint my eyes as I imagine myself looking down at this street rather than up from it.

I look down at the note in my hand again, double-checking the time Theo has scrawled out onto the paper next to "Rose City Designs." Not even a full year after graduating from college, I've secured an interview at the company I thought I'd never have a chance to work at. At least not until five years into my career. Theo's list has thrown my plan wildly off course but in the best way possible.

I try not to think about what else my parents might have been right about as I fold the note and shove it into my blazer pocket.

Straightening my button-down shirt, I push open the glass doors of the building. My eyes squint again as they adjust to the lighting change from outside. The lobby smells of coffee and pastries, the scent wafting in from the shop next door. My shoulders loosen ever so slightly at the relief of not having to serve coffee anymore.

"Good morning," the young woman at the front desk greets me as I approach her. Though she doesn't look up from her cell phone until I speak.

"Good morning," I say with a smile, "I have a meeting with Mr. Emerson at eight thirty."

I watch as she taps her long pink fingernails on her keyboard. A star gem hanging off the pinky nail clinks against the keys as she types. Picking up the phone, she brushes her blond waves off her shoulders as she begins to speak. Setting down the phone, the woman raises her hand, motioning toward the elevator to my left.

"Head up to the twelfth floor. Mr. Emerson will be ready for you shortly." I'm not able to get a thank you out before she's back to typing away on her cell phone.

It's the longest elevator ride of my life, and I lose track of how many times the elevator stops on its way up to the twelfth floor. By the time I reach the top floor, my nerves are more shocked than before.

You can do this.

The pep talk I give myself ends when the elevator doors ding, opening to reveal the lobby of the twelfth floor. The lobby feels as though it's growing in length as I make my way to the man sitting at the large oak desk. The front of it, one long piece of oak, smoothed and shaped into a swooping curve, the right side coming to a point almost as tall as I am. I take in the design as I pass the black leather loveseats lining the lobby. Architectural magazines lay out on the tables next to them. Behind the man at the front desk hangs the Rose City Designs logo: a rose in place of the "O," the whole illuminated by a light carefully hidden in the ceiling.

Before reaching the man at the front desk, he holds his hand up to me, motioning me to take a seat on one of the nearby loveseats.

"Mr. Emerson will be out in a moment." I nod to him as I take a seat as instructed.

My foot taps lightly on the dark wood floors. Not wanting to be caught with my phone in my hands, I fidget with my clothing. Smoothing out my button-down as though the heat from my fingers can further iron out already straightened silk. The clock hanging on the wall opposite me ticks by. The sound grows louder in my ears by the second.

The clock goes silent when Graham Emerson steps into the room. He's instantly recognizable from the many magazine covers I've seen him on. I wasn't expecting him to be this good-looking in person. His suit, tailored to his body down to the centimeter, stretches only slightly over his muscles. I'd guess by his build that he and Roman aren't only best friends but workout partners too.

"Ms. Parker, it's nice to meet you." Graham's tone is warm as he throws a charming smile my way.

His smile doesn't compare to the one I find myself missing. The smile made of pure sunshine that I've grown to love over the summer.

Reaching my hand out, I intertwine my hand in his, giving a firm, professional shake. The feeling is far from that of Theo placing his hand in mine, the now permanent pit in my stomach growing even larger at the thought.

"Likewise, Mr. Emerson." I follow him when he waves me down the hallway. We pass a few doors with names I can't catch and a conference room before reaching his. Walking into his office, I'm amazed by the view of the city, showcased by the floor-to-ceiling windows spanning the entire wall behind his desk. The black furniture and dark wood accents are bathed in sunlight, brightening what would otherwise be a fairly dark room.

Bookshelves line the wall to the right, adorned with

brass sculptures, books of all sizes, and a few personal photos in frames that blend seamlessly with the shelves. The black leather furniture rubs against my slacks as I take a seat, making an awful screeching sound. The noise reminds me of the first time I met Theo.

Get your mind off Theo, Sienna.

Easier said than done.

I shouldn't be surprised by such a beautifully designed office. Graham Emerson was given the unofficial title as the king of architecture, after all.

As Graham takes a seat at his desk, he gets right to business. "So tell me about yourself..." With that, the interview is off.

I match each of his questions with a carefully rehearsed answer, having spent all week prepping for this interview. Graham nods his approval as I speak, leaning in when I talk about the inspiration behind my portfolio. Roman did say he likes his ego stroked, after all.

When he speaks highly of my portfolio in response, a smile spreads across my face. The feeling is strange, and my stomach churns again when it's not Theo who is the cause of my smile.

"To be honest, I don't have any associate positions available right now. But I'd be more than happy to hire you on as one of the architecture assistants. It doesn't pay well at all, but it'd be full-time, with plenty of growth potential."

My smile spreads wide as I lean forward, reaching my hand out to him. "Thank you, Mr. Emerson. I'm very excited to contribute to the success of Rose City Designs in any way that I can."

Graham chuckles lightly, giving a firm shake of my hand. "I'm sure my entire team will greatly appreciate your contributions. I'm very excited to see what you bring to the table. Steven out front will get you set up with instructions for your first day."

Rising from my chair, I nod toward him. "Thank you again for your time."

I head toward the door, feeling on top of the world.

That feeling doesn't last long when Graham says after me, "Anything for a friend of the Kanes."

I hesitate for a moment. His words hit me like a gut punch to the stomach. While I appreciate Theo's help in setting up interviews. I don't think I could accept a job if I knew I didn't rightfully earn it.

"Would you mind if I ask a question?" I ask, hoping he doesn't count that as my question.

"By all means." He motions for me to continue.

"Am I only being offered this position because of my connection to the Kane family? Because if that's the case, I'm not sure I can accept." He looks surprised by my words.

"I can assure you, Ms. Parker, that I don't allow anyone to tell me how to run my company. I won't lie to you, I set this interview up as a favor for Roman. When he told me his party animal little brother had fallen in love, I had to meet the woman who changed his heart for the better. But after reviewing your portfolio and our interview today, I actually believe you'd make a great addition to my team."

I stare at him, unmoving and unspeaking, trying to process his words. Did he just say Theo was in *love*? He must be mistaken. If Theo loved me, he would have told me so. God knows he's had plenty of chances to.

Graham stands from his desk chair. "There's no shame in using connections. You are clearly talented, and I'd love to have your talents on my team for the benefit of my company. If I thought you'd be a poor addition, there's no way in hell I'd hire you. Not even for the Kane brothers." He levels me with a look that suggests my initial question didn't need to be asked.

"In that case, I look forward to working here, Mr. Emerson." And with that, I exit his office, my head and heart once again at odds.

I'm standing in the elevator, holding a packet of instructions for my first day of work at Rose City Designs, as I ride it down to the lobby floor. Logically, I should be happy. I stand here holding everything I've wanted in a career and five years sooner than when I thought I'd have it.

But my chest aches when I think back to my father's words.

Success means nothing if you have no one to share it with.

That must be what I'm feeling. The pit in my stomach that's been there during each interview. The lack of excitement I feel knowing I've secured my dream job. As I stand alone in the elevator, I realize my father was right. There's only one person I wish were here right now. One person I wish I could celebrate with.

I think back to my mother's words as I exit the elevator. Walking out of the lobby, I shove the papers into my purse, ignored by the blond woman sitting at the front desk still typing away on her cell phone. My mother was right too. Love isn't something you can plan. It's something you feel when the time is right.

When I push open the glass doors, making my way out onto the sidewalk, I'm met by the man I haven't been able to get off my mind since I first met him in that diner all those months ago.

The man who I know with absolute certainty, I've fallen in love with.

Theo stands tall, leaning against his blue Mustang. I take note of the back bumper, where no sign of our accident is found.

As I approach Theo, he holds out a bouquet to me. The same bouquet from the night of our first date.

"Hi," he says, smiling as I take the flowers from his hands. One inhale and I'm transported back to this summer. My own smile spreads across my face at the memories.

"What're you doing here?" I ask.

"I thought you might want to celebrate getting an offer to work at your dream company." He shrugs, as though it shouldn't even be a question as to why he's here.

"Oh, you just assume I got a job offer?" I raise an eyebrow at him in question. As people move past us on the sidewalk, I'm forced to stand closer to him. The only object separating us is the flowers in my hands.

"Of course you got a job offer. Not offering you a job would be a bad business decision. You're too talented."

I smile at him, but Graham's words still haunt my mind as Theo stands before me. I know without a doubt that I'm in love with this man. If there's even a sliver of a chance he loves me too, I can't walk away from him without knowing for certain.

"Just a friend here to support another friend?" I ask, trying to gauge his reaction to my question.

His eyebrows furrow, his only response a slight nod of his head as he looks toward the flowers. It's the reaction I need to continue.

"It's interesting because Graham seemed to be under the impression that we were more than just friends." My heart beats faster as I get the words out, testing the waters.

"What'd he say? Actually, let me go ask him myself. He always did have an issue with knowing when to keep his mouth shut." Theo moves around me, taking a step toward the front doors, only to be stopped by the foot traffic in front of him.

I chuckle, grabbing his arm in an effort to stop him from creating more distance between the two of us. "I'd actually prefer you didn't threaten my new boss after I just accepted a job offer."

Theo turns toward me, that blinding smile spreading across his face as he throws his arms around my waist. He picks me up, and as he spins us around in a celebratory hug, some of the angelica from the bouquet in my hand flies off onto the ground. I squeal at the sudden movements, and Theo's laughter echoes in my ear. The hug is a warm embrace, confirming my suspicions that this is what I was missing on my ride down in the elevator.

Setting me down gently on the sidewalk, he keeps his hands wrapped around my waist. "I knew you'd get the job. I'm so proud of you, Angel." My breath hitches as he rests his forehead against mine, as though the physical connection between us gives him the strength he needs to ask his question.

"Friends is what you wanted, is it not?" he asks me.

"Only because it's what you wanted."

I'm holding my breath, waiting for his response, when he says, "Only an idiot would want to be just friends with you, Sienna Parker."

As though his resolve snaps the moment my name releases from his lips, he pulls me in even closer, crashing our lips together. Immediately feeling at home, I melt into the kiss as our tongues collide. Only breaking apart when the flowers I'm holding tickle our cheeks as I try to pull him closer.

Theo's smiling when he releases me from the kiss. "I want to be worked into your plan. Any way you'll have me. Just work me in. This last month without you has been excruciating. I'm sorry for everything. The only thing I regret more than walking away from you that night is not realizing sooner that I've fallen deeply, hopelessly in love with you, Sienna Parker. If I had known then, I never would've let you leave."

With my free hand, I cup his cheek, staring into those beautiful green eyes as tears begin to spring from mine. "I never would've left if I knew then that I was deeply, hopelessly in love with you, Theo Kane."

He pulls me in for another kiss, but I cut it short as I continue, "I don't want a plan. You've shown me that even when things don't go according to plan, it doesn't always mean it's bad. Sometimes the things we don't plan for are the best things that could ever happen to us."

He chuckles. "Then I propose an idea. One year. Let's plan for one year together. No more, no less."

"You've got yourself a deal." With another kiss, the morning melts away as I'm held in the arms of the man who I love.

EPILOGUE

THEO

Six Months Later

We're back at the lake house, lounging on the couch in the living room as we watch the fire crackle. Beth has joined us. She and Sienna engaged in a conversation about a newly released rom-com movie they recently went to see for "Galentine's Day."

Roman sits next to me as he taps away on his phone, finishing up last-minute business before putting it away to spend the weekend with the rest of us. We've decided to come up here for a long weekend to spend time as a family before our schedules get hectic in the spring. As the weather gets nicer, it's prime time for construction.

Being here with Sienna again, with her on my arm as my real girlfriend this time, feels right. As if everything in my life has officially clicked into place.

We've drafted our one-year plan, leaving room for flexibility, of course. Which I'm thankful for, considering

I have something planned for later that will throw our plan completely out the window. Something tells me she won't care too much about that, though. The thought of building a life with Sienna gives me a newfound purpose I didn't know I needed.

I've spent most nights at her place, but when Beth really needs to focus, Sienna comes over to my place. Although that usually ends in Matt and me fighting over some dumb shit he ends up saying, and we have to hide out in my room for the rest of the night.

I throw my arm over Sienna's shoulders as we wait for Alex and Leo to join us. Slipping my free hand into my pocket, I rub my finger along the small blank key I've tossed in there. I run through my plan again of how I'm going to ask Sienna to move in with me.

Beth and Sienna's lease is up at the end of the month, making it the perfect time for us to look for something together. It wasn't exactly in her original plan, but the other set of keys weighing down my other pocket reminds me that, with Beth inevitably moving out, Sienna will be looking for a new roommate anyway.

I wish I could take credit for us all meeting back here, but it was Alex's idea. When he found out that Sienna and I made things official, he lost it. He was excited that we were finally together, of course, but more than that, he was excited at the chance to crown a winner of this year's Kane Family Games. After all, we never did play that last game of Uno, and he always did hate leaving things unfinished.

Leo joins us from the kitchen, setting a plate of meats

and cheeses on the coffee table. He takes a seat next to Beth as I start a conversation.

"I still can't believe you and Alex tied this year," I say to Leo. Out of the corner of my eye, I see Roman empty the box of Uno cards onto the table, preparing to shuffle them as we wait for Alex to arrive. After a few table flips and food fights over the years, Roman became the designated shuffler.

"I can't believe it either, but I'm ready to beat him this time," Leo rubs his hands together, "That asshole needs to be taken down a few pegs anyway." I smile at Leo. After our last trip to the lake house, I checked in on him so frequently that he eventually told me to fuck off (lovingly). We were able to talk things through, and I eventually stopped apologizing for triggering his anxiety.

Beth snorts. "You can say that again." She high-fives Leo. "Where is Alex anyway?"

"He should be here any minute," Roman says.

Beth and Leo discuss their Uno strategy when Roman turns to Sienna and me. "I'm happy to see things worked out between the two of you."

Sienna gives my brother a soft smile, one that makes me resist the urge to plant a kiss on her soft lips in front of everyone, "I truly am sorry for this summer. We didn't really think through our plan entirely, and I—"

Roman raises his hand, and Sienna stops mid-sentence. "It's all in the past, Sienna. You don't need to apologize. I'm sorry for the things I said that night. My brother tells me that I come off a bit grumpier than I intend to be."

"A bit?" I snort at his downplaying of his own attitude.

Roman throws a glare my way before looking back toward Sienna. "See how happy you've made Theo." He gestures in my direction. "And I'm certain you're the reason he's actually made it to work on time every day these past few months."

Sienna laughs, jutting up her nose in playful confidence. "I might have a thing or two to do with that."

Roman smiles at her, and I'm happy to see the two of them getting along. She's warmed up to him over the past few months, reinforcing my sentiment that she fits in well with my brothers and me. Which is a good thing, considering I have no plans of ever letting her go again.

A cold rush of air runs through the living room when the front door bursts open. Alex barges in, wearing the winner's belt. "Who's ready to lose to me again?"

Once he settles down, Roman deals out the cards. We decide to play a few rounds among all of us before Alex and Leo play their tie-breaker game.

Sienna wins the first round, taking all of us by surprise.

"What? I may be uncoordinated, but I'm excellent at card games." When she smiles at me, I kiss her until a chorus of "boos" sound around us.

"Don't rub your happiness in our faces, Theo. It's unbecoming," Alex says.

"You're one to talk." I motion toward the belt he refuses to take off.

"Alright, tie-breaker round. If I don't get food soon, I'm going to get grumpy," Roman says as he deals the cards between Alex and Leo. We all chuckle at his words until he levels us with a glare that has the laughter tapering off.

It's a close game between Alex and Leo. One that's kept all of us on the edge of our seats. Roman doesn't pick up his phone once as we watch in anticipation.

"Uno," Leo says as he drops a draw four, wild card onto the deck.

There's a collective chorus of gasps as we all hold our breath, watching Alex draw four cards to add to the three already in his hand. He stares at his cards in deep concentration, thinking about his next move.

"You can never go wrong with red," Beth says, breaking the silence.

Alex tips his imaginary hat to her and sets down a red number six card onto the deck.

Beth laughs before any of us can process the events that unfold. Leo sets down a red number four card onto the deck, winning the game of Uno.

"Hand it over." Leo holds out his hand, waiting for Alex to hand over the belt as the rest of us burst into laughter, cheering at Leo's win.

Alex, being the good sport he's always been, stands up and pulls Leo into a hug, then turns to all of us. "I'd like to remind all of you that I've won the last three years, and I plan on winning next year." Alex pulls the belt from his hips and hands it to Leo.

"Sure you will." Leo pats him on the shoulder, and Alex brushes him off, laughing. "Who's ready for dinner?"

"Me," Sienna says, raising her hand enthusiastically. "I've had dreams about your food, Leo."

Leo laughs as he and the others move toward the kitchen. I stop Sienna before we follow. "What about my food?"

"Oh don't worry, baby." Sienna places her hand on my chest. "Nothing will ever compare to your sandwiches." She winks at me, and a warmth fills my chest at knowing this woman is mine.

"My ego appreciates your lies." I kiss her on the forehead. The giggle she lets out prompts me to land a small slap to her ass as I follow her to the kitchen. A reminder of the many things I plan on doing to her tonight, assuming she says yes to my proposal of moving in together.

Dinner is full of laughs and embarrassing stories I wish Sienna never knew about me. She says she finds them "endearing," but I'm reminded to ask Sara to see her baby photo album next time I see her so I can give Sienna a taste of her own medicine.

We've spent every summer here since I was a kid, but tonight is the first night since my parents' passing that the table has felt full. My heart feels the same with Sienna by my side.

"Give me ten minutes before coming upstairs," Sienna says to me as we stand in the kitchen after putting away the dishes. Roman and Leo have retired to the firepit out back, bundled up with a couple of beers, as Beth and Alex finish their portion of cleanup in the kitchen.

"Do you have a surprise planned for me?" I say to her in hushed tones.

"Yes, but you don't get it if you come up early. Ten

minutes, no more, no less," and with that, she heads upstairs. Knowing how punctual she is, I set a timer on my smartwatch.

"Hey, Theo." Beth approaches me from the dining room. "Were you able to turn in my signed lease forms to the owner of that shop?"

After Sienna and I became official, Beth expressed interest in the abandoned shop I had dragged Sienna to. Over the past few months, I've been helping Beth sign lease agreements. Getting her set up so she can begin the process of opening her bookstore. It was easy considering I'm close with the owner. I don't blame her for wanting to rent the space. It's in a great part of town, and it has potential. Something I hope she remembers when she realizes I've been lying to her.

Grabbing the set of keys that rest in my pocket, I hand them to her. "It's all yours. I turned in the agreement last week, and the landlord gave me the keys this morning." I pause. "Beth, there's something you should know about—"

She raises her hand to shush me. "Unless you're about to tell me that the lease agreements didn't go through, I don't want to hear it. This is the only usable place I've found at a price I can afford. I don't want anything to ruin this celebratory moment."

"You really don't want to hear what I have to say?"

Beth grabs the keys from me. "Nope," she responds. Jumping up and down slightly as she says thank you, I try to shove down the guilt that I feel as she all but prances off upstairs.

Alex approaches me in the kitchen, placing a hand on my shoulder. "You give her the keys?"

I shove his hand off me. "Yes, but I still don't like this. Sienna is going to tear me to shreds when she finds out we lied to Beth." I lower my voice to avoid anyone over-hearing.

"You didn't tell her?" Alex looks surprised. "You were supposed to tell her before you gave her the keys."

"I tried. She wouldn't let me. She said she didn't want to ruin the moment."

"Well, at least you tried." Alex shrugs.

"Beth is going to kill you when she finds out,"

"And I would happily die by her hand." Alex fakes getting stabbed in the chest, tumbling back as though he's hurt. I take that as my cue to walk away, leaving him alone in the kitchen.

The only reason I agreed to help him in the first place was because he helped me in my time of need. I just hadn't fully thought through the repercussions of my actions until he gave me the keys this morning. Alex doesn't just own his gym. He also owns the other two buildings attached to it. With the coffee shop next door closing, I appreciated him letting me use it to build a bridge between Sienna and me.

The plan was to offer Beth a killer deal on the place she fell in love with to house her bookstore. We were going to tell her Alex is the landlord when I gave her the keys, but since she refused...this is getting way more complicated than I signed up for. But it's a problem for another day.

Today, I focus on heading upstairs to find the woman

I love and the surprise she has waiting for me. Excitement courses through my veins at the thought of spending each of my nights falling asleep by her side.

With a deep breath and a smile on my face, I pull the blank key from my pocket and head upstairs.

Thank you for reading *Fake It with You*, your support means the world to me. If you enjoyed this book, I would be forever grateful if you posted a review on the platform(s) of your choice. Reviews, posts, and word of mouth go a long way for authors.

Until next time,

Makenna

THE KANE BROTHERS SERIES WILL CONTINUE...

Preorder *Hate It with You* today. A spicy enemies to lovers romance between Alex and Beth full of tension, heat, and drama you won't want to miss!

ACKNOWLEDGMENTS

Thank you to every single one of you who has read Theo and Sienna's story! I hope you loved reading their journey as much as I enjoyed writing it.

Thank you to the amazing team over at English Proper Editing Services for your beta reading, sensitivity reading, and proofreading expertise. The feedback I received was invaluable to the progression of this story. Not to mention how much fun I had reading back the comments left on my manuscript.

Thank you to my wonderful copy and line editor, Jenny Sims, for working with me to meet close deadlines and keeping great communication in the process. Without you this book would be a mess of commas and unreadable sentences.

Thank you to Emily Wittig for making my cover design dreams a reality. I had no idea what I wanted and yet the design you created is exactly what I was picturing for this story. I can't wait to design future covers with you.

Thank you to Vic and Lero for working with me on character artwork that surpassed all of my greatest expectations. You both brought Theo and Sienna alive through your art and I cannot wait to work with you on future projects.

An infinite amount of gratitude goes to my husband;

my alpha reader, my support, and my muse. Thank you for making sure our lives didn't fall apart while I was consumed with writing and publishing my debut novel. Without your belief in me, this story would never exist and for that, I will always be eternally grateful.

Thank you to each and every one of you who has supported me on my journey to release my debut. Without your support, this book would not be where it is today. Finished. Published. In your hands. I cannot thank you enough for the love and support you've shown for this story. I'm so excited to share many more with you as I continue on this author journey.

Lastly, thank you to my younger self. With everything you've been through, your continued resilience still amazes me. We fucking did it babe.

ALSO BY MAKENNA CLEAVER

<u>**Kane Brothers Series**</u>

Fake It with You

Hate It with You

ABOUT THE AUTHOR

Makenna Cleaver grew up an avid daydreamer with a fascination for storytelling. It didn't matter if it was a TV show, a movie, a book, or a play, she found herself captivated by the characters, plot twists, and settings that made up an unforgettable story. Romance storylines in particular never failed to grab her attention.

She currently lives in the Pacific Northwest with her husband and dog, Scout. Having gone through a few hardships in early adulthood, she's passionate about telling real stories with raw emotions and complex characters that reflect life itself. Although, knowing there's a light at the end of every tunnel, she never leaves her characters without their happily ever after.